A Grand Exposition

Kim Idynne

A small article in the Reader's Digest volume *Strange Stories, Amazing Facts* describes a mysterious disappearance during the 1889 Exposition Universelle: an English woman checked into room 342 of a Paris hotel and soon fell ill. Her daughter alerted the hotel doctor and was sent on a long, elaborate journey to get medicine. She returned to find no trace of her mother. The hotel manager and doctor denied any knowledge of her; the guest register showed that the girl had checked in alone, and the room itself was not as she described it. She was dismissed as delusional, and her mother was never found. This story began as an exploration of how such a disappearance could have been staged—and more importantly, what impulses could have driven someone to such a crime in the first place.

1

QUEENS, NEW YORK: MARCH 9, 1889

An hour before dawn, Katharine woke and bolted upright in bed. She struggled for perception, scanned the room for looming shadows. The vague moonlight guided her to a bedside lamp that she lit with shaking hands.

In the opposite bed, her young cousin slept soundly.

The room was in its usual state. Again, Katharine checked the room for an unwelcome figure—particularly, for a stocky figure with dark brown hair and a height of five foot ten. She leaned over to look beside the bed. Then stood and gazed through the window to the empty street.

The drawing room, too, was vacant. Katharine carried the lamp and a small book to the chestnut table at the window—and paused, surveying the breadth of the room. All was still, though the flame of the lamp cast erratic shadows across the quiet space, agitated by Katharine's trembling hand. Her aunt and uncle's clean, perfectly inoffensive room seemed unduly threatening; her fear fed itself through the shadows it created.

Katharine set the lamp down and watched as the flame steadied. She took a fountain pen from its stand and tapped it against an old newspaper.

"Katharine," a voice whispered.

The sound hissed phantom-like in her ears. The pen and book fell from her hands as she whirled around.

Her cousin stood in the entryway. Startled by Katharine's reaction, Helen jumped, then clapped a hand over her own mouth.

"For God's sake, Helen," Katharine breathed. "You scared me."

"I scared *you*? What are you doing up?"

"Nothing. I woke up."

"I figured that much for myself." Helen sat on the sofa, looking searchingly into Katharine's eyes. "Were you having nightmares?"

Katharine hesitated, remembering her dream: Helen, her delicate features lit with excitement, telling Katharine about the wonderful stranger she'd met. *He told me he has a little cottage right by the pond, and it's all underground, with glass windows on one side so you can see the water from below.* Helen, heedless of others' warnings, descending into a muddy tunnel—into a place with no air, no light, nothing but the stranger's foreboding assurances: *It's just a little farther. Pretty soon you'll be down there with all the pond life, watching the moonlight cascading through the water. . . .*

"Yes, but I'm fine," Kathrine replied.

"You're going to stay awake again?"

"It's almost morning."

"No, it isn't."

Katharine was silent.

"Do you want me to stay up with you?"

"Go back to bed," Katharine said. "And do me a favor—don't tell your parents I was up."

Helen didn't move.

Stifling a sigh, Katharine sat beside her and spoke earnestly. "I'll be married soon, and it will get better. I won't get scared when Paul is beside me. All right?"

Helen nodded. Katharine studied her cousin's fine, wispy hair and delicate features—features that suggested vulnerability, perhaps making her the subject of Katharine's nightmare. Helen had grown tall and broad-shouldered in her seventeen years, but was otherwise delicate in stature; and though she was not lacking in shrewdness, she was by nature gentle and quick to offer help, with candid eyes and a soft, unassuming voice, all of which evoked Katharine's yearning to protect her.

"Go on," Katharine prodded her. "I'm going to write for a while."

Helen stood and left the room, turning to look at Katharine for a moment before exiting. Katharine waited until she was gone before opening the book—her personal journal. She moved the pen across the page, then paused to look up at the empty doorway through which Helen had disappeared. Her eyes scanned the room. Finally she resumed writing.

Saturday, March 9, 1889: I dreamed about the bog monster. It's the same monster I always dream about, but he always comes in a different form, and in increasingly realistic settings. Conversations make sense, and details fit together, so that I don't suspect I'm dreaming; he pulls me in and scares me half to death before I finally manage to wake. This time he was preying on Helen. He seduced her at a party, lured her into his swamp, and smothered her. For more than five years he has haunted me, both in the waking world and in dreaming. I've watched him move through my dreams like a gilded devil, wooing people with a shrewd, flawless charm; I've watched the same monster creep up on people and scare them out of their wits with foul-breathed malice. He knows that I am watching. In every dream, he looks directly into my eyes and gives me that same smug, knowing look.

He bragged to me once that he makes himself people's fears, and can frighten anyone out of their wits to get what he desires, always getting stronger and more skilled in the process. And I am scared—but not of him. The monster, after all, is just one entity—like a demon jumping into body after body, one mobile specter that thrives on the responses of the people he encounters. If others didn't respond the way he wanted, then he wouldn't have any power, but people make themselves incapable of seeing him for what he is. And ultimately, I realize he's not the one I'm afraid of.

She paused, remembering the latest nightmare. Helen beaming, starry-eyed, at the stranger. The smile breaking unabashed across her glowing face.

She finished: *It's everyone else, and the way they react to him.*

2

QUEENS, NEW YORK: MARCH 9, 1889

Helen screamed with delight at the edge of the pond, struggling against her captor.

"Stop!" she cried through peals of laughter. "Katharine, help me!"

Paul, Katharine's fiancé, grinned at her for a moment as he carried Helen closer to the water. The pond at the edge of his yard was still frozen, but covered with a wet sheath on the sunny day.

"Yes, Katharine, help her!" Paul swung Helen lightly back and forth, as if gaining momentum to throw her onto the ice. "She's having some trouble getting into the water. What we need is another person to help us break through all this ice. Maybe if we jump on it. Ready?"

"Paul, don't, you're mad," Helen gasped.

Katharine leaned against a nearby tree, smiling vaguely as she watched them.

"You're certainly in no position to judge." Paul set the young woman down and peered at her mud-caked shoes. "You're the ones who walked here in all this filth. How are we going to get you cleaned off?" He turned to Katharine. "You must have been desperate to see me."

Helen tried unsuccessfully to scrape the dirt from her shoes. "She's always desperate to see you."

"Go ahead and run inside." Paul waved Helen away, adding: "Leave your shoes at the door, please."

Helen retreated toward the house, a modest cottage in the center of a snug, snow-patched lawn.

"Don't you dare," Katharine said as Paul approached her.

He feigned surprise, but couldn't suppress a grin. "Don't I dare what?" He put his arms around her. "What?"

She shook her head. "You have that look on your face."

"What look?" He waited, but Katharine only smiled. "Have you seen the state of your shoes and your clothes? We should take them off and

4

have them washed right away."

Katharine glanced toward the house.

"Your shoes, I meant. On the other hand, you could use a good bath after tramping through all that mud."

"I'm tempted. We're lucky if we can get warm water at my aunt's house."

"Tell you what, I'll heat some for you if you share it with me. We can save time that way."

She appraised him coolly. "I hope you'll keep yourself in check while Helen is listening."

"Don't I always?"

"No."

"I can't help it. I like teasing you." Paul took her chin gently in his hand. "Tell you what—give me a really good blush, and I'll behave myself in front of the kid."

Katharine grabbed him suddenly, closing her grip around his index finger. "Tell me I'm the most wonderful woman in the world, and I'll let go of your finger."

"Don't imitate me. It makes you less attractive." He grabbed at her with his free hand, but she twisted out of his grasp.

"I can't think of any other way to show you how annoying this is," she said.

"It doesn't bother me. I like being close to you. You're the one who's squeamish."

"It'll bother you if I do it for as long as you. Promise me you'll behave in front of Helen, and tell me how wonderful I am, and I'll let you go."

Paul squirmed for a few moments, and abruptly stopped. "I'll behave myself in front of Helen. Just in front of her, mind you. And I think you're the most wonderful woman in the world."

"You have to say it more convincingly."

He chuckled. "Fine, it's annoying. I get it."

"I'm waiting."

Paul leaned forward and kissed her. Her grip slid from his hand.

"You're too gullible," he said as he withdrew. Paul grabbed her hands and gently pulled them behind her back, kissing her again before releasing her. "Come on."

From the parlor window, Katharine stood watching as her cousin skated alone across the icy pond. Helen was sure-footed on the ice, but Katharine couldn't stave off feelings of dread as she remembered her nightmare. *Pretty soon you'll be down there with all the pond life . . . .*

"Come away from the window, would you? She's fine." Paul sat on the sofa, patting the space next to him. "Can we talk?"

"Of course." She sat beside him, offering her full attention, but he looked at her silently. "What is it?"

"I have a birthday gift for you."

"Really. My birthday isn't until Friday."

"I know that, but I can't wait."

"One of your defining characteristics."

He smiled, but spoke with seriousness. "I want to take you to Paris. In May, for the World's Fair."

"Are you serious?" She shook her head.

"I hope you'll say yes, because—are you saying no? I can always go alone if you're not interested."

"I'm not going to say no."

"Good, because it's already arranged. We'll be staying at the hotel where Nathan works."

"Nathan Neville?"

"Yes."

Katharine lowered her gaze.

"He offered to entertain us while we're there. Will that be all right? If it's not, I can always make an excuse . . . ."

She hesitated, then met his eye. "No, it'll be fine. I can manage it."

"Of course, you and I would be sharing a room."

"Oh, I see. I think Mr. Neville might see that as somewhat inappropriate."

"No, Nathan wouldn't."

"If it involves me, he will. Is this really some elaborate plan to get me into bed with you?"

He smiled, putting an arm around her waist. "What, do you still want to wait until our wedding night?

She hesitated. "Yes."

"Oh, you had to think about it this time."

"Paul . . . ." She put a hand on his back in a vague embrace. "Why don't we get married earlier?"

"Earlier, when?"

"Soon. Now, before we go to Paris. We can take a few weeks to get settled in together. We could still have a reception with everyone, later on . . . ."

"Well, well. Miss Proper wants to elope." He grinned. "Are you sure you want to marry me? If we wait, you'll have a couple months to change your mind. If we do it now, you're trapped."

"We've already waited this entire winter."

"By your own choosing. I would have married you immediately."

"I'm done waiting." Katharine smiled back at him, and added gently, "I want to start my life with you."

"Good. I was going to suggest marrying early, so I could take my wife to Paris. I'm glad you did it for me. Problem solved. How would you like to spend your twenty-fifth birthday marrying me?"

"Well, it was your idea to celebrate my birthday. You can decide how we celebrate."

"That's a dismissive thing to say about your wedding."

"Not if I'm saying that I want to marry you as soon as possible." Katharine paused. "Your parents will be disappointed about the wedding plans, but . . . ."

"No they won't." He kissed her and stood up. "Stay here. I'll be right back."

He fled from the room, leaving Katharine to stare after him in mild bewilderment.

3

DELHI: MARCH 15, 1889

Charlotte Morgan's birthday was a bittersweet occasion. She had arrived in India with her mother only days before, making a virgin tour across the country with conflicting feelings of excitement and guilt. She quickly became enchanted by the vast landscapes and exotic cities, the strange animals and unfamiliar blends of humanity, even the complications of foreign customs—so different from the London neighborhoods where she'd passed her nineteen years. Her uncle's bungalow stood in the heart of Delhi, embellished throughout with the British style but still fascinatingly alien. The room in which she dined had high white-washed walls and a sweet-smelling grass-matted floor, and around its perimeter was a large assemblage of Indian servants who stood at silent attention; Charlotte initially found their presence uncomfortable and intrusive, but was surprised at how quickly she forgot them. She relaxed and yielded to her feelings of excitement, but any glimmer of happiness was kept fiercely at bay. A journey through India had been a longtime dream of hers. It was a dream she'd shared with her elder brother, Walter, before his death; and, ironically, it was because of his death, and the death of their father, that Charlotte had finally been summoned here.

Her family's London estate had been passed into the hands of her uncle Howard, who subsequently invited Charlotte and her mother to join his own household in Delhi. He regarded his niece with the air of someone who wished to become a second father. Charlotte tolerated his intentions with quiet appreciation. Howard's wife, Diane, was equally welcoming, though her attentions were morose compared to those of her husband. Often, during conversation, she would become swept up in a moment of merriment—and then stop, remembering with dread the awful tragedy that had befallen the two women. Charlotte's father and brother had been killed when a London inn caught fire and collapsed. The wound was deepened by other impending losses: the abandonment of a life-long

8

home, and of servants who had lived long with the family. Seeming to think it inappropriate to laugh and be merry, Diane resigned herself to being forlorn, and would often look at Charlotte and Mrs. Elizabeth Morgan with pity in her eyes, as if to let them know that she had not forgotten their sorrow.

Also among the dinner guests were Howard's daughters, Minnie and Blythe. Minnie was tall with ruddy flesh and sharp eyes, energetic and voluminous; Blythe, the younger, was smooth and pale in contrast, with reddish-gold highlights in her fair hair. Blythe was naturally pretty, but Charlotte noticed that she had been made up very carefully tonight, her hair pinned with delicate flower ornaments and hints of color added to her already healthy-looking face. She wore a blue chiffon gown that complemented her eyes. Blythe had spent well over an hour being prepared for the dinner, and there was a design to the efforts: of the two remaining guests, James and Maitland Asher, the latter was a well-to-do bachelor. James, an established medical doctor, was recently engaged to Minnie, and Charlotte understood that the family hoped to arrange another marriage between Blythe and Maitland.

Wine and champagne were poured as the dinner courses succeeded one another onto the table. Howard led the guests in a toast to his niece: "I wish you an eventless year, my dear."

Diane, acknowledging the unspoken tragedy that lied behind his words, threw a sympathetic glance in Charlotte's direction.

"You mustn't wish it to be eventless," Blythe interjected. "Let us at least hope that you take to Delhi. The neighborhood needs more British—especially women. We have so many gentlemen in want of a proper wife."

"It would ease my mind if Charlotte found a good man to marry." Charlotte's mother, Elizabeth, spoke without looking at her, perhaps not wanting to see the reaction. Her daughter gave her a tolerant smile anyway.

Howard appraised Charlotte with amused interest. "What do you say to that, Charlotte?"

"I should appreciate an uneventful year."

"I hope that's not entirely true." Elizabeth smiled at her—a smile full of uncharacteristic cheer, as though some fantastic secret hid behind it. "I think that you and I should travel a bit more, if you'll not refuse another adventure before our return to London."

James Asher spoke dryly: "All the ladies could benefit from staying out of London, so long as Old Jack is in town."

Minnie scowled, momentarily forgetting her food. "Oh, do stop going on about Jack the Ripper."

"At least wait until we have finished eating." Diane glanced nervously from Charlotte to Elizabeth. "Anyway, I expect that his spree has come to an end."

"Last November, was it?" Howard asked casually. "Or was there another in late December?"

James shook his head. "The police determined that she died as a result of being a blundering drunk."

"And what drink should induce her to accidentally strangle herself?"

Blythe regarded Elizabeth with eager interest. "If there *has* been another, we have not heard of it. Come, aunt, tell us: has there been any more ripping in White Chapel?"

Elizabeth's face was drawn; her cheer had vanished. "Let us talk of something else. It may be intriguing to some, but I have a young daughter to worry over."

"He wouldn't harm a girl like Charlotte," Howard assured her. "The Ripper preys on street walkers, and it would surprise no one if he was only a police agent trying to frighten the rabble into submission. They crawl over one another like rats in the east end, and operate as victims of their own vices, and it's just as well if a few are put under. Someone has to clean the filth from the streets."

Charlotte froze.

"Well," Elizabeth said, flustered, "I have some exciting news about—"

Charlotte interrupted tonelessly. "Howard, would you please apologize for your vulgar comment."

A brief silence ensued. The guests looked on Charlotte in surprise.

"You and I were born into money," she continued, "but not everyone is so fortunate. If you had been poor and ended up a street walker, I would hate to think that—"

"Charlotte, really," Elizabeth cut in. "Don't trouble yourself, Howard. Charlotte upsets easily."

Charlotte shook her head in silent protest.

"No, it's no trouble." Howard was red in the face, clearly thrown off by Charlotte's words. "I don't wish to upset Miss Charlotte on her birthday. I apologize. It is a grisly manner by which to meet one's end."

The comment was met with silence. Howard looked around the room, checking faces, then gestured to Charlotte with his glass. "It's a fine thing for a woman to maintain some sensitivity," he insisted. "I am certain Charlotte will put it to good use."

Diane prodded the conversation along with a forced expression of interest. "Tell us the exciting news, Elizabeth."

"Well . . . ." Elizabeth collected her nerves, straightened her posture.

"I have a surprise for Charlotte. Howard has helped me arrange a trip for myself and Charlotte to the World's Fair in Paris."

The comment raised a few eyebrows. Charlotte, though quiet, was clearly taken aback by the news.

"To Paris?" she asked at last.

"The Paris Exposition?" James Asher scowled. "You had better keep a tight lip about that. The entire affair is an insult to Britain."

"A perceived affront is no excuse to miss the World's Fair," Howard replied. "Especially in an age like this."

"And to the church," James added as an afterthought. "Not that it matters much in these parts."

His brother, Maitland Asher, had been remarkably silent; but now he smiled with amusement. "Yes, it is a terrible insult to the Raj," he said, and chuckled. "And the two of you are going by yourselves?"

"With each other." Elizabeth smiled at Charlotte; and the young woman, recovering from the shock of the announcement, managed to smile back at her.

Night had plunged the hotel suite into darkness. The weak paraffin lamps seemed to give little power to the eye, and Charlotte could see her mother's gaze moving nervously round the bedroom, looking in vain for hidden predators. The bed sat in the center of the floor, enveloped by a canopy of fine netting, its four legs resting in bowls of shallow water. Through the small windows, Charlotte could see the low border that had been raised around the hotel verandah; and she knew that in the water-closet just down the hall, the drains had been covered for the night.

Diane had explained to them: *The beds cannot be pushed up against the walls because animals sometimes get into the buildings, and they hide behind the beds. The water is to drown the ants, and the netting is to keep the mosquitoes out. It really is unlikely that one would catch malaria—it happens rarely in the city—but the bites are irritating. Oh, yes, they cover the drains at night to prevent snakes from crawling up. It really is unlikely, but we must avoid any possibility. And take care if you step outside at night. The servants set up borders around the buildings to keep the snakes out. No, you must not leave that in the open—it makes too good a hiding place for scorpions.* And so on. Carpets couldn't be put on the floors, nor wallpaper put upon the walls. Wood floors were out of the question; the white ants would eat them. Meat had to be inspected carefully because it rotted easily in the tropical heat. A cholera outbreak had recently encroached on the neighborhood, and only days earlier a woman had succumbed to dysentery.

But these were, for Charlotte, not the most troubling specters. Just a few decades past, the settlements had been sacked by rebels. On Charlotte's first tour of the neighborhood she had noticed a number of memorials to the British victims: plaques on the old houses, monuments at places of slaughter. Howard had removed such a plaque from his own house upon purchasing it, claiming that it would make the house "haunted." Minnie and Blythe spoke of visiting the well at Cawnpore, where the hacked-up bodies of more than two hundred British women and children—some of them still alive—had been dumped. British soldiers discovered the remains, and in their outrage they looted and maimed the city. They forced a number of sepoy rebels to lick clean the bloodstained walls and floors at Bibigarh, whipping them, exposing them to various acts of physical and spiritual degradation before executing them. Violence spread like a plague; interconnected episodes of rage and revenge, of indiscriminate terrorizing and killing, were so many that Charlotte wondered how they had ever ceased. As the tales unfolded, gruesome scenes crept into her nightmares. She dreamed of broken bodies crawling the streets in weeping despondence, trying in vain to lap crusted bloodstains from cracks and crevices. India, once a vast and lovely land of ready adventures, had become a looming specter of poisonous stings, of disease and danger and sweltering discomfort, of undead phantoms that haunted in the night.

Elizabeth loathed it. Charlotte knew without asking, and her mother refrained from discussing it, perhaps because she felt doomed to stay.

"Perhaps we could rent rooms in London," Charlotte suggested softly. She stood behind her mother at the dressing table, removing pins from Elizabeth's hair. "We have enough money to last a few years. One of us will have made a marriage by then."

"I cannot marry again, Charlotte." Elizabeth's face became pained.

"No . . . I suppose it would fall on me to marry." Charlotte paused, thinking over potential suitors, a succession of uninteresting faces. "It really is a shame I wasn't born a boy. Then I would inherit, and Howard couldn't sell the estate from under us . . . and he *will* sell, regardless of whether we return to India. He has been generous enough in his welcome, but he is likely to leave us to the streets should we reject his hospitality."

"Charlotte . . . ."

"And then he can scorn us with the same contempt he expresses for the rest of the poor."

"Howard meant no harm. You know how the men behave when they discuss such things."

Charlotte met her mother's eyes in the mirror, but said nothing.

"It was good of him to help make our arrangements. Howard is fond of you. He wants to see you happy, just as I do."

"Yes, I know, and I appreciate his help," Charlotte replied. "It is a wonderful gift. But such a gift cannot excuse him."

"Howard is a good man."

"Being 'good' gives us no leave to behave like monsters when the opportunity arises."

Elizabeth's hair hung loose now. She sighed and rose from the table.

"I am more than tired of listening to the way people talk about a deranged killer as though he's no more than a drinking companion who got a little out of hand." Charlotte continued with mocking sarcasm: "'Oh, it's just Old Jack, it looks like he got carried away with the street rabble again, haha.' I was tempted to tell Howard that your sister was an 'unfortunate' who ended up—"

"Charlotte," Elizabeth whispered sharply. Her gaze flicked toward the doorway, as if in fear of eavesdroppers.

"Mamma, I would not have said it. I was merely tempted."

Elizabeth took her arm roughly. "You must never mention Emily to anyone. Ever. Understand?" Her voice was low and strong. In the grip of her fingers and the glittering of her eyes, Charlotte could read the intensity of an emotion—not quite akin to anger, but to something more fragile and desperate.

"Yes," Charlotte said quietly.

"Do you? Emily was my sister, Charlotte—my family. You never met her; it is *my* burden to bear, not yours, and I forbid you to use her in any of your self-righteous speeches."

"I know." Charlotte lowered her eyes, wincing. "I'm sorry, Mamma."

Elizabeth stared at her, then relaxed her grip and sighed. The fire receded from her gaze. "No, I am sorry. Howard was being an ass. And we must not bicker about the past. You and I . . . ."

Charlotte looked up at her, saw the woman's eyes becoming wet.

"You and I are on our own now," Elizabeth continued. "We need to support each other."

Charlotte nodded.

"We have much to be thankful for. Your father was a good man, and I had twenty felicitous years with him." She smiled, her eyes glistening with sudden happiness. "And two bright, stellar children. I am lucky to have one of them still with me. I don't wish to begin taking you for granted."

The women stood in silence. Charlotte found her focus drifting, receding into the past, easing out of the alien surroundings. She vividly felt the way her home had been with her father and brother inside of it— the comfort of their presence, the routine sounds of their existence. The house had since become stiflingly quiet. In the absence of half her beloved family, Charlotte discovered that silence made its own noise: a jaundiced sound, relative to what preceded it, buzzing in all the spaces of the house where heavy footsteps had fallen and baritones once sang. So many things about those two men she had depended upon, never guessing how suddenly they would be snatched from her.

Elizabeth shook herself out of her own reverie. "So . . . we are supposed—"

A sharp knock sounded at the door. Charlotte looked at her mother anxiously.

"That must be Nikhil, come to tell us goodnight," Elizabeth reminded her. Her hands rose quickly to her hair; she twisted it into a loose braid as Charlotte crossed the room.

Charlotte was struck silent by the pair of austere, penetrating eyes that awaited her on the other side of the door. Nikhil, the servant who'd been hired to attend to the women, gazed at her for only the briefest moment before addressing Elizabeth. "Good night, Memsahib. Do you need anything before I am asleep?"

"No, thank you, Nikhil," Elizabeth replied.

He nodded and vanished. Charlotte gently closed the door. "He has such an intense gaze," she told her mother quietly. "If I didn't know him, I would think him dangerous."

"We do not know him," Elizabeth replied.

"No . . . I suppose not." Charlotte was still staring at the door, remembering. "Nikhil's eyes are a different color than those of everyone else. They are . . . such a shade that they soak up an extraordinary amount of light. They blaze when the sun hits them."

"Is that so," Elizabeth said lightly.

"He always has such a hard look in them. It is a shame—"

"Come, dear. Let us plan our trip." Elizabeth pushed aside the netting and sat on the bed, beckoning for Charlotte to sit with her. "Which places should we visit in Delhi?"

"I would like to see the emperors' mausoleums, and the gardens. Could we not return to Agra, to see the Taj Mahal?"

"Howard advised against it. I imagine it is less worth seeing than the Delhi mausoleums. At least those places haven't been sacked."

Charlotte paused contemplatively. She sat with her chin resting in one hand, looking at nothing in particular, while Elizabeth gazed on her with renewed admiration. Charlotte had been graced with the same large brown eyes and long lashes as her father, and in those eyes shone the same quiet, earnest thoughtfulness that had drawn Elizabeth to the man—the trait that had first fixed her attentions on him. That his daughter expressed that same lovely quality, that a piece of him lived on so beautifully in her manners, was a blessing.

Charlotte, noticing her mother's inspection, looked up at her inquisitively.

Elizabeth put an arm around her. "We are going to have such fun," she said, squeezing her in a gentle hug.

"Are we? I know that you hate it here, Mamma."

"Delhi is not all bad. It chases other thoughts from my mind." She paused, watching her daughter with melancholy tenderness. "You and I have had a difficult year. We deserve an adventure—something to clear our heads. Then we can return home refreshed, and decide how to manage our affairs from here on. Agreed?"

"Agreed."

"Good. Let's go to bed."

Charlotte stood and began to exit into the hall. Her own bed was in the adjacent room, and she would have to perform her own nightly check to ensure that the bedroom was critter-free; but she hesitated at the door, looking back at her mother. "Mamma?"

"Yes?"

"I love you."

The words stirred tender bliss and shearing agony, feelings that clashed deep in Elizabeth's being. She recognized both love and fear behind those words.

Unable to speak, she smiled and nodded. Charlotte left the room quietly.

4

NEW YORK: MARCH 15, 1889

"Congratulations, my dear." Paul's mother locked Katharine in a delicate embrace, instinctively taking care not to crush her wedding gown. "You're like a daughter to us now." She released Katharine and stood close. "If you ever need another woman to talk to . . . ."

Katharine smiled, a bit sadly. "Thank you."

Evelyn moved across the parlor, approaching her son. "And congratulations to you, too." She gave Paul a brief hug. "It's been good to see you happy."

Paul lowered his eyes.

"How long before you leave for Paris?"

"May twelve—after the fair starts," he said. "I wanted to take her to the opening, but the hotels were all booked up."

"That should give her plenty of time to settle in." Evelyn paused; her voice lowered a notch. "Are you sure you want to stay at the house?"

"We're sure," Paul replied. "It works better if we stay. Mrs. Adelaide can keep her job, Katharine won't be left alone when I'm gone, the Levinski boys can have their work, I get to see all my same patients . . . anyway, I love that house. We both do."

"I wish that you would let us publish a wedding announcement. Even if it's—"

"Neither of us wants an announcement."

"Oh, really, Paul. I can't imagine how it could be such a big deal."

"I'm glad you feel that way," he replied lightly. "If it isn't a big deal, let's drop it." Paul wrapped an arm around his mother in a friendly embrace.

Evelyn sighed. "Never mind, then. We'll have to keep our happiness to ourselves."

They looked across the room at Katharine, who was talking quietly with her cousin Helen. Paul couldn't resist smiling at the sight of Katharine in her gown. He had been present while Katharine debated with her aunt and cousin about the dress she should wear; she had chosen a dark blue gown, absent of frills and intricacies, but the other women were offended by its plainness. They had talked her into adding lace around the off-shoulder neckline and at the edge of each sleeve, and now Katharine was fumbling absently with the lace, as if still resisting the idea of it. She had confessed to Paul that the material was harsh against her skin and that she couldn't wait to take it off.

He'd replied that he couldn't wait either. He expected a flush of nervous anticipation from her, but she only smiled back at him.

"She's a good woman," Evelyn said. "You've done well for yourself."

"I got lucky."

"Does she want children?"

He shrugged. "Maybe. It's not definite. I don't particularly care about that part, but I figure I'll have fun finding out."

"Paul."

"What?"

"You're too much like your father."

"I don't want to know the details."

"Be a gentleman." She patted his arm and walked away.

Opposite them, Helen was leaning closer to Katharine, murmuring in a low voice. "Does Paul want to try for children right away?" Without hesitating, she added slyly: "I get the sense he won't wait."

"Oh, you got that sense, too, did you?"

Helen chuckled. "Never mind that. I think he'll be a good husband."

"I think so too. I hope I can be as good a wife."

"You will be. You have an advantage to begin with. Anyone can see that he loves you."

Katharine studied Paul, watching his mannerisms closely. "Why do you suppose that is?" she asked quietly. "I don't think I ever made myself out to be very amiable—not in the beginning. I don't have connections, and he doesn't know that I have money . . . ."

"Yes, he does. Father told him about your inheritance."

"Did he? Are you certain?"

"Yes. He was trying to sell you off—" Helen cut herself off abruptly. "I'm sorry, I didn't mean it like that—but you know how Father is."

"I do." Katharine paused. "Paul never mentioned it."

Helen looked up at her, speaking with uncharacteristic caution. "You don't see your own good qualities. I hope you don't think that Paul is after your money."

Katharine's gaze was still fixed on her husband. "No, I trust him," she replied softly.

"Good. Mother and I are excited for you. And we both envy you going to Paris, even if you have to meet with someone you dislike."

"I don't dislike Nathan. I just . . . ." Katharine spoke hesitantly. "I'm aware that he has a poor opinion of me."

"He doesn't know you well enough to form an opinion, does he?"

"No. He lived near me in Troy, but he's at least ten years older than I am. We rarely moved in the same circles."

"Then what does it matter?" Helen looked at Katharine searchingly, but received no answer. "How does he know Paul? He's a doctor?"

"They graduated from Bellevue together."

"If Paul likes him, he must not be so bad."

"No, he isn't 'bad'," Katharine agreed quietly.

Paul was approaching now; he put an arm around Katharine, pulling her close. "How are you holding up? Are you panicking yet?"

"You know I'm not. What about you?"

"Only because I know I don't deserve you."

"You don't have to flatter me like that anymore, you already have me."

"Really. You shouldn't persuade me to take you for granted so quickly."

Paul's stepfather uncorked a champagne bottle, carefully filling glasses as he addressed the small gathering. "Let's have a toast. Come and grab a glass. It's not the best, but we got it on short notice."

"It's all right, there's still going to be the reception when they come back from Paris," Evelyn reminded him. "We'll have everything in order then."

Paul accepted a glass from his stepfather, who addressed him lightly: "Just make sure you come back in time. I understand the Exposition is on 'til late October, and there's enough distraction to keep you there for the full six months."

Paul's half-brother, George Jr.—a tall, thin man who looked the spitting image of his father—agreed. "It's Paris. They might do like Nathan and never come back."

"Ah, it can't be as charming now, with that eyesore in the middle of it."

"The tower?" Paul asked.

"I hear it's hideous," George Sr. replied.

"We'll let you know."

"My bet is they'll take it back down before the year is up."

"Well I think it all sounds fantastic," Evelyn said. "What a great time to be newlyweds, and to have the opportunity to go to Paris."

"We're mostly excited to see the miniature cities—the reconstructions of places we'll probably never get to go to," Paul said. "Katharine wants to see Cairo Street in particular."

Katharine, still discreetly tugging at her gown, lowered her hands before speaking. "I want to see all of it—the music and dancing, and the theatre, and the artwork and crafts that we don't get to see here."

"And we'll look at the inventions, but there are so many new machines popping up everywhere that it's getting overbearing."

"Be grateful for it," George Jr. said. "We're living in a real golden age."

"We'll see. Let's have a couple of toasts . . . ." Paul raised his glass and pulled Katharine close beside him with his free hand. "To my lovely wife Katharine, and our future together."

As the guests raised their glasses to the couple, he added: "And to *Le Exposition Universelle*!"

5

DELHI

Charlotte's excitement about Paris dissipated as she eased into an affection for India. The climate, though uncomfortably hot, complemented her usually sensitive skin, and the air seemed especially easy on her lungs—and all around her were new marvels that never ceased to pique her curiosity. At Charlotte's insistence, Nikhil took the two women on a brief excursion around Chandni Chowk, the famous "moonlit market" that stretched westward from the massive Red Fort on the banks of the Yamuna River. They began at the Digambar Jain temple, where Elizabeth held back with half-hearted protests of "Surely we're not welcome here;" but they were welcomed after removing their shoes, and Elizabeth's concern about the fate of those shoes was quickly forgotten. The temple's vast interiors were stunningly ornate, eliciting astonished silence from the women. They moved quietly from room to room, where people prayed before lit candles and altars; each shrine bore such intricacy and profusion of rich colors, glittering from floor to ceiling, that Charlotte never knew where to rest her eye.

The peaceful effect was shattered upon stepping outside. The market's narrow lanes were increasingly pressed with throngs of people. Charlotte caught a brief glimpse of intricately decorated booths stuffed with lovely hangings, cloths, jewelry, shoes, and garments of all colors—and farther on, dolls and masks and statues, and more types of dishes and musical instruments than could be counted. As she gazed on her surroundings, a small cloud drifted before the sun, momentarily subduing the colors and bringing out a somber richness in the blues and purples; and then the light was again cast full on the market, overwhelming the eye with the mad glittering of silvers and golds.

But Nikhil ushered the women away from the crowds, back toward the tanga and the hotel, while Charlotte protested heartily.

"You do not need to be at the market," he said, waving her onward. Nikhil followed a few steps behind the women, and Charlotte walked with her head turned around, pleading with him while Elizabeth gently pulled her onward.

"Perhaps not, but I *choose* to go," Charlotte argued. "It isn't for you to decide."

"I have a gift from the market. If you want anything more, I will go for you."

"Come, Charlotte," Elizabeth coaxed her. "Another day, perhaps. We have not enough time today."

Before they reached the tanga, Charlotte insisted on stopping at the fifteenth-century Jama Masjid. The trio ascended the north-side steps which cascaded from the mosque like a massive angular waterfall, with Elizabeth once again lagging behind uncertainly. "You don't mean to go inside, do you?" she said anxiously. "Really, we don't belong." As an afterthought, she added: "People are praying."

Charlotte stopped and turned to Nikhil. "It's lovely enough outside. May we sit for a while?"

Scattered on the mosque's lower steps were a few vendors with piles of fruit and fried vegetables. Two men played a melancholy raga on sitar and sarangi. Charlotte sat beside her mother, and they gazed out at the Red Fort, a residence of Shahanshah Shah Jahan—the same Mughal emperor who had commissioned the Taj Mahal in honor of his beloved wife. The Fort's reddish sandstone hues glowed vibrantly in the afternoon sunlight. Nikhil had explained that during the Mutiny, the Fort was occupied by the last Mughal emperor, Bahadur Shah Zafar. The emperor had surrendered to the British general William Hodson at Humayan's Tomb—one of the mausoleums Charlotte was so eager to lay eyes upon—and was subsequently exiled. Two of his sons and a grandson, leaders of the rebellion at Delhi, also surrendered. Hodson transported them to one of the southern gates of the walled city, personally executed them, and put their corpses on display. Rumor had it that after some time the bodies were decapitated, and the heads sent to the grieving emperor.

Despite his infamy as an enemy of the British, Bahadur Shah Zafar retained a reputation as a gentle man; he had, after all, been regarded gentle enough to pose no significant threat to British endeavors. Charlotte came away from Chandni Chowk with a single souvenir: a small book of Urdu poetry, written by Delhi's last emperor. Nikhil had taken an earlier trip to the market to purchase it for her.

Charlotte discreetly studied Nikhil's profile from beneath the brim of her sun hat. He sat close enough that she could see the slight dimple in his chin and the tiny moles scattered across his face, now etched neatly in her memory. He was young, probably not yet thirty, but his demeanor had a sternness about it that made him seem decades older. For weeks he'd looked after Charlotte and Elizabeth with surprising thoroughness. He was unfailingly committed to their welfare, yet his demeanor always seemed unattached, and he often sat gazing into the distance as if immersed in his own thoughts. At such times Charlotte would stare at his eyes, trying to figure out what made them so startlingly lovely. His eyebrows arched and thickened toward the center, giving him a look of perpetual seriousness, and his retinas were wide pools of dark amber that blazed deeply in direct light. Charlotte despaired at the thought of forgetting his eyes, and had made several attempts at sketching them in her journal. She had stared at Nikhil's face for such long periods that he had finally demanded to know what she was looking at, and she sheepishly explained that she was trying to draw him. He'd peered at her latest attempt, then flashed a puzzled look at her and said: *You are sitting and working all this time, only to make two eyes? You are very slow. I feel that you should be practicing a different skill.*

Now, Nikhil abruptly turned toward her. The evening sun flamed in his eyes, and Charlotte saw the eyelids curve closer to the retinas as he looked on her with something like suspicion. Her fingers fumbled with the pages of her book.

Nikhil nodded at her. "How is your reading?"

"I confess I do not read very well." Charlotte examined a page uncertainly. "I do know the language a little, although—" She hesitated, chanced another look at him. "I suppose you read Devanagari."

"Yes, and Urdu also."

"Do you? Then perhaps you could help me . . . ."

He settled beside her and studied a page. "There—read there," he said, pointing.

For some time they worked together, with Charlotte translating what she could and Nikhil correcting her, but the emperor's poems imparted such stark despair that Charlotte could hardly bear to read them. He grieved over his murdered family and shattered livelihood, mourned the pervasive emptiness of his being. Charlotte became increasingly quiet as Nikhil gave a voice to the heartbroken and dispirited man, while the sorrowful duet of the sitar and sarangi added power to emotion. *Not the light of anyone's eye am I, not the solace of anyone's heart am I; of no use to anyone, a mere clump of dust am I. I am not the song that gives life; no one would wish to hear me. I am the cry of separation; I am the cry of great sorrow. . . .*

Nikhil's voice was impassive as he delivered the poem's final lines. He spoke slowly, moving his finger along the print. "That which is ruined, I am that fate. That which is destroyed, I am that place. *Pae*

Faatihaa koi aae kyuun? Koi chaar phuul charhate kyuun? Koi aake shamaa jalaa kyuun? Main vo bekasi kaa mazaar huun." He looked expectantly at Charlotte, but she shook her head.

"Will you just translate it?" Her voice trembled.

"Why should anyone come to say the *Fatiha* prayer? Why should the offering of four flowers be made? Why should anyone light candles? I am that deposed one's tomb."

Charlotte pretended to study the writing, but her eyes burned with tears. "I think that is enough for now."

Nikhil saw her tears and chuckled. "You are weeping for old Zafar?"

She looked up at him curiously, let herself become immersed in his amber eyes as she searched for some sentiment. "I know what it is to lose my family," she said at last. "I suppose I am lucky only to have suffered that much."

Nikhil's smile vanished.

Elizabeth stirred herself and cleared her throat. "We should return to the hotel. We have preparations to make before dinner."

"Yes, Memsahib."

As Charlotte retreated through the streets, Zafar's sorrowful tone continued to move within her. And it came upon her again: the surreal, jolting knowledge that she was a colonist. It was a realization that appeared in panic-ridden flashes, sweeping over her just as quickly as she was inclined to forget it. Her own people had caused the misery of Zafar and countless others like him; they had ravaged, murdered, plundered, stayed on through violent rebellions, aroused the most intense suffering. Charlotte's brother had always meant to take her to India, and she had reacted with nothing but the anticipation of adventure. But thinking of India and being in it were very different things. Her arrival had filled her with anxiety and dread, for she suddenly had to acknowledge that it was aggression and greed that made it possible for her to stand here; it was bloody opportunism that cut a gash through Egypt and created the Suez Canal, that colonized India and drove out its leaders beneath a pretense of superiority. Everyone here knew it. And yet Charlotte moved easily among these people, admiring their crafts and eyeing the women in beautiful, bold saris—and not one had looked back at her as though she was borne of monsters. Such a thing could change at any time, of that she was certain; rage and violence set upon human beings in often unpredictable waves. But Charlotte had endured the city's fortune and was grateful for it.

Her anxiety dissipated by the time she reached the hotel, replaced once again by an excited yearning. The hotel was a quaint dwelling near the western bank of the Yamuna River, set amidst a landscape of gardens

and ponds, with high ceilings and touches of the Mughal style that
Charlotte found so exquisite. Charlotte had yet to see any of the local
mausoleums, and the architecture of the hotel invigorated her desire to
explore.

"You must take us to the market again tomorrow," she begged Nikhil
as they approached the room. "We have hardly seen it—and we must
choose a day to tour the mausoleums."

"You will have tea with Mrs. Brook tomorrow."

"But we have already sat with her twice this week," she protested.
"Surely she doesn't expect us every day."

"You must go, Miss Charlotte. If you will be returning to Delhi, you
must satisfy the memsahibs."

"But I—"

Nikhil raised his eyebrows severely, and she fell silent.

"Come, dear." Elizabeth unlocked the door with some difficulty.
"Perhaps we can tour the market day after tomorrow."

"Perhaps, but we will surely receive more invitations. Could you not
decline them?"

"And what shall we say; what reason should we give? Should we say
that you want to run loose in the market rather than behave like a proper
English lady?"

"That is unfair. We are in India, not England; and if we must be
confined to one painfully dull neighborhood, then I should never be
happy living here. I would much rather tour as I please, and offend the
neighbors, than subject myself to such imprisonment. The temples and
mausoleums are a thousand times more interesting than all of Mrs.
Brook's boasting about her furniture and fine things, or the same old
dances and gossip at the neighborhood balls. Minnie will be married this
Saturday, and then we shall have her old bedroom to stay in—and once
we settle there, we shall never be allowed to leave." Charlotte followed
her mother into the room, pausing to glance at Nikhil. "And worse, we
shall lose Nikhil."

"We will see the market day after tomorrow," Elizabeth promised. "If
anyone—good God!" Her eyes went wide with sudden alarm. She
pointed to a weathered cane chair near the window. "Nikhil, look there!
Is it a snake?"

Nikhil stepped inside and followed her gaze. He made an attempt at
remaining expressionless, but Charlotte saw a rare glint of amusement in
his eyes. He moved to the chair, where a thin, motionless form
meandered out from behind a front leg.

"Well?" Elizabeth asked.

He picked up the object, letting it hang limply in his hand as he carried it to Elizabeth. "It is a stocking, Memsahib."

"Oh, for . . . ." She snatched the stocking from him.

He allowed himself a tiny smile. "I will wait in servants' quarters, Memsahib."

"Yes, thank you, Nikhil."

The women readied themselves for another evening in the British quarter, and at length Nikhil returned and announced that the driver was ready with the tanga. Charlotte and Elizabeth rode a few miles to Mr. and Mrs. Eastlaw's modest bungalow; they saw at once that it was nearly identical to Howard's, but with larger, more colorful gardens surrounding the house.

Mrs. Eastlaw welcomed them warmly. She announced that dinner wasn't quite ready, and used the opportunity to give her new guests a tour of the grounds. Other guests arrived: Diane and Blythe, Mrs. Brook and Mrs. Tipton. They joined the tour and offered the obligatory compliments. It was difficult, Charlotte had observed, for the *memsahibs* to impress one another with their homesteads; each had the same whitewashed walls and matted floors, the same Indian furniture covered with English linens. At dinner, she found herself faced with the same fowl and vegetables she'd become accustomed to seeing at every table. But each home had its token signature. Mrs. Brook had her few pieces of English furniture; Mrs. Tipton had her fine dishes; Mrs. Eastlaw, her lush gardens. There was something about the limited manner in which the women spoke that disturbed Charlotte. She'd said as much to her mother: *You must have noticed it in my aunt and cousins, at least. I'm starting to dread living here; there's something about colonial life in India that turns Englishmen into caricatures of themselves.*

"Elizabeth, you must take tea with me tomorrow," Mrs. Tipton proclaimed over dinner. "It offends practicality, to have such a fine tea set so rarely used."

Charlotte cast a wary glance at her mother.

"We have promised to take tea with Mrs. Brook tomorrow," Elizabeth replied.

"Indeed. And the day after?"

Elizabeth hesitated.

"We plan to tour the Chandni Chowk market day after tomorrow," Charlotte replied hastily. "We have been meaning to go for some time."

"What—you mean to go yourselves?" Diane asked. "Surely it would be better to send your servant."

"I think I would greatly regret leaving India without seeing it. I hope to come away with a poetry collection; I understand there are many talented poets who write in Urdu. And I would like to taste the food, and perhaps buy some sari silk."

"Sari silk?" Mrs. Eastlaw looked aghast. "For what? Surely you would never wear it."

"No . . . I suppose not."

"The sari silks *are* lovely, though," Blythe said. "If you are determined to have one, you can easily buy it at the fair in Paris. And you really must not eat from the bazaar. The food, surely, is unclean, and might cause all manner of illness. The natives are accustomed to it, but I am certain it would do you harm."

"And surely you don't read Urdu," Mr. Eastlaw added.

"I do. I studied it with my brother."

"Really. How unusual. None of the women here can read Urdu—nor most of the men, excepting those of higher rank."

"There was a woman who could read Urdu," Mrs. Tipton said. "Mrs. . . . what was her name?"

Mrs. Eastlaw shook her head, quickly swallowing a bite of chicken. "We never speak of that one."

Charlotte looked curiously from face to face: Mr. Eastlaw with his thick mustache and prominent eyes, Mrs. Eastlaw with her paper-like skin, Mrs. Tipton with her high cheekbones and sleek nose. "Why not?"

"She turned out badly," Mrs. Eastlaw replied. "She had trouble adapting to life in India."

"She was unfaithful to her husband." Mrs. Tipton said the words quietly, as if to prevent the servants from hearing. "Wanted to run off with an Indian."

Mrs. Eastlaw, too, lowered her voice. "It was only suspected. Her husband disapproved of her behavior—thought it rather wild. She was always running off with this servant or that, to all kinds of places, and without his approval. He had her charged as a deviant and shipped back home. He moved on to Lahore, and we have heard nothing of him since."

Elizabeth stared at her in consternation. "Charged as a deviant?"

Mr. Eastlaw clarified: "A lunatic. Not right in the head. Dr. Asher wrote up the diagnosis, and the husband hired an escort to return her to London—to Bedlam Asylum, though I doubt she stayed long. Her family likely secured her release."

Elizabeth turned to Diane. "The same Dr. Asher to whom Minnie is engaged?"

"Yes, the same."

"It was a nightmarish journey for her, I imagine," Mr. Eastlaw continued. "They had to sedate her to get her onto the ship. We can only imagine what transpired afterward."

"How horrible," Charlotte said in amazement. "All that, because she wanted to tour India?"

"You must take it as a warning, my dear. If you mean to stay in India, and want to see so much of it, take care that you marry a man who wishes to do the same."

Dinner was followed by recreation. The older women went to sit under a garden canopy, while Blythe and Charlotte practiced archery in the rear yard. The compound wall had several targets affixed, and Blythe had hardly drawn the bow when a booming voice sounded behind her: "GOOD EVENING!"

Maitland Asher had joined the party under the canopy. He took a minute to greet the other women before advancing on Blythe and Charlotte.

Blythe was all smiles at the appearance of her secret intended. As he stood beside her, Charlotte couldn't help noting how mismatched they seemed: burly, red-faced Maitland and dainty Blythe. It seemed that the two could more easily pass as father and daughter than as a courting couple. Asher made himself all the more imposing with a loud, boisterous commentary on Blythe's performance—a gesture that Charlotte found rude, though he meant it as a compliment. Blythe released a couple of wayward shots before giving Charlotte the bow. "I can never aim properly," she said with a small laugh. "You take it, Charlotte."

Charlotte drew the bow taut and fixed her eyes on a target. Moments later the arrow struck near the target's center. She set the bow up again.

Asher stood close by, stopping her with a gesture. "You have excellent form," he said, "but you might improve your aim with a few small adjustments. If you would lower your elbow just so—may I?" He gently guided her arm into position. "Just there . . . now let go."

Charlotte hesitated, letting her focus adjust to a fine point, until she saw nothing but the center of the target. She aimed and released her grip, standing statue-like as the arrow sped through the air.

"Bulls-eye!" Mr. Asher cried. "Well done, my girl. Very well done."

Blythe looked on with substantially less enthusiasm. "Very good, Charlotte," she said. She raised the back of her hand to her forehead. "It *is* intolerably hot. I wonder how you can focus."

"Take another shot," Maitland insisted, but Charlotte handed him the bow.

"The heat is rather overbearing," she replied. "I think I shall sit in the shade."

She left Blythe and Asher for the shade of a large Kadamba tree. Charlotte settled herself near its trunk and picked up the book she'd left there, but she abruptly dropped it. "Damn," she said, standing.

Mr. Asher perked up. "Is something the matter?"

She stared in consternation at the Zafar text. "The white ants are eating my book!"

Blythe let out a peal of laughter. "Serves you right for leaving it on the ground."

Asher approached. "Allow me," he said again. He picked up the book and slapped it a few times against the tree, then flicked the remaining insects from it. "There. Not too damaged, I think." He studied the binding, flipped through pages, and raised his eyes to Charlotte. "You can read Urdu?"

"A little. Our . . . our friend, Nikhil, is helping me translate it."

"Your servant, you mean," Blythe said as she drew near. She flashed a smile at Asher. "Charlotte is striving to achieve familiarity with the natives."

"And well she should, if she studies the language. What other books are you reading?"

"Just this, for the moment—but I would love to read more Urdu poetry," Charlotte replied. "I have studied Hindustani these four years past. I wanted to ask Nikhil—"

"Really, you want to know India that badly?"

"Charlotte studies all things native," Blythe answered. "She is determined to have India figured out by the end of the month."

Asher kept his eyes on Charlotte. His questioning expression never changed.

"My elder brother studied to be a missionary in India," Charlotte said evenly, "and he wished me to come along. I never developed a love for the church, but I took to the language."

"That is very practical on your part. Missionaries, particularly women missionaries, are unappreciated in India—by Indians and most certainly by the British."

"Why?"

"The British are preoccupied with loyalty to the Raj, and Hindus don't understand the concept of women missionaries. Pardon my being frank: their own temple women are prostitutes."

Charlotte blushed.

"A great many have developed a legitimate distrust of the church. The masses are hungry, and the missionaries say 'You need Christ more than you need earthly food.' If a person is starved close to death, the church says 'Do not despair; you are going to meet Christ.' Indians are in want of food and justice, but the church will only give Bibles, saying 'Your real justice is here.' What little food they do provide is given to converts, and only as a daily charity. What India really needs is a stronger, more intelligent, more engaged Raj. You shall fare better knowing some of the language. For that matter, our society would be enriched by women inclined to study."

Blythe looked genuinely surprised. "A singular opinion. How could such a woman run a proper household?"

"Rather efficiently, I would think. She would have to run it well if she wanted any freedom from it. The Raj is populated with women who consume themselves with household and society duties; they stay in their tiny encampment and scorn anything outside of it, and become feeble in their confinement. The more adventurous women keep their vibrancy. For my part, I could never marry a woman who hates India."

Blythe's eyes seemed to glaze over. Her look of surprise became flat and cold. She was quiet for a moment, and then murmured: "How fortunate for Charlotte" before heading back to the gardens.

Charlotte watched her cousin's departure with dread. Blythe's back seemed unnaturally stiff, her steps hard and stilted.

The day's heat finally made its way into Charlotte's body, forming drops of sweat beneath her clothes. She stammered: "I am—I am not interested in 'all things native,' sir. I only learned the language to follow my brother, and now I am only here on account of my uncle's hospitality."

"Yes, and now you think you've slighted it, I see." Asher, too, was watching Blythe's departure. "The women in these parts are impractically sensitive. You needn't pay any mind to her."

"I think it would be best if I joined the others, sir."

"Certainly. Please, allow me to accompany you." He paced himself beside her as she started away. "Have you read Mirza Ghalib?"

"No, sir."

"I would very much like to bring you my own collection of his poems. You will soon be staying at your uncle's house, I understand."

"Yes, we shall have Minnie's room."

"I will come and call on you. And you must allow me to give you a tour of the mausoleums. Your cousins will never take you, nor allow a man-servant to escort you."

"I am unsure of our plans," Charlotte replied hesitantly. She was painfully aware of the volume of Asher's voice, which had certainly reached the guests ahead. Beneath the canopy, they were turning in Charlotte's direction—Blythe with a stony expression, Diane with a look of suspicious disapproval, her mother with a line of concern on her brow, Mr. Eastlaw with an amused smile. "My aunt will be busy with preparations. They are moving house to the Himalayas for the summer."

"Of course," Asher replied briskly. "I would be delighted to help you stay out of their way. I have invited your aunt and cousins time and time again to accompany me to the Mughal sites, but they consistently refuse. If you and your mother would do me the honor, it would please me immensely."

"Perhaps, but as I said, I am unsure of our plans."

"Of course," he repeated. "I shall stop by early next week for an answer."

Charlotte felt her heart sinking.

6

Saturday, May 11: The departures in my life seem strangely abrupt. We have endured the train ride back to Bombay and settled into life on the steamship, and already I find it difficult to maintain a vivid memory of India. For days I watched its landscapes pass by, like a miniature life flashing before my eyes, and now the whole continent seems to fade behind the Indian Ocean and all that lies ahead: the Red Sea and Suez Canal, the Mediterranean, France and the World's Fair, and finally, Home.

I stopped writing in my journal after discovering that Blythe had been reading it—she caused quite a scandal by reporting to all the neighbors that I was drawing pictures of "Indian men" on the pages. I earned her wrath by unintentionally stealing the interest of Mr. Maitland Asher, an unmarried gentleman of the Indian Civil Service. The family wanted him for Blythe, though she does not particularly like him. Needless to say, the family was displeased with me, and the neighbors followed in suit. Mr. Asher sensationalized the gossip by delivering me a book of rather peculiar Urdu love poems. The servants saw it and reported its contents to Aunt Diane. It seems certain now that Mamma and I will not return to India.

For my part, I found Mr. Asher quite displeasing and did what I could to avoid him. Lovely Nikhil helped by taking me and Mamma on tours of the markets and mausoleums, so that Mr. Asher had no opportunity to do so. Mamma paid Nikhil for his time, of course, but on our last day in Delhi he came as a friend to see us off at the station. Diane set him to work with our luggage, and then demanded that he be paid. When he declined, she insisted on paying him herself, saying something to this effect: "Who hires a servant and then refuses to pay him? No Indian will want to work for us when they hear of it." Of course, this was merely a maneuver to put Nikhil back in his place. Blythe was also rude and childish. After boarding the train, we stood at an open window and heard her exclaim "Wait until Mr. Asher hears that Charlotte has passed him up

for a Negro!" Nikhil was well within hearing range, but of course he did
not react. I was irritated with Blythe's antics, but Mamma put her hands
on my shoulders and said "Don't mind her." Then she waved at Nikhil
and smiled, and turned away without waving to the women—and I did
the same. I was rather proud of Mamma then.

I had planned courteous ways in which to part company with our
relatives, but found it most difficult to say goodbye to Nikhil. Mamma
thanked him for looking after us so well. I surprised myself by thanking
him for being like a brother to me. I had not realized until then how
isolated I have felt, or how he, to some extent, soothed the loss of my
brother's companionship. It was a rather painful thing, of course, because
although I had that feeling for a short while, I am ultimately left with a
sense of loss, as I shall never see Nikhil again.

"You are writing?" a voice asked.

Charlotte looked up to see a young Chinese woman standing before
her on the promenade. "Oh, yes—I was writing about our journey." She
patted the seat beside her. "Would you like to sit?"

She had befriended Lai Ping earlier, in the game parlor, where she'd
been spending time of late. Charlotte had long since tired of translating
Zafar's bleak couplets and Ghalib's cynical love poems, and had made
several shy attempts at breaking into the little communities that had
formed on the ship. Lai Ping was her own age, and Charlotte had found
her approachable and sweet-tempered. The two young women basked in
the fresh ocean wind and bursts of evening sunlight as they resumed their
conversation, moving from the subject of their homelands to their recent
travels.

Charlotte enunciated carefully, still unsure of Lai Ping's
understanding of English. "We spent some time walking through the
Victoria Terminus."

"Yes, Victoria Terminus, it was made finished last year. Did you like
it?"

Charlotte shrugged. "Well, it is . . . elegant, but I didn't come to India
to see British buildings. I preferred the places at Chandni Chowk, in
Delhi—and the mausoleums just to the south of it, along the river. Did
you visit any mausoleums?"

"Mmm . . . yes, we went—I think it is said Qutb Minar, you know
this place? A big tower?" Lai Ping gestured with her hands, raising one
palm high above the other to indicate height.

"No."

"The most tall, tallest, brick tower of the world?"

"I have not heard of it. When we arrive in France, we shall see the
world's tallest metal tower—the Eiffel."

Lai Ping grinned. "It is strange . . . people pay a lot of money to build the tallest towers; and people travel the sea and the railroad, and pay money, to see the tallest towers."

Charlotte laughed. "I suppose you are right. People are strange."

Elizabeth greeted them, pausing next to their perch and nodding to Charlotte. "Dinner will be served very soon, dear."

Charlotte stood and smiled at Lai Ping. "I shall see you again soon."

"Yes, goodbye."

As they retreated, Elizabeth lowered her voice. "Who was that?"

"Her name is Lai Ping. She lives in Lijiang in China, and she is traveling with her family. Her father is a tradesman."

"What kind?"

"She neglected to say."

"Opium dealer," Elizabeth muttered.

Charlotte rolled her eyes. "You mustn't presume such things, Mamma."

"She speaks English?"

"Yes, rather well. She said that China is filling up with Christian missionaries who teach English and Bible classes. Lai Ping has invited us to join her family for dinner tomorrow. What do you say?"

"I suppose you would love to."

"I would."

7

MONDAY, MAY 20, 1889

For Katharine, the arrival in France was all but refreshing. She'd been awash in sea sickness and was still unsteady on her legs, though relieved to be on stable ground. The eight-day journey across the Atlantic had been placid enough at first. It was on the third day that the steamship's passengers were introduced to the stormier moods of the sea. Merciless gales rocked the ship so violently that the kitchen stopped serving meals. Katharine, who had been queasy throughout the journey, didn't mind fasting; it means less to vomit. At night, Paul moved the mattress onto the floor to prevent being tossed out of bed. Katharine sat at the edge and clutched a small bowl, often aiming poorly as she retched and dry-heaved.

The newlyweds stayed a quiet night in Le Havre before catching the train to Paris. Katharine spent the morning convalescing, and then, dreading the captivity of the moving train, she took an hour beforehand to wander the port town with her husband, anticipating some pleasure in the hard immobility of the streets. She found instead that ocean sprays made the roads perpetually muddy. Discarded trash became lodged in the soft ground and was systematically picked over by birds and rodents, while the day's weather cast an aura of gloom over the cargo-cluttered port. At last, with mud-caked shoes, the Gardiners rode the railways to the Pont-Cardinet station in the seventeenth arrondissement of Paris.

In the late afternoon, not knowing their way around the city, they hired a fiacre for the final leg of the journey. Katharine arrived at the Hotel Clément exhausted and encumbered by headache, and grimy, and foul-breathed, and hungry; she'd vomited most of what she'd eaten that day.

Katharine was momentarily relieved of her headache when she stepped into the hotel. The lobby was vast, with high vaulted ceilings and ornate columns, tall windows elegantly draped, marble floors, and expansive white walls with gold-tinted molding that housed glowing electric lights. A statue of a woman—or perhaps of some forest nymph—stood with gilded leaves arranged about her hips, gesturing to a broad white staircase lined with twining black and gold railings. A few of the moldings hosted large paintings; a heavily bearded gentleman in a top hat stood before a portrait of Jacques-Louis David, giving a biography of the French painter and reformer to a young English couple.

The reception desk was opposite the doors, puny in contrast to the pillared expanse that could easily have passed for a lavish ballroom. Katharine stood gazing while Paul checked them in.

"Just a moment," the clerk said, and waved to the man at the David portrait.

The man, stout and distinguished, was introduced to them as Mr. Arnaud, the hotel's manager. He shook Paul's hand cordially. "Yes, Mr. Gardiner." He spoke slowly, as if to compensate for his heavy accent in the ears of foreigners. "Dr. Neville wished, to pass a message to you. He is not here, at present; he will call on you, when he returns. In the meantime, you will find our restaurant, here, on the first floor . . . ." He commenced a brief explanation of the hotel's amenities. Katharine's attention perked up when he mentioned the bath rental; she immediately put herself on a waiting list for a tub.

Arnaud rang for the porter. "If you need directions, or other assistance, feel free to inquire at the desk. Our boy will help with your luggage." He pulled a novel-sized book from under the desk and handed it to Paul. "And this belongs to you, compliments of Dr. Neville—a complete guide to the Exposition."

"Ah, how thoughtful. Thank you."

As they ascended the stairs behind the porter, Paul leaned toward Katharine and spoke in a hushed voice. "The awkward greeting is postponed. You'll have to brace yourself for Nathan tomorrow."

"Can I see the guidebook?"

"Good luck. It's almost three hundred pages of French. October will have come and gone by the time you finish trying to decipher it."

They situated themselves in a room on the third floor—one of the smaller rooms, Nathan had warned them, but elegant nonetheless. Paul relaxed on the plush golden bedspread while Katharine tried to freshen up. She went to relieve herself in the water-closet down the hall, then returned to the room and made do with a pitcher and sponge, trying to scrub away the lingering stench of sweat and vomit. At length she dressed herself and stretched out beside Paul.

"Can I lie next to you? I smell much better now, I swear it." She propped herself up on her elbows, lazily paging through the Exposition guide.

"You always smell like fresh daisies," he murmured.

"I always smell like fresh daisies?" Katharine chuckled. "Did I smell like fresh daisies on the ship? Really, Paul, if you want to pass for anything more than an insincere flatterer, you'll have to stop telling such blatant lies."

He smiled. "Is that the guidebook?"

"Yes."

"Let's wait for Nathan," he advised, closing his eyes. "We'll never figure it out on our own."

"I'm reading it rather well, thank you. 'Rain, earthquakes, and time above all have affected the old houses. When we . . . browse . . . an old district of Cairo, one finds most of the facades . . . crumbling and patched . . . as best they could. If the neighborhood is a merchant neighborhood, it has been rebuilt in the Frankish style—that is to say, in the worst taste.'" Katharine raised her eyebrows at Paul. "Well I hope the Paris version is in the old style."

"I'm impressed. I thought you couldn't speak the language."

"I can read it to some extent. I'm just terrible at conversation. The pronunciations throw me off."

Paul sat up with an air of renewed interest. Between the two of them, they figured out the maps and identified places they'd most like to see.

"I need to walk," Katharine insisted at last, and so they went out directly, heading toward the Pont d'Iena, the bridge that crossed the river toward the fairgrounds. The site could hardly be missed. On the opposite bank, it was marked by the colossal mass of iron that was the Eiffel Tower.

"Let's look at the restaurants first," Katharine said as they approached the bridge.

"You're feeling better?" Paul sized her up cautiously.

"I'm much better—don't worry. But I am not looking forward to the return trip to New York."

"Neither am I. I'll have another week with a nauseated wife." He put an arm around her waist. "Don't worry; we'll have such a great time, it'll make up for it. A week in Paris makes up for two weeks on a steamer."

"It had better," she murmured.

They began to pass east of the Trocadéro Palace, a newer establishment which had been built for the previous World's Fair, and stopped at a kiosk to buy tickets. As they traversed the bridge toward the massive iron tower, they were joined by a surge of visitors headed for the fairgrounds. Katharine's eyes were at first fixed on the statues that graced each side of the bridge: two noble-looking, muscular stone men, each leading a magnificent stone horse, perched on platforms high above the walkways. Her gaze settled across the expanse before her and became riveted, out of habit, on a splotch of dark brown hair that curled out from under a gentleman's hat. It was the right shade, the right style—the very type that always caught her eye—and she kept him in view until she had a chance to see his face. She did so automatically, but with the casual expectation that she was fixating on a stranger.

The man turned then, looking back toward the right bank, gesturing as he addressed the two young men who stood before him. Katharine saw his face and froze.

Sound became muted; her vision blurred at the edges, while the center of her focus became more vivid, more pronounced, the details etching themselves painstakingly into her memory. Without meaning to, she dug her fingertips into Paul's arm.

"Paul?" she said, beginning to withdraw, hiding behind him.

"What's the matter?" He looked into her terrified face, then followed her gaze. At first he simply looked on in bewilderment; but at last he spotted the man in the black top hat, and he understood. "Is that who I think it is?"

Katharine pulled on his arm, forcefully leading him away. "Come on." Her own voice shook so, and with such a strain, that she didn't recognize it.

8

TROY, NEW YORK: SEPTEMBER 1883
(6 YEARS EARLIER)

The real nightmare with John Damgaard began after the human zoo. Later, Katharine would see how the spectacle had provided him with ample opportunities against her; but at the time, all she knew was that the man was paying her more attention than usual.

She was sitting on the grounds of Troy Female Seminary when she caught sight of him heading down Congress Street. He had long since passed, but turned his head to stare at her with a peculiar expression of satisfaction. Katharine met his eyes. Damgaard lifted his chin; his smile widened.

"What on Earth does he keep grinning at?" she muttered.

Her schoolmate, Sophie, turned with a puzzled glance. "Is it someone you know?"

"My father's business partner. He's gone now—probably on his way to see my father." Katharine shook her head. "Strange man."

"How so?"

"Lately, he's been . . . ." Katharine paused, thinking back. "He showed up at our human zoo and stood in the audience for some time, and watched me with such a strange smile on his face. He's been looking at me that way ever since, with a sort of . . . boastful expression. As if he's laughing."

"Let him laugh. He wouldn't be the only one." Sophie sifted through the lists and essays piled beside her on the bench. "What should we do about the invitations? We could send them all at once, but I thought it might be better to secure at least one notable figure first, and use that as an incentive to lure the others."

Around them, dying leaves created an ever-shifting kaleidoscope of colors on the lawn of Seminary Park. Summer was giving way to autumn, and the air carried a crisp freshness that had long been lacking.

Gentle breezes seemed to dispel the light haze of industrial smoke that perpetually wafted over the city of Troy. While many were drawn outside to bask in the weather, the two young women were focused on securing the attentions of prominent social activists—at the moment, Harriet Tubman.

More than two decades had passed since Tubman, the famed heroine of the Underground Railroad, helped stage a daring rescue at the Commissioner's office on First and State Street—a mere block away from where Katharine now sat. It was there that Charles Nalle, an escaped slave and legal property of his younger half-brother, waited in shackles for his return to a Virginia plantation. When anti-slavery crowds flooded State Street, Nalle's peers rushed into the building and wrestled the man away from police. Wild tales of the event abounded, with the spotlight often turned on Tubman: she was said to have knocked down police officers, to have carried Nalle to safety while dodging bullets and pro-slavery mobs.

"All we have locally," Sophie said, "is Anna speaking on Oneida women's sovereignty and their influence on the suffragist movement, May on the New Vigilance, and Rachel on the legacy of Emma Willard and the need for education for women of all means."

"We have all winter to plan for it," Katharine said. "I still want to try for Douglass. We could have Douglass and Anthony talk about reconciliation between the black men's movement and the women's movement. I know it's a lofty hope."

"The best kind," Sophie replied.

The women connived for some time about means of attracting notable figures. At last Katharine looked up from her paperwork to the elegant, rising granite walls of Gurley Hall, and beyond it to the factory-cluttered banks of the Hudson River. Two other women were approaching—May and Anna. Katharine greeted them and hastily added, "I hope you're early."

Anna gave her a knowing look. "No, we're late."

"Then it's time for me to go." Katharine gathered her papers. "I promised my father I would be home for dinner."

She hurried north across the park and along Congress Street, in the direction of her father's house. Though Katharine boarded at the seminary, the house on Fifth Avenue was only ten blocks away, and she often spent the weekend at home. The longtime absence of her mother made it all the more pressing for her to be there. Katharine's mother, Jana Reinhardt, had come to America from Cologne after the failure of the 1849 revolutions. Her family sailed across the Atlantic with a number of human rights activists, and Jana had often spoken to Katharine of her admiration for the endeavors of so many who were flushed out of Europe. After she married Charles Eliot, Jana committed herself both to motherhood and to community work; but she endured difficult pregnancies after Katharine's birth, and died along with a newborn daughter in 1872.

Katharine attributed her own interest in social activism to her mother. Her father, meanwhile, had additional ambitions for her. As a young man he'd worked his way to a management position in an iron works, providing munitions for the Union army and helping supply some of the country's first ironclads. By 1870 he'd converted the mill into a steel works; he raked in higher profits, and helped pull the mill through a major economic depression. As the economy recovered, Charles' business partner sold his share of the company to John Damgaard, a New York socialite who had inherited much of his wealth.

Because Katharine was his only heir, Charles Eliot made the unusual choice of adding business management to her education. He pored over old economic journals with her, explaining how he'd anticipated the depression. Katharine lacked his enthusiasm and maintained only the vaguest notion of the steel mill's harsh environment where women, men, and children as young as nine drudged for twelve hours a day in intensely concentrated heat, overbearing smells, and bone-grinding lifting. Katharine was interested in her father's economics lessons only because of their relevance to the social order; she dreaded ever having any responsibility for the mill. Surely there was another future available to her—and it was at the Seminary, where she began to connect with people and explore other ways of living, that she began to formulate her own plans.

The house emptied after Katharine left for boarding school; now there was just Hannah, who kept house for a few hours a day and provided Charles with home-cooked dinners.

"Hello Hannah," Katharine said breathlessly as she ascended the two steps to her father's home. She paused to smile at the gentle, thick-skinned woman who had served as her confidant for the past few years.

"You're looking well, dear." Hannah greeted her with a brief embrace. "Your father and his guests have started in on dinner. A plate is ready for you on the table."

"That's fine, I'll take it from here. Thanks for your help."

"Enjoy your time at home."

Katharine found her father dining with Mr. Damgaard—a frequent dinner guest—and Edward Casey, a young man with whom Katharine had been acquainted for many years. Katharine addressed the older men first: "Hello Father, sorry I'm late. Hello, Mr. Damgaard."

Edward stood politely as Katharine moved to sit at the table. He was much the same as he'd been two years ago, on their last meeting: neatly dressed, with his light brown hair slicked close to his head. Katharine saw the slight dent in his hair where his hat had rested; she recognized his nervous habit of trying to push his spectacles up the bridge of his nose, though they could move no farther.

Katharine's father addressed her mildly. "Katharine. You remember Edward, James Casey's son."

"Of course. How are you, Edward?"

"Very well, thank you," he said, sitting. "Are you enjoying school?"

"Very much. And you?"

"Well . . . very much, but I haven't been in school lately. I've just returned from working in Bloomingdale. My uncle owns a logging company there, and has a house near the Saranac."

John Damgaard chuckled. "That's unfortunate. He's likely to go bankrupt. The entire logging industry is moving south. They've got great, thick ones down in the south, not the spindly forests we've got up here."

"It's nothing to do with the trees," Katharine said. "We have logging railroads shipping so much of our timber to other states that we're running out, and—"

Charles shook his head. "No one's saying we're running out."

"—the local papers publish lies about our diminishing natural resources," Katharine continued, speaking through her father's attempt at interruption; but now she addressed him. "Exactly, no one's saying we're running out; all the reporters are rubbing elbows with industrialists. They publish false public opinion about how proud everyone is to have such rich natural resources, and how much everyone loves to see all those resources dug up and chopped down and carried off to other states. Reporters can never quote anyone in particular—"

"Katharine has been reading Thoreau," Charles explained.

"—because it's all a bunch of made-up horse manure."

Damgaard missed a beat, and said, "Well. I see you've come to show off your schooling."

Katharine looked at him without response.

"Go ahead, put some practice in," he encouraged her. "Now you can boast that you're educated—and you've got an esteemed businessman for a father. You could secure a successful husband, or scare him off, depending on how you apply yourself."

"I have no interest in applying for a husband," she replied. She turned quickly to Edward, adding: "Edward, I do hope your uncle is doing well, and that his business isn't being affected by the decline."

"No husband?" Damgaard said lightly to Katharine. "You don't have your sights set on anyone?"

"Katharine wants to study nursing and run away with the Red Cross Society," Charles said.

"Really." Damgaard spoke with disinterest, but continued to question her. "And you're going to forfeit a family? No children to see that you're taken care of when you're aged?"

"If I married, I wouldn't be free to travel and work of my own volition," Katharine said.

"You'll need money for that," Damgaard replied. "But I suppose you have that sorted as well."

"I do—and I've sorted my goals. I want to work for a better society, so that by the time I'm old, I'll live in a place where the elders are looked after by the community. Anyway, Mr. Damgaard, you've never expressed an interest in marrying; I wouldn't have thought you would scoff at the idea of remaining independent."

"No, I admire your decision. All that is potentially sentimental should be observed from a distance and brought close only when it allows practical leverage, whether it's one's family or one's labor force. And while we're on that subject—"

"Not now, Damgaard, please." Charles' expression went sour.

Damgaard pointed his fork at Charles with an air of accusation. "We don't have an eternity to consider selling out. Other entrepreneurs are grabbing all the land along Lake Michigan, and have set up so well that it's becoming near impossible for new enterprises to succeed. Think, Eliot: you could remove yourself as far as possible from the brunt of the labor while reaping the highest benefit. That is the trend that the world is moving into, and if you want to keep your place, you must move with it."

"Agreed, but we have options aside from selling out from under our workers. As long as business is profitable in Troy, we have no reason to change our proximity or our payouts."

"That is *sentimental*, sir." Damgaard turned his attention to Katharine and Edward, leaning toward them imploringly. "Help me persuade him. In the beginning of a business endeavor, you must amass the most money possible in order to compete; correct? Only much later, after you establish success and resources, can you organize benefits for your laborers." He let his attention drift back to Charles, passing it evenly between his host and his plateful of potatoes and salmon. "We must stay competitive, and yet here you are, treating workers like helpless children under your tender guardianship. And the effect is the same as with one's own children: You let them suck the energy and vitality out of you."

Katharine responded: "Perhaps you simply lack energy that is readily available to others.”

“Me? You’re saying I lack energy?”

She ignored him and addressed Edward. “What do you think, Ed, do you agree with Mr. Damgaard’s opinion on family?”

The young man spoke tentatively, glancing around the table and meeting each person’s eyes. “No, I think I would one day like to have a family, after I settle on a career.”

Damgaard’s eyes lit with wry amusement. “Well, Miss Eliot is out of the question. Perhaps you should have gone somewhere else for dinner.”

“Don’t be presumptuous,” Katharine scolded him. “Ed and I are old friends. Right, Ed?”

“Of course,” he said lightly, pushing his spectacles farther up the length of his nose.

“And the same goes for his family.” Katharine nodded to Edward: “I’ve been crossing paths with your brother Carl near the Seminary. Last week I caught him passing the park; I introduced him to my friend Anna.”

Charles spoke up: “Which one is Anna?”

“The Oneida woman. She’s the one who started sewing pants for the women’s movement at the Seminary.”

Damgaard checked his tone, but allowed a mocking fire to burn in his eyes. “Pants for the women’s movement?”

“Yes, pants, so we don’t have to drag ourselves around all day in layers of ridiculously heavy skirts.”

“I see. And you consider it practical to dress in such a way? Would you do so in public? In *this* neighborhood?”

Katharine hesitated. “I have.”

“Really, to what reaction?”

Again, she paused. Charles raised his eyebrows, gesturing for her to answer.

“Sometimes none—but there were some boys who threw rocks and vegetables at me,” she confessed. “I decided it’s best to begin by wearing pants with a mid-calf skirt. People are less volatile about that.”

“Less volatile about seeing you dressed like a child?”

“Like a sensible woman. I think it’s hypocritical of men to expect women to dress in a way that you would find impractical and hindering if you had to do it yourself. Working women dress like this—”

“Impoverished women,” Damgaard muttered, and chuckled. “I think it unwise of you to believe that society will take any notice of such antics, except to mock them.” He turned to Edward, his eyes gleaming with mischief. “Mr. Casey, I wonder if you’re aware of the great spectacle that Miss Eliot has made of herself lately—and I don’t refer to her manner of dress. She was dressed quite nicely a few weeks ago, when she appeared in a zoological exhibit at Liberty Street Church. Surely you've heard of it?"

Edward seemed befuddled, and didn't reply.

Katharine interjected: "But you must know what a human zoo is. Wealthy Americans and Europeans kidnap people from African and Asian nations and put them on display, and abuse them, and make a mockery of them. Some of the women at the Seminary decided to make a statement about the practice by holding our own human zoo—but with Troy society on display. We played cards, and had tea, and danced—"

"And they allowed the audience to reward them for their performances by throwing biscuits through the fence," Damgaard said.

"We had good reason for what we did. There was an article in the *Freie Deutsche Presse* last year about five men who died in Carl Hagenbeck's ethnological exhibit. You must have heard of Hagenbeck; he travels the world collecting wild animals for zoos, but he also exhibits humans. He arranged a kidnapping expedition in Chile, and his captives were displayed in Europe for a short time. The paper said that they died of 'weak constitutions,' but everyone knows what that means: they died from exposure to European diseases."

Damgaard smiled. "Miss Eliot has plenty to say on the subject. She even had her own opinion piece published in the *Daily Times*."

"She did," Charles said evenly, "and I thought it very smart, even if it was unnecessarily sarcastic in tone." He nodded at Katharine. "But the attention must be wearing on you. I haven't seen you going about in trousers lately."

"Oh, but you have. I'm wearing them now." She stood, moving back from the table just far enough to afford them a view of her skirt, which she raised—rather high—to reveal the trousers she wore beneath. "See?"

Edward immediately covered his eyes, as if by pure impulse; Charles put his fork down and subtly shook his head.

"Katharine . . . ." Her father's voice was uncharacteristically pained. He said to the guests, particularly Edward: "You'll have to excuse my daughter; the suffrage movement prides itself on being improper." Then, to Katharine: "At dinner, Katharine, do refrain from being so indiscreet."

She lowered the skirt and sat with an air of defiant self-righteousness. "My clothes are no less indiscreet than the pants you're all wearing. I could throw my skirt off and still be fully clothed."

Edward was standing now, flushed and nervous, attempting once again to adjust his spectacles. "Um . . . Mr. Eliot, as I said, I have to be home early tonight . . . thank you very much for dinner. Katharine, it was good to see you."

Charles nodded with cordial understanding. "Thank you for being our guest, Edward. You know you're welcome any time."

"Yes, thank you . . . good night."

The young man hesitated, looking uncertainly at Katharine. She started to stand.

"Can I see you out?" she asked.

"No, please don't trouble yourself." Edward's eyes moved inadvertently toward her skirt, as though he felt mortified by the thought of seeing her pants exposed again. He mumbled "Goodnight" to Damgaard, began to exit; nodded another "Goodnight" in Katharine's direction as he left the room.

Charles waited until Edward was gone. His eyes were fixed steadily on his daughter.

"Looks like you'll have your way about never marrying," he said at last. "I believe you scared him off."

"At least he didn't throw his food at me like the other boys. Anyway, Edward knows what I'm like."

Damgaard grunted his disagreement. "I think that even your father is surprised by what you're like."

"It's a shame about his uncle's business," Charles said. "I hope Edward didn't abandon school to invest in the timber industry. I didn't want to ask"—he looked pointedly at his daughter—"especially after you gave him an earful about the innate evils of industry and logging railroads."

"I don't think industry is innately bad."

Damgaard's eyes shone with vain amusement. "Only when it turns a profit?"

"When it's not sustainable. I'm not flatly opposed to it, and anyway, reformists use the new technology as well as entrepreneurs. With the trolleys, telegraphs, the railroads, and even with people traveling here from different lands by boat, we can create so much dialogue," Katharine said—to her father, rather ignoring Mr. Damgaard.

"Good God, Charles, what have you raised up in this house?" Damgaard chuckled. "People don't get on with their own neighbors, and yet you imagine peace and equality with every savage and nitwit on the planet."

"You forget that I have friends and family who've been dismissed as savages and nitwits," Katharine said. "My mother and uncles were dismissed as drunken heretics when they arrived here. And you, you have managers who began life as slaves."

"And so it follows that you and your uneducated masses will fix the world," Damgaard said blandly. "Go out into it, Katharine; make your way, and come back in a few years, and then we'll talk about ideals. Even Carnegie gives his infamous idealist speeches because of their appeal to the masses—not because of any fanciful idealism on his part. In private, he earns the friendships of entrepreneurs. He's always thinking of the return."

"But he also claims that an important part of the return is the bliss that's inherent in compassion and integrity. If you're so insistent on following the example of millionaires, perhaps you should try to understand his sentiment."

"Oh, I understand it perfectly—from a businessman's point of view."

"Then it follows that you express your own opinions based not on their truth, but on a formula crafted for a selfish return. And it also follows that my father shouldn't trust the advice of someone whose professed aim is to garner riches and opportunity for himself at the expense of others. If you'll sell out anyone, surely you'll sell out my father."

Charles chuckled. "Ah, she has you there, John."

"Oh, I doubt that." Damgaard smiled strangely; his lips seemed to tremble, as if in an attempt to restrain the smile. "I doubt that."

"Hm," Charles said shortly. His eyes were lowered, his fingers carefully forking up the last of his meal. "Perhaps you should be satisfied with the limits we've managed to retain."

"What limits? You have long-timers whose wages you've raised, and for no reason except to pat yourself on the back for your own thoughtfulness." Damgaard shook his head. "You see, Katharine, how your father's sluggish compassion is destroying our leverage in the world?" He grinned again, his coffee-and-tobacco stained teeth flashing yellow in the glow of the gaslight, eyes gleaming with cryptic mendacity. "If your father isn't willing to make a killing in this game, I might just have to do the job myself!"

It was that moment—the moment in which Damgaard's eyes and teeth flashed like shining yellowed stains, in which his tone and demeanor contorted in the ominous shadow of some excited and unknown thought—that stayed in Katharine's mind even after the weekend passed.

Her father began to talk of trouble at the mill. Her next weekend visit found him dull-eyed and tired, with vague murmurings about quarrels and drama at work. As the situation intensified, Charles' normally easy tone became hardened with real anger. Damgaard had been firing people on grounds that were likely false; the workers, fearing unemployment and upset by the treatment of their peers, were increasingly perturbed.

When some of the employees arranged to take Damgaard to court, Charles Eliot agreed to testify on their behalf. Damgaard, meanwhile, was banished from the Eliot home. Instead of finding him at the dinner table, Katharine sometimes came home to find her father hosting meetings with senior workers.

She got a shock one Thursday on campus, as she and Sophie walked into Gurley Hall and nearly ran into Damgaard himself. He was walking arm in arm with a soft-spoken, pale-skinned young woman with a swan neck and thin brown hair: Miss Bell, the science teacher.

Sophie said something that further astonished her: "Hello, Mr. Damgaard."

"Well hello, Miss Taylor." Damgaard half-tipped his hat to her. "How pleasant to see you! I was just talking to Moe Davies, who spoke at our meeting last week. We passed him not more than fifteen minutes ago."

Sophie's smile never diminished. "Oh, yes, Mr. Davies lives close by. I see him often."

"What an animated man—and very inspiring. He lends good qualities to his cause. I look forward to talking with all of you again—but my stopping to converse now will put a dent in our schedule." He smiled apologetically at Miss Bell, who beamed up at him in flushed silence. "I've promised to take Miss Bell to the orchestra."

"How lovely. I'm sure you'll both enjoy it."

Damgaard flashed the briefest glance in Katharine's direction, his eyes burning with a secret, unspoken exchange. "Miss Eliot," he said in polite acknowledgement. "A very good day to you, too." With that he led Miss Bell away.

As the door closed behind them, Katharine turned to Sophie with a demanding air. "How do you know Mr. Damgaard?"

Sophie looked surprised. "I've seen him around. He was at a meeting on immigration reform this week, defending new immigrants from attempts by the nativists."

"Mr. Damgaard is my father's business partner. He's the one who's been accusing the workers of stealing and tampering with equipment."

Sophie frowned and looked back at the doorway. "That's him? He doesn't seem the type . . . ."

"He *is* the type. Trust me, I've known him for years. What is he doing with Miss Bell?"

"He's her beau. I'm surprised you didn't know. Mr. Damgaard has been here off and on; he's become a contributor to the Seminary."

"A contributor?"

"He gave us a considerable donation, though I don't know how much. Miss Bell seems very fond of him."

Katharine stared at her in disbelief.

The following day she went home early and found her father in the drawing room with Thomas Beckett, one of his long-time employees. She saw their faces drawn and somber, and dreaded knowing the cause.

"Hello, Mr. Beckett," she said, and turned to her father. "Has Hannah arranged something for dinner?"

"Yes, but you'll be dining alone," Charles replied. "We're not particularly hungry."

She hesitated. "What's happened?"

The two men exchanged glances. Charles paused for some time, and calmly stated: "A riot occurred at the factory."

Katharine gripped the arm of a chair, seating herself near her father. "Today?"

"Yes. Property was damaged, the police made arrests, and things are none the better for the workers. Twelve are in jail, and Damgaard is using the event to fire most of the others."

"*Most* of them? How can he do that? Does he want to shut the place down?"

"Oh, no. There's another piece to the story," Charles said dryly. "It's been found out that Damgaard has been in touch with labor hunters in Europe. He paid them to persuade a sizeable group of Austrian immigrants to come here for work. They've already agreed to the wage he offered—which, I need not point out, is considerably low."

"Good God—I thought he was vile before, but I had no idea. You're sure it's true?"

"Absolutely."

"Are they on their way here?"

"They arrived yesterday. Damgaard brought them on a tour of the factory, to see the jobs they'd be replacing. The workers realized what was happening—and, naturally, they rioted."

"*Some* of them rioted," Mr. Beckett put in grimly. "A few of them started in, and it didn't take long for others to follow."

Katharine was nearly frozen with anxiety. She sat with her back arched, her fingers digging into the fabric of the chair. "What about the immigrants, were they hurt?"

"No, they were well out of the way by that time—along with Damgaard. The rioting started after they left, and the overseers were powerless to stop it. Of the people who were injured, most were supervisors—including Mr. Beckett." Charles nodded to his companion. "He's had both his arms stitched up."

"Barely," Beckett said. "It's nothing serious."

"Good God," Katharine said again. "But Damgaard—can he get away with it? You have an equal share of the company. Surely he can't do these things without your consent."

"I've been in touch with my attorney." Charles' voice became heavy with exhaustion. "I've quite a mess to deal with, Katharine, so you'll have to spend the evening on your own. I have some details to work out with Mr. Beckett, and Mr. Delaney should be here shortly. Perhaps you would be better spending the weekend at school . . . ."

"No, I'll stay; I won't interrupt. I'll be here in case you need anything. And you should eat, both of you—I don't mean to lecture, but it will sap your strength if you go hungry."

The hint of a smile touched her father's lips. "Perhaps later, but there's no need to solicit to us."

"I'll leave something out in case you get hungry—but I'll finish my own dinner and stay upstairs the rest of the night." She turned to Beckett. "I'm sorry you were hurt. I hope the wounds are as trivial as you say."

He managed a smile. "Goodnight, Miss Eliot."

Katharine sat in her room late into the night, until the men's voices faded from the parlor and she heard her father shuffling around in the kitchen. She went to the top of the stairs; listened; descended quietly. She found her father standing near the stove, staring at the plate she'd left for him.

"Still not hungry?" she asked.

He looked at her silently for some time, then beckoned her. "Come here."

In the drawing room, he sat with his gaze fixed on the floor, not speaking, while Katharine studied him with growing concern. Often, when he was lost in thought, his eyes would move subtly back and forth, and he would absently stroke his moustache; but now he sat motionless, his eyes seemingly vacant. Charles was quiet for such a long spell that Katharine was startled when he suddenly said: "Tomorrow morning, I want you to return to school and spend the weekend there."

"No," she said in surprise.

"I'm not asking," he replied in an unusually hard tone. "I don't want you here when . . . these things are happening. Don't argue," he said as she began to speak. "This is not something I will debate with you."

"Father, I wish you would—"

"You'll go after breakfast. Understood?"

She felt her heart sinking, looked at him with helpless concern. "I understand. But I need to tell you something that may change your mind."

"What's that?"

"John Damgaard was at the Seminary today. I ran into him at Gurley

Hall."

Her father's gaze took on a strange gleam; his voice was thick, as though his throat had suddenly become cloaked with cobwebs. "He was at the Seminary, doing what?"

She repeated everything Sophie had told her: Damgaard's courting of Miss Bell, his active support of new immigration, his financial contribution to the school.

"I don't doubt that I'll run into him again," she said. "And—"

"Don't talk to him," her father interrupted. "If you see him again, please refrain from acknowledging him."

"I'd really like to tell him what a vile excuse for a human being he is."

Charles' voice took on a peculiar edge. "Katharine, again, I am not asking. Do not speak a word to him. If you see him, turn and go the other way."

Katharine was surprised. "I know he's wicked, but I don't think he's likely to drag me into any of his scheming."

"Really. Why do you suppose he's at your school?"

"He seems fond of Miss Bell."

"Does he? If Damgaard is 'fond' of a woman, it's for her money and status alone. I can't imagine Miss Bell possesses any of the qualities that would draw him in." Charles watched his daughter intently, then let out a tired sigh and rubbed his eyes. "Katharine, I do hope that you will marry someday. The world isn't safe for a lone woman."

"I don't intend to be alone."

He frowned at her.

"Really, I may not be out in society, but I *am* socially active. Right now you think me safer at the Seminary, surrounded by women. It won't be much different in the future."

Charles emitted a short, humorless laugh. "Yes, Katharine, it will, because you won't be in school much longer. And I don't think you particularly safe at the Seminary. It just seems more practical for the time being."

"Other women are able to make their own way—perhaps not many, but those who do are determined to support other women who choose the same path. I won't be on my own."

"I think that as you get older, and go out into the world, you'll find that your peers are often not as supportive as you anticipate. If your mother was still here, I think she would be better able to explain why a woman must be careful about society."

"Mother excluded herself from society. She certainly wasn't a conformist."

"No, she wasn't. And you're like her in that way. You have your mother's spirit, but not her shrewdness. You don't have her quietness."

"I don't remember her being quiet."

"Not to children, no. You wouldn't have noticed it."

She stood and kissed his forehead. "Don't worry, father. Please save your worries for the factory. And if you need me, please don't hesitate to send for me."

He said nothing. Katharine squeezed his shoulder and retreated upstairs.

Katharine's weekend stay at the Seminary seemed to her a gross mistake. Damgaard was back on the grounds on Saturday, wandering through the park with Miss Bell on his arm—at mid-day, and again in the afternoon. Katharine kept from his presence as her father had asked. But after some hours, she had one of her schoolmates pass a message back to the house: *Father, please allow me to come home. Mr. Damgaard is at the school again and I do not want to be here.*

In the evening she attended a local function, with the understanding that some members of the old Vigilance Committee (who, led by Harriet Tubman, had helped rescue Charles Nalle back in the sixties) could be introduced to her there. Katharine entered the gathering with a dreadful suspicion that she would find Mr. Damgaard there as well, touting his support for the New Vigilance; but to her relief he was absent. She spent some time interviewing a woman who had been involved with the Committee, but could not muster much enthusiasm in doing so. Thoughts of her father—of the demise he might be facing—permeated her being. When her own party left, she asked to be brought back to the house, and was taken by carriage along Congress Street. They dropped Katharine at the corner of Fifth Avenue, leaving her to walk the last few blocks.

There was something about the streets at night that she loved—especially at the turn of the season, when the air was fresh with the ardor of transformation. Fall was becoming winter now, and the air bore a new, cold current, clean and clear, but not yet strong enough to make a person shudder. The gas lamps had been lit for the night, and the near-full moon cast the neighborhood in mellow shades of blue. A passing trap broke the subdued silence as it passed along Fifth; Katharine kept to the sidewalk, glancing up at the lone figure who commanded the horse, and realized with a start that the driver was Mr. Damgaard. His top hat was perched on his head, covering his brow, casting a shadow just above his eyes. He looked at Katharine and she saw the flash of recognition there; in the vague light his expression seemed terribly dark and shadowed, the eyes glowing a greenish-yellow as they reflected the gaslight. He smiled a small, tight smile as his face passed beyond her sight.

The sound of hooves clattered away. Katharine found herself unable to enjoy the late-night silence of her walk. The gentle breezes in the dark leaves above her bestowed ominous foreboding instead of the usual soothing rustle, and the idea of solitude was suddenly unwelcome. Damgaard must have been to see her father. They had probably argued, exchanged bitter words. Again she would find her father fatigued and worried.

She could see from the street that he had not retired to bed; the gas lamp was still lit within the front parlor. Katharine climbed the two steps to the porch.

At the doorway, she inexplicably stopped. Her fingers hovered just over the knob as some impression washed over her—a shadow, a malignant stain that flashed like dark lightning across her mind. Katharine frowned and opened the door, placing her foot into the deep-red puddle that spread beyond the threshold.

Her mind struggled for some time to reconcile what she was seeing: her father, crumpled on the floor, facing away from her, and lying in— what?

"Father?"

But at the moment she said it, the sight and scent sank sharply into her being, and she knew that he would not answer, that she would never hear his voice again.

9

TROY, NEW YORK: SEPTEMBER 1883

It was exactly a week after Charles Eliot's death that Mr. Damgaard paid another visit to the Eliot home.

The decision to send Hannah, the housekeeper, home for the night had been spontaneous. Hannah's youngest son was overcome with fever, and Katharine thought it best to persuade Hannah to return to him. Had Damgaard known of the illness, and predicted that Hannah would leave because of it? Katharine couldn't be sure; but Damgaard's bold gesture that night filled her with the fear that he had some clairvoyant power over the Eliot household, over the entire neighborhood, that allowed him a successfully clandestine night-time visit.

At the time, she was in the drawing-room, re-reading a telegram from her uncle, who represented her last remaining relation in New York. Her mother's family was long gone; Jana's two eldest brothers had been killed in the war, while Gernot, the youngest, had died during the depression-era protest at Tompkins square. On her father's side there remained only a sister, her uncle's wife. Katharine had met the family on occasion and found them pleasant; and as she was a grown woman, she figured she had little to fear from the move. Staying, on the other hand, became ever more fearful.

Damgaard had been investigated for the murder of her father. He was detained briefly for questioning, and released. All of Katharine's testimony against him, all the testimony of the workers, could not prove his guilt as a murderer. And so it was that Damgaard still walked the streets of Troy.

Katharine had no idea how long he'd been standing at the window—only that she looked up, and in the vague light spilling from the front window she could see Damgaard's face, split with a wide grin, the green eyes dancing in perverse merriment at the sight of her. It seemed so incongruous: the cozy drawing-room, her mother's pretty lace curtains framing such a loathsome specter.

She started, froze, thought she must be imagining him. But after some time she realized that she and Damgaard were staring at each other.

Her mind raced over the interactions they'd shared over the past few years: conversations over dinner and occasional outings, which, no matter how self-interested or peculiar on his part, could never have clued her in to what he would become. And now she knew; and she stared at his strange, smiling face with the certainty that he had come to kill her.

He raised a glass bottle and tapped the window with it.

Damgaard is outside; the door is locked, and if I simply get up and drape the window, he will not be able to see where I am; and then I can sneak out the back. . . .

But Damgaard was wedging the window open from outside, causing Katharine to jump to her feet in alarm.

"Good evening," he said, with an obvious slur in his speech. "I just wanted to apololize, apologize . . . for the trouble I've caused. Ah, Katharine; you know how it is with these things." He spread his hands in a gesture of feigned helplessness, of blamelessness. "The predator has the advantage, you see. I am at work, and I have . . . I have the *big picture* in mind. The prey's only choice is to run, never knowing the best retreat, never having access to the grand scheme." He sighed as he gazed at the petrified woman before him. "I had to apologize for what I did. I know it caused you pain, but I intend to remedy it within the week, you see. A dead woman doesn't grieve—and I'll have you dead in no time, no time at all."

The grin spread on his face so that he could barely speak the last words; he broke off into a choking sort of laughter, then withdrew from the sill and raised the bottle in her direction, singing softly as he danced a stumbling jig on the lawn: *"Oh these words I kindly speak: I'll have you dead within the week!"*

Katharine tipped her head back, squeezed her eyes shut, and screamed as loudly as she could.

Within minutes, as the neighbors began to appear, she was devastated to learn that they had seen and heard nothing aside from her screams. She fled to the police, but on investigating Damgaard they found him sitting comfortably at home, perfectly sober and neatly dressed, and apparently amazed at the new accusations against him. He had, in fact, been in another interview with the police that evening; he insisted he couldn't have been anywhere near the Eliot home, which was not on his route.

The second week brought no more of his physical presence, yet he had developed ways of being vicariously present in Katharine's life. Her journal entry for that week read:

Evil is not a strong enough word to describe Mr. Damgaard. The police are convinced that my story about his latest visit was a fabrication, or at the least a case of mistaken identity exacerbated by "nerves"—and the more I've insisted that he is the culprit, the less I am trusted. Damgaard has had the nerve to insinuate that I'm accusing him to cover up my own guilt (this should be thought a ludicrous claim, but I'm not sure that everyone rejects it). He spreads wild and insulting rumors about me, under the pretense of being concerned for my well-being. Every move I make is grossly distorted—first by Damgaard and then by others—to make me seem unworthy of credibility and support.

For instance, I wear trousers at times, and I showed a pair to Mr. Damgaard and Edward Casey a few weeks ago at dinner. Damgaard gave a colorful account of the event. Ed, unfortunately, chose to corroborate it. Thus it was quickly spread around that I laughingly lift my skirt to display my "undergarments" at men of all ages and classes, along with many other expressions of inappropriate behavior. Ed also corroborated the idea that I was after my father's money so that I can live independently, though I never said such a thing; it was Damgaard who suggested it. And there has been plenty of gossip about my antics at the human zoo. I could go on and on with examples and would be writing all weekend.

The end result is this: where once people thought me calm and collected, I am now thought prone to expressions of bizarre and loose behavior; where once I was thought honest and civic-minded, I am now untrustworthy and selfish. Mr. Damgaard succeeded in isolating me from acquaintances, and then from neighbors—and the most active gossip among the neighbors is Mrs. Swift, who has been exposed to Damgaard at society parties. Though I have only suspected that her animated whispering to other neighbors is focused on me, her children confirm it for me. I have been back and forth to the house to put things in order, and on Wednesday the littlest girl (Kitty) said hello to me; her brother James quickly took her arm and said "Don't talk to her, mother says she's bad." I'm sure that some of the neighbors are glad to avoid me, as I was never a favorite. I didn't go out in society enough; I didn't follow social rules. I went to Reform meetings. The human zoo, of course, completely did me in.

I have no community to help protect me from Damgaard. I will have to leave not only my home, but every group I believed in and put so much faithful effort into. Damgaard even seems to have sway over larger social causes to which I am committed. For instance, because of my interest in nursing, Damgaard has added fuel to the notion that women who pursue a study of medicine—even of nursing, or of midwifery—are mentally ill and a bane to both medicine and proper society.

I suppose he means to kill me. Damgaard has my old friends and acquaintances reporting my movements to him; he claims that he needs to be "protected" from me in case I should try to make further false reports against him. My so-called community has left me utterly exposed to all the dangers he poses. I cannot sleep; I cannot focus; I am not living. I cannot even grieve properly—but though others seem to have abandoned me, I must not abandon myself. I will not let him take my health and my mind; for my father's sake and mine, I will not let the man steal my spirit. . . .

After a hard and lonely week Katharine returned in a stormy mood to the house—and to Hannah's friendship, one of her sole comforts.

"No one has come forward to report seeing Damgaard that night. How can it be that the man can move through the streets like a phantom, so that no sees him? How is it that he knows when to come here?" Katharine's voice was raw with anger. She sat down hard on the sofa and lowered her head into her hands. "And to think that the workers are completely under his power!"

"I'm afraid the man has gotten away with great crimes," Hannah said with a sigh. "Katharine, I wish you would return to school for the weekend. Surely it's a safer place to be. You'll be surrounded by people, and you have your friends—"

"I don't have friends at the Seminary," Katharine said flatly. "Damgaard has them."

"What do you mean?"

"I mean that Damgaard has been wooing all my connections. He's a philanthropist now. He donated money to the school—not just within the past days, but a couple of weeks *before* my father's death. You understand? And he's taken up an interest in the Reform movement. In fact, while I was away from school—when Damgaard was first being investigated for *murder*—he spent time alone with Sophie; and now she's trying to persuade me to come to an 'understanding' with him."

"An understanding of what?" Hannah gazed at her with amazement. "You mean your friend Sophie? The one who's been organizing the Reformist meetings?"

"Yes, that Sophie. She's been criticizing my unfair behavior toward him, and thinks there has been some great misunderstanding between us."

"I don't believe it," Hannah said, with an unmistakable note of fear.

"Nevertheless, it's true. I've been working with her for almost two years, and it's as though she doesn't know me. She heard about Damgaard's visit here, and—" Katharine choked on the words. Hannah looked on her with empathetic misery.

"She didn't believe you."

"She thinks I made a mistake—or I'm so convinced of Damgaard's guilt that I'm willing to lie to get him arrested."

"Did she say that?"

"She warned me against it. Don't look surprised. I always thought Sophie was smart—she *is* smart—but apparently people become stupid in Damgaard's presence, and only have any hope of knowing his nature if they've spent considerable time viewing his bad side. He goes around smiling and talking it up, and people think, 'Ohhh, what a pleasant man! He couldn't have killed anyone.' And then they talk to me and I seem mad. Of *course* I'm mad!"

"Oh, Katharine."

"And the more I go after him, the more he'll try to pin my father's death on some poor worker. As soon as I informed the police of his visit, he implicated a metal wheeler—a man named Mayes who rioted at the mill. A riot that *Damgaard* started." She looked sharply at Hannah. "I'm not lying. Damgaard came here and threatened me."

"I know you're not lying, dear. Why he did such a thing, I can't fathom; but I know you haven't made anything up."

"I don't understand it either, and that's why it scares me so much. He's *up* to something. Maybe he just wants to discredit me; maybe he's trying to break me, to make it easier to get my share of the mill. I . . . I don't know."

Katharine's voice was strained with sudden exhaustion. She stood and went to the windows, clutching her hands over her folded arms, as if at a sudden chill. "Can you imagine, Mr. Damgaard sympathetic to the Reform movement? Only an idiot would believe it, you'd think; but . . . ."

A long, heavy silence hung in the room. Hannah broke it tentatively: "Mrs. Swift came by earlier. She—"

"Mrs. Swift, really? I'm surprised she was willing to taint herself by coming to the front door."

"She said that if you feel like staying away from the house, she'd be willing to look in on it until—"

"I don't want that snake-tongued wretch in my house—or anyone else in that family!" Katharine erupted.

"Katharine!"

"Do you know what she's been telling her children about me?" Katharine turned on Hannah with wild eyes.

Hannah was aghast; she stepped forward with a hand held out in protest. "Please—the neighbors will hear!"

"I don't give a damn about the neighbors!" Katharine roared. "I care as much about that entire lot of vile, simple-minded, pathetic gossips as they care for me. I've just seen my father murdered; and after they've delivered their neighborly supply of fish and vegetable platters, all they have in response to my nightmare is their complete gullibility to Mr. Damgaard—and only because he has money and contrived social standing, while I am far easier to spit on. And they spit as though it's their God-given duty."

"Katharine!"

"They make a show of going to church on Sundays and condemning anyone outside of it, and of professing their belief in the gospels, and then they go home and behave in the most anti-Christian ways. They enjoy one another based solely on one's standing, and feast on one another the moment that standing falls. They let themselves be mastered by the most indolent gossip as if they've taken some sort of pledge to be hopelessly vile and stupidly malleable."

"Katharine, Katharine, sit! Calm yourself, please."

"Fine, I'll sit," Katharine acquiesced in a low tone, "but you know that I'm calling it what it is. Human beings are hopeless. I'm tired of being among them; I'm tired of being one of them."

"Please, dear, you mustn't say such things." Hannah remained pale, but her voice was soothing; she had conquered the strain of panic and stood protectively over her charge. "You mustn't give in to such thoughts."

"No, I won't. Believe me, I've thought it over already, a dozen different ways at least. But I can't give in to such thoughts because it would mean a morbid victory for that monster of a man." Katharine's voice was toneless, her eyes fixed vacantly ahead of her. "I could never allow that, no matter how much I might suffer. It would mean . . . ." She shook her head; her eyes welled with tears. "The man wants to triumph in breaking my spirit. And I will never let him have it, no matter what I have to do, or how long it takes. He has frightened my spirit off somewhere and I mean to get it back," she concluded softly.

Katharine's brooding meander was interrupted: a knock sounded at the front door. The women looked at each other with trepidation before Katharine rose to answer it.

"Let me," Hannah offered, but Katharine peered through the front windows and said "No, I'll get it. I think it's Mr. Beckett."

Thomas Beckett's face was wrought with concern. Katharine noted a sickly pallor in his flesh.

"Hello, Mr. Beckett. Please come in."

Beckett's weary tone matched her own: "Thank you."

As the door closed behind him, he asked what she'd seen of Damgaard. "Is it true he came here to taunt you?"

"He was here last weekend, but I dare you to believe it. Everyone else thinks I'm lying."

Beckett's eyes darkened, clouded with troubled thoughts. "Miss Eliot, you shouldn't stay here—even when someone else is with you. I know it's your home, but . . . ."

"I know."

"It's just been the two of you?" Mr. Beckett addressed Hannah: "Mrs. Petren, would she be welcome to stay with you?"

"Of course," Hannah said, but Katharine shook her head.

"No, I won't stay with her. Damgaard will find out, and he'll come to her house. I don't want to cause trouble for Hannah's family."

"But Katharine, you must stay *somewhere*," Hannah protested, "and not in this house, not anymore. It's dangerous, and it's terrible on your nerves."

Mr. Beckett beckoned them to the drawing-room. "Come, sit down. Let's figure this out."

Katharine narrated a lengthy account of her week. She struggled to condense the tale, to give examples rather than run Beckett through every misfortune she'd endured. Beckett listened quietly as she ended with the spectacle of Mr. Damgaard singing and dancing at the window: *Oh these words I kindly speak: I'll have you dead within the week!*

"I know it sounds improbable," she added hesitantly, "but . . . ."

He held up a hand. "I believe you. When are your aunt and uncle expecting you?"

"We haven't set a date."

"You should go now—and without telling anyone, save me and Mrs. Petren. If you'll trust me to act on your behalf, I can work with Mr. Delaney to manage the rest of your father's affairs. I can forward your address, or communicate between the two of you, whichever you prefer."

Katharine hesitated, gazing steadily into Beckett's eyes, making a quick review of her memories of him—of every expression, every word her father had said on the man's behalf. The scenes rushed through her mind at high speed; they arranged themselves into neat calculations, determining Beckett's trustworthiness even under pressure.

She nodded. "Yes, I'll do that—and you can communicate between me and Mr. Delaney. I don't want people to know where I am. People have acted so strangely that I haven't wanted to tell anyone . . . ."

"Good. Let me send a telegram to your uncle, explaining that I'm sending you to him. I'll wait until I hear back, and then I'll see you off at the train station." Beckett's gaze moved to Katharine's hands as they clasped tightly in her lap. "Tell you what: I can bring my daughter and we'll escort you as far as Greenbush. In the meantime you'll have to set aside the things you don't want to sell. You can take a few things with you, and Mrs. Petren and I will pack up the rest. I'll have them delivered to your aunt's house."

Gratitude swelled in Katharine's throat. "I would appreciate that."

"Delaney and I will do what we can to see that the rest of your father's affairs are handled. You don't have to directly involve yourself if you don't want to."

"Thank you, Mr. Beckett. I'm not sure there's much you can do . . . ." She hesitated, and said in a sharper tone: "Don't do anything to cross Mr. Damgaard. I don't want him fixing his attentions on you. If he can legally take my father's share of the company, let him have it."

Mr. Beckett looked surprised. "Let him have it? I don't think so."

"I know it's harsh for the workers, but that damage has already been done. I just . . . I don't want you doing anything that will get you killed."

Beckett frowned. "I'll see what we can do. Let the attorneys handle it."

She nodded reluctantly.

"Now, I'm a boarder at Walter Perkins' house, and . . . ." He hesitated, and continued apologetically. "I was going to invite you to stay there, to give you more time, but on second thought it may not look good for you to be there . . . ." He struggled for words.

"I understand," Katharine said.

"Why don't you sneak on over to Mrs. Petren's for the night, and come back here tomorrow morning?"

"I don't know . . . ." Katharine regarded Hannah with fear in her eyes.

"Just one night," Hannah assured her. "It'll be fine, dear." She stood abruptly, before Katharine could object. "I'll fix dinner in the meantime. Why don't you work on getting your things arranged?"

Katharine watched her go with trepidation. She felt sinews straining, muscle tissue crunching with anxiety.

"I know you have reason to worry," Beckett said gently, "but you'll be safe soon. You just have to pull through these next couple of days."

Katharine stared at Beckett with renewed intensity. She scanned him with some newly developed mechanism—barely conscious, yet alert and highly intuitive. And she didn't analyze him to determine trust; she had already established that. She was seeking something else now, attempting to detect every part of the man's soul. Beckett had weathered a difficult life. He had known terror, anger, helplessness, heartbreak. And yet there was a peace about him. Katharine wanted to know the root of that peace, to mimic and absorb it into her own being.

"I have worse problems than fear, I think," she said, making a covert study of Beckett's haggard face. She imagined him as a young boy, running from a southern plantation in the dead of night while gunshots felled the woman running next to him. An ugly event preceded by other ugliness, other crimes, unfathomable to her imagination.

"Mr. Beckett, I have to ask you something," she said. "I know that . . . ." She left the thought unfinished.

"What is it?" he asked gently.

"It's just that . . . it may sound strange, but maybe you'll understand what I mean when I say that I'm afraid of succumbing to rage."

Surprise registered in Beckett's face.

"Not against Damgaard," she continued, "but at people who I expected justice from. The police detective; the neighbors; other people. I keep thinking of the things the detective said to me—that he couldn't implicate Mr. Damgaard based on the unlikely claims of an emotionally disturbed girl, that I was 'obsessed' with Damgaard, that it seemed like I wouldn't stop making things up about him until I got him arrested. . . ."

Beckett was nodding absently. "Justice doesn't come easy in this world. It's a hard part of life."

"Yes, and I thought I knew it, but I didn't realize what it could do to me." She hesitated; felt a lump in her throat, a swell of grief as she thought over the past few difficult nights. "Something is happening to me. I can't explain all of it, but . . . ." Katharine wiped at her eyes as the vein of sorrow pushed upward, and quickly apologized for her tears: "I'm sorry; it's just that I don't have anyone else to talk to, except Hannah."

"Don't apologize," Beckett said gently. "Go on."

"I can't stop thinking of all the things people have said. I think of what the detective said, and I end up wanting to find him and . . . smash his face in. And I won't, of course, but I can barely restrain myself from lashing out at other people. There are little children living along this street, and I see them and have an urge to hit them. And I think I understand the impulse: it's easy for people to trample on me because I have no social power. I'm not vengeful, I'm not conniving. People can discard me without worrying about the consequences. But now that it's been done, I have this urge to turn around and crush someone who's . . . ." She paused, searching for the word. "Vulnerable. Someone who can't fight back. A child. A kitten. Maybe it's just that I see these children smiling, and I want to teach them that there's nothing to smile about. I wouldn't actually do such a thing, but it's so strong an urge. I'm ashamed to admit how strong it is. I feel like I've been given a disease, and I'm not sure how to fight it off. Do you understand what I mean?

I've talked to Hannah about it, but she doesn't understand . . . ."

Beckett was listening quietly. When he spoke, his tone gave away nothing, but Katharine saw that his eyes were sharp and clear. "I think I understand," he replied carefully. "You have someone who's done you wrong, and you can't get justice with that person. They've been put too high above you, and there's a temptation to take that anger out on someone else—someone you can reach."

"Yes—but what do you do about it?" Katharine pressed him. "How do you fight it? I mean, I'm asking what *you* would do, personally. I don't mean to make assumptions, but I do know that you've been through hell. You've seen innocent people tormented and killed, and the murderers treated like kings. Didn't it make you feel outraged?"

"Well, look. This country is *full* of killers walking around free, and I never forget it. I've felt plenty of rage. Mostly, I've prayed to God for strength. Any time I felt that kind of rage, I would stop and pray. There's no guidance in rage, and I needed guidance."

Katharine lowered her eyes. "I don't think that will work for me," she said dryly. "I have trouble believing in God."

"Well, do you believe that you have a spirit?"

"I must've had one, because it feels damaged."

"Then believe in the strength of your spirit, and don't ever give up on it. Your spirit came from somewhere. Wherever it comes from, that's what you pray to. You don't have to call it 'God'."

Katharine was silent.

"I'm not sure what to tell you," Beckett continued. "You know yourself better than anyone else. You just have to find something that reminds you to be strong. I pray, and I remember the people who raised me and what they prayed for. When you start to pray, you take power away from your own demons, and you give more power to your own faith."

He waited, but Katharine stared mutely at the floor, so he tried again. "Mrs. Derricks, the woman who brought me up here—she used to talk to me about that kind of rage. I would get to talking about revenge, about burning people alive and so on, and she would say, 'That's your demon talking. You may think it's not the same demon as theirs, but that's just another trick that the devil plays on you. He'll have us all tearing one another to pieces if he gets his way.' She would say that the devil isn't a bogeyman who lives under the ground; he's a disease that gets under people's skin. And he's contagious. You have to remember who you really are, and that's how you know the difference between your own spirit and the one that's trying to devour it. You create something else— integrity, kindness, courage. Those things are contagious too. Hate and love both have the power of inspiration. You understand?"

She nodded.

"There's no solution in rage. You can pursue justice through other means, and sometimes you have to pursue it through fighting, but you can't fight in a rage. It clouds your judgment."

Katharine met his eyes. In his gaze she could see the desire to help, and everything behind it: a bond with her father; simple compassion; a personal vendetta.

"You have a hard journey ahead," he said. "But you have to find strength somewhere, or . . . ." He shrugged.

"Or the monster wins," Katharine finished.

"Well, yes. I guess that's it."

Katharine slowly leaned forward, resting her chin in her palms, covering her face. A tumult of feelings rolled through her. She had a desperate, dangerous desire to throw all of her trust into this man, to amplify the bit of comfort he'd given her—to find in him all the friend and family that no longer existed for her. To hug him rather than shake his hand. Once again she became aware of her unbearable loneliness.

I had better let him leave, lest I start trying to hug the man, Katharine told herself, and almost chuckled at the thought. She uncovered her face and spoke calmly. "Well. I suppose I should start arranging everything. I'll pack at once." She stood and regarded Beckett with the most grateful look she could muster. "Thank you, Mr. Beckett."

She walked him out onto the front step, and thanked him again. "You've no idea how much you have helped me. I'm greatly indebted to you. If you ever need anything from me . . . ."

"You don't owe me anything, Miss Eliot. I'm indebted to your father. He was a good friend."

"Was he?" Katharine asked. "It struck me . . . you live with your daughter, and she's my age—isn't she?"

"She is."

"And yet our families have never met."

Beckett took his time in responding. He glanced across the street, where Mrs. Swift's two youngest sons stood looking on with obvious interest. "Never mind that now, Katharine. I'll meet with you and Mrs. Petren as soon as I can."

Katharine spent the weekend with Hannah's family and left them for good on Monday morning.

Troy Union Station was within walking distance of the Eliot home, but discretion and Katharine's luggage necessitated that they travel by carriage. Beckett helped Katharine load her bags, helped her inside, and introduced her to his daughter. Sarah and Mr. Beckett accompanied Katharine on the first leg of her trip, traveling by train to Greenbush, where Katharine would board the New York Central. Sarah sat beside Katharine on the train. Mr. Beckett sat nearby, alone.

As they stood together on the Greenbush platform, Mr. Beckett handed Katharine a neatly printed sheet of paper. "I know you have a lot on your mind, so I wrote everything down."

Katharine scanned the list with a tiny surge of gratitude. Beckett had written a detailed travel itinerary, including the time and exact place where she could expect to meet her uncle. At the bottom he had included her uncle's address along with his own.

"The rest of the journey will take you straight to Grand Central Depot," he said, "so you can just set your mind at ease from here on."

"Yes, I've done it before; I know the way. Thank you for—" She broke off. Katharine had looked aside, aware of the fact that someone had stopped nearby and was watching her—and was startled by a familiar, unwelcome sight.

Standing well within listening distance was a woman with thin brown hair weaved elegantly above a swan neck: Miss Bell. The woman had stopped there on the platform, bag in hand, staring at Katharine and her companions with obvious interest. Katharine's being filled with fearful dismay. *Miss Bell—of all people.* She recollected that the schoolteacher had family in Greenbush and took the train there regularly.

Katharine quickly averted her gaze. "Mr. Beckett . . . ."

"What's the matter?"

"Come with me for a moment, please." Katharine drew away, and the others followed warily.

"It's Miss Bell—the teacher I was telling you about, the one Mr. Damgaard has been courting," she explained shakily. She stood out of the teacher's view, with Mr. Beckett situated between the two of them. "She's standing nearby. I won't point her out, but she overheard us."

Beckett was quiet for a moment. His eyes remained locked on Katharine. "She heard me saying that you're on your way to Grand Central," he said, and let out a long sigh. "Well . . . at least I wasn't more specific than that."

"She's going to ask after me," Katharine replied in a low voice. "If she approaches you, I want you to tell her that I'm on my way to the psychiatric pavilion at Bellevue Hospital."

Sarah's eyes widened. Mr. Beckett looked aghast. "Tell her *what?*"

"Tell her that I'm going for psychiatric care at Bellevue."

"No," he said flatly. "You've—"

"Please, you must—*if she asks*, and I'm certain she will. She already knows I'm on my way to that area. She'll ask you about me, and act concerned, and then she'll go and tell everything to Damgaard. If he thinks I'm on my way to Bellevue, then maybe he won't search for me. I can't afford to have him find out that I'm going to live with—" She hesitated, checked for eavesdroppers. "If he thinks I'm checking myself into the insane pavilion, he's likely to think he's broken me, and he might leave me alone."

"I doubt that he would go looking for you in—"

But Katharine was shaking her head fervently. "You're wrong about that," she insisted, taking care not to raise her voice. "He *will* come after me. I'm still my father's heir. He has something to gain by . . . ." She couldn't finish the idea. "You'll see: I'll hardly be out of sight, and Miss Bell will come to you. She'll explain that she's my teacher, and she'll express concern for my well-being—and then she'll ask where I'm going. I'll be safer if Damgaard thinks I'm locked up, with no hope and no credibility to my name."

He lowered his eyes, looked distant.

Sarah gave her a slight nod. "I understand. I'll do it."

Katharine lightly squeezed Mr. Beckett's arm before walking away. "Thank you for everything. Thank you, Sarah."

Beckett sighed and called after her. "Take care, Miss Eliot. Have a safe journey."

10

MONDAY, MAY 20, 1889

"Quick, Mamma—we must get rid of the third chair," Charlotte said in a hushed voice, glancing stealthily around the half-empty saloon. "It will keep Mr. Kint from joining us."

The Morgan women were less than a day's length from the port at Marseille, preparing for a light dinner on the steamer. Rows of long tables filled the elegant dining room, but Charlotte had secured a small, private corner place with only three seats. She rose and pushed the extra chair across the floor, crowding it into a space at another table.

Elizabeth sighed as she returned to her seat. "Really, Charlotte. You talk of being married, and yet you run from any proper suitor who takes an interest in you."

"Mr. Kint is not proper," Charlotte replied. "He is boorish, and has only taken an interest in us after being rejected by ten other women—at least. He must think us the plainest women on the ship. And even if he had any genuine interest, he lives so far from London that I would wonder at his intentions."

"Perhaps you should have settled for Mr. Asher. At least you found him intelligent and engaging."

"I did not."

"Diane said that you did."

"I never said any such thing!" Charlotte protested. "I am sure it was an accusation on her part, rather than an observation. Mr. Asher is old enough to be my father. He is your age, Mamma—just two years shy of you. And I . . . ." Charlotte lowered her voice discreetly. "I was offended by his odor."

Elizabeth raised her eyebrows.

"Did you not notice? He smelled like . . . like . . . I cannot describe it, but he had such a strong, unpleasant scent about him."

"Well . . . ." Her mother looked thoughtful. "I suppose he did have a certain odor. It must be the Indian food. I know he is fond of the cuisine.”

“Impossible! None of our Indian acquaintances smelled like that. And the food cannot be the culprit, because his brother had the same odor.”

“I see.” Elizabeth leaned back in her chair, resting her gaze contemplatively on her daughter. “And is that the sum of your complaint? You found him old and odorous?”

“I disliked the way he spoke to me. He was always so certain of himself, and if he learned anything about me, he had to tell me whether he approved or not.”

“I think you exaggerate.”

“Hardly. And I disliked the way he insulted the missionaries, especially after he learned that Walter wanted to be a missionary in India. I can think of other objections, but the odor alone was enough. Think of it: if we had children together, our children would smell that way.”

Elizabeth smiled. The gesture deepened the lines around her eyes, and Charlotte studied her for a moment, noting the placidity of that smile. Other people interpreted it as peaceful, indicative of a calm and collected persona, but Charlotte knew better. Six months ago, that smile had been exuberant, full of life; now it appeared calm because there was so little energy behind it, so little peace. The voice, too, had quieted. These things seemed to fade along with her mother’s youth. Grief had aged her; the light hair was graying fast, the face rapidly collecting new lines, the body becoming slow and restful.

The steward appeared, sliding two plates of food onto the table. Elizabeth turned her smile on him with a soft “thank you,” but Charlotte didn’t move her gaze from her mother’s face.

“Anyway,” Charlotte continued, “I suppose we shall settle in London, and it will be better for us if I met someone there.” She thought over the young men she knew at home, but her mind quickly wandered back to Nikhil. She thought of his lovely eyes and dark lashes, the intensity of his gaze, his pleasant face—a stark contrast to Maitland Asher’s splotchy and perpetually sun-burnt guise. She remembered how she had dreaded meeting Maitland Asher on Howard’s verandah, only to see Nikhil waiting there instead, his eyes glowing in the early morning sun, his palms pressed together in the *anjali* greeting.

In the privacy of the yard, he’d wasted little time in explaining the reason for his visit: *Miss Charlotte, you are causing gossip among your neighbors. The memsahibs say that you are trying to marry yourself to Mr. Maitland Asher . . . .*

He had come to put her in check, and did so with his somewhat harsh directness—a trait that had initially intimidated Charlotte, but that she

soon found endearing. Nikhil's brow had furrowed sharply at the sight of
the Ghalib text, which Charlotte had carried from the house. He snatched
it and shook his head in amazement as he scanned the pages, reading
aloud: *Years have passed since the excitement of love caused me to tear
my clothes; again my spirit burns to release the fires of . . . hot
disturbance.* He'd regarded Charlotte admonishingly, waving the book in
her face. *You should not be reading Ghalib. If you wish to read Urdu,
fine—but not* this *Urdu, not this love ghazal. Why do you read this?"*
    I like poetry.
    *You would do better to stop liking it. It is fortunate for you that the
other ladies cannot understand it.*
    "I wonder why Nikhil never married," she mused. "He is very
handsome, is he not?"
    Her mother gave her a peculiar look, then lowered her eyes to her
plate. "He *was* married—when he was young. His family arranged it. But
his wife died in childbirth."
    Charlotte's heart throbbed with grieved astonishment. "Did he tell
you that?"
    "Yes."
    "When? I never heard you discuss personal matters with him."
    "Oh, we spoke a few times. I never dared mention it in Delhi. It
would have caused trouble with the neighborhood." Elizabeth lowered
her head and coughed feebly, then cleared her throat. "Nikhil is supposed
to be our servant, not our friend."
    Charlotte mulled that over. "And his child . . . ?"
    "The child died," Elizabeth replied quietly, picking up her fork.
    "How awful." Charlotte thought back over the times she'd confided in
Nikhil about the pain of losing her own family. "I wonder why he never
told me, when . . . what is the matter, Mamma? Are you ill?"
    Elizabeth's face had gone pale. She abruptly put down her fork. "I
can't eat," she said. "I'm going to the cabin to lie down."
    Charlotte looked at her in surprise. Her mother had endured the
journey without much complaint, and was only now beginning to feel
strange and fatigued.
    "It must be sea sickness," Elizabeth said, and forced a nervous smile.
"Except . . . ."
    "Except what?"
    Elizabeth paused. Her eyes glinted strangely. "Perhaps it was
something I ate—or perhaps I have caught something. I feel like
something is *wrong*." She put a hand to her throat, as though testing its
sensitivity.
    Charlotte studied her mother's wan face and felt a sting of concern. "I

hope you haven't caught a fever from Mrs. Fung." Other passengers, too, had fallen ill—mostly from sea sickness, Charlotte imagined, as they had been characteristically nauseated throughout the journey. But both of Lai Ping's parents had been stricken rather suddenly with exhaustion, and were spending the day in bed; and the mother had succumbed to fever.

Elizabeth's eyes were distant as she focused on the workings of her own body. "No, I don't feel feverish," she said. After a moment, she added in a strange tone: "Not yet, anyway."

11

PARIS

Katharine suppressed a groan as Paul's fingers pressed into her shoulders. He stood behind the wingback mahogany chair, his muscles straining against hers in an unsuccessful attempt at relieving the knots that burned beneath her flesh.

"Wait," she said. He paused long enough to allow her a sip of red wine, letting his palms rest lightly on her shoulders until she lowered the glass.

"Of all places," she sighed. "We cross the ocean to see the fair, and on the way there, the first thing we see . . . ."

"Don't worry." Paul kissed the top of her head. "There are thousands of people milling around. We probably won't run into him again."

She knew he was wrong.

Katharine sipped steadily on the wine, let it work its way through her strained muscles. She imagined its fluidity saturating her frazzled nerves.

It wasn't until evening that Nathan was released from work. He had sent a message asking to meet Paul and Katharine for dinner, and was waiting with his wife in the hotel lobby. Katharine, by then somewhat relaxed, couldn't restrain a surprised grin on seeing them: the two could have easily passed for brother and sister. Nathan was thin and tall, with frosty blonde hair and white eyelashes, and pale skin that flushed easily. His wife almost matched him in height and bore the same pale flesh, with white-blonde hair piled thinly around her head and a slight, slender figure, and merry blue eyes that matched the shade of her dress.

Nathan shook Paul's hand heartily and exchanged pleasantries. He didn't acknowledge Katharine until it was simply unavoidable. "Katharine," he said, and gave her a cordial—though slightly awkward— nod of his head. "It's been a long time. You look well."

"Thank you."

"This is my wife, Annette."

Nathan's wife greeted them with a warm "Hello."

"Bonjour," Paul replied.

She smiled. "Ah, parlez-vous français?"

"Yes, it's lovely."

"Paul doesn't speak French," Nathan explained, and Annette laughed.

"Oh, that's all right. I lived in America for three years." She looked at Nathan, wrinkling her brow. "Four years."

"Annette speaks excellent English," he assured them. "So what do you say, shall we have dinner?"

He introduced them to a restaurant down the street—one of the best in the area, he insisted—and helped them order a three-course meal. Nathan led the conversation; he was relaxed and polite, but kept his attentions fixed on Paul.

"So what's new in the so-called United States of America?" he asked. "I hear it's bigger than when I left it."

"Cleveland signed in four new states just before he left office. People keep spilling in from all over the world to grab more land."

Nathan gave him a knowing look. "And the industrial world keeps spilling all over the planet to grab even more," he said. "The U.S. is certainly no less ambitious than France in that respect. Have the states had any skirmishes with their European competitors lately?"

"We almost got into it with Germany on our wedding day."

"Over what?"

"You didn't hear?"

"I've been wrapped up in local events."

"It was over Samoa. We sent a few naval vessels to scare away the Germans; we had three ships, Germany had three, and there was a British ship floating nearby. Our vessels were about to fire on the Germans, but a cyclone blew in and sank all but the British ship. The battle was called off."

Nathan swallowed his soup with difficulty, perhaps fighting off a spasm of disbelief—or laughter. "A cyclone?"

"Mother nature."

"So, what, they just dropped the confrontation?"

"All's forgiven for the time being. A lot of people died, and everyone is taking time out to deal with the losses, but they'll get riled up over the Pacific islands again in no time."

"Yes," Katharine said, "but they're also planning to hold a civilized conference on divvying up Samoa, instead of shooting one another over it."

"Yes, we impress the world with our civility," Paul agreed dryly. "What about France? Still spreading?"

"Of course—but don't ask me for details. I really haven't picked up much in the way of national news lately, unless it's related to the Exposition. This part of Paris has really been worked over for the last few months. The Eiffel wasn't opened until just a few days ago."

"It actually isn't finished yet," Annette said. "You can only visit the first and second levels, and only by foot. The elevators are still being worked on."

Nathan nodded to Paul. "Have you had a look at it?"

"From the opposite bank. It's hard to miss."

"And what do you think?"

"It's tall."

Annette smiled at Katharine. "What about you, Katharine?"

Katharine was distracted; she turned to Annette, only knowing she'd been addressed. "Sorry, what?"

"What do you think of the tower?"

She hesitated, shrugged. "It's . . . tall."

Nathan grunted.

"We haven't had a good look at it yet."

"Do you think you'd like to explore it?" Annette pressed her.

"Well . . . I'd like to go inside and see how Paris looks from the heights."

"We should go together, tomorrow, and have lunch," Annette suggested with enthusiasm. "There are restaurants on the first level of the tower. Nathan will have to work, but the three of us can go. Our friend Leonard is working at the tower. He's an Arab—from Algiers. He might let us in free of charge. Otherwise we can buy tickets for the first level."

"I'll go," Katharine said. "Paul is afraid of heights."

Paul didn't comment, but gave Katharine a tight-lipped smile.

"Still nervous about heights, are you?" Nathan chuckled.

"We caught part of President Carnot's opening speech in the papers," Paul replied coolly. "He seems pretty optimistic about France's recovery. Things must have settled down quite a bit, politically . . . ."

"Yes. Boulanger left for Belgium last month, and people have accepted it as a sign that the Republic will stand. Economically, we're . . . ." Nathan hesitated. "We're certainly not at the top at the moment."

"France ranks fifteenth now, I think, among the nations."

"Oh, you're interested in economics now, are you?" Nathan asked with mild amusement.

Paul chuckled. "I can't help it; I read newspapers. The fair has made France subject to an intense study."

"We're fourteenth, and moving back up. That's what the fair is meant to demonstrate. We have some impressive entries in the machinery hall. France contributed Tesla's work—some things he completed before we lost him to New York. And Thomas Edison will be here, at some point, in person; he has his own pavilion behind the Liberal Arts building. Has Tesla done much for him?"

"Plenty, but now they hate each other."

"But they must still be coming up with all kinds of wonders back in the States."

"Actually, Edison's latest famed invention is the electric chair," Paul said. "There was a press release about it a couple months ago."

"An electric chair, for what?"

"For executing criminals by electrocution. There was another messy hanging a couple years ago—a woman, Roxanne something . . . ."

"Roxana Druse," Katharine said softly.

"She was too lightweight for the rope, and it took her a long time to die. The state decided to look into other methods. Edison was supposed to build the thing, but he had one of his employees do it instead. Probably didn't want to go down in history as its inventor."

Nathan was nodding. "I remember that woman, Roxana Druse. She killed her husband—and made the kids help. *That* was a grisly tale."

Katharine was looking around at nearby tables, shifting uncomfortably. "Let's not talk about that while we're eating, please."

"No, I want to know." Annette's face was lit with curiosity. "What did she do?"

"She chopped him up and put him in a stew." Nathan raised his soup spoon in Annette's direction before putting it in his mouth.

She reacted with disgust, but quickly recovered. "That's nothing. If you want to see some real cannibals, you can find them at the Exposition."

"I don't doubt that," Paul said.

"The first day the fair opened, we went to see the Fan cannibals."

"What's that?"

"They're savages from the French Congo. You can see them at the Village Nègre."

"The Negro Village," Nathan explained. "France imported four hundred Negroes from primitive tribes in Africa, and put them on exhibit at the Champ de Mars."

Katharine started. "On exhibit?"

"In a temporary village on the grounds," Annette explained. "It's part of the History of Human Habitation exhibit. The primitive category shows how the savages live outside the colonies. The Negro Village has received the most visitors. They give demonstrations on how to make their village crafts, and they perform tribal songs and dances. People have hardly been able to turn away from it—though it seems scandalous at times. The way the females dress can be a bit shocking."

"Or don't dress, rather," Nathan murmured.

"Even the way they hold their babies is peculiar. When you see the comparison, you realize that they're hardly more civilized than animals."

Katharine pressed her lips together, glanced at Paul with clouded eyes. "Which animals would those be?"

A splash of color caught her eye: Black above brown, near the front doorway. A black top hat over curls of dark brown hair. The man had just entered the restaurant, but turned toward the door, as if waiting for someone. Katharine stared at the back of his head. Everything seemed to go silent around her; the conversation at the table, the din of the restaurant, slipped into a void.

The man's companion joined him, moving through the doorway with a smile. A woman in a burgundy dress and feathered hat. And the man, turning toward the dining room, presented a long, slender nose, little dark eyes, and a thin-lipped mouth. *Not Mr. Damgaard.*

"Katharine?"

Her eyelids fluttered. She focused on Paul. "Yes?"

Nathan turned to see what had so consumed her attention, and saw nothing of interest. "Paul said that you think of the southern Democrats as animals with fine clothes and forks," he said, still gazing toward the entryway. "Is that right?"

Katharine looked at him silently.

"Pitchforks, in some cases," Paul said. "And I consider the northern industrialists to be more of the same. It's a matter of personal prejudice."

Katharine composed herself, still watching Nathan. He lowered his head to his bowl and tried to scoop the rest of the soup, catching the broth that dribbled down his chin. *Speak, Katharine. Say something coherent.* "What seems practical to some is easily made animalistic to others. For evidence, Annette, see how your husband is eating."

Paul made an effort to keep from choking.

Nathan dabbed with his napkin, unaffected. "Why the industrialists, Paul?"

"It's the northern animals backing the southern animals. They're helping to maintain the old south."

"Both the north and south have replaced slavery with convict leasing," Katharine cut in. "Police kidnap Negroes off the streets and sell them off to people looking for free labor."

"Hm," Nathan said shortly. "Abolition still isn't going as planned?"

"It's become a problem even in Troy," Katharine continued. She eyed Nathan, and he abruptly lowered his gaze. "We don't commit the kidnapping, but some of the local factories have benefited from it."

Nathan's voice took on a peculiar smoothness. "Oh, you still keep up on the happenings in Troy, do you?"

"We do," Paul answered curtly. "The owners know full well about the kidnappings and everything else. Southern politicians are fighting hard against change. They keep drafting new laws to prevent non-whites from owning land, and they enforce new voting regulations to prevent non-whites and the poor from voting—and they're not above openly terrorizing and killing their opponents."

Nathan nodded. "There's a lot of anger in the south. People lost their homes and loved ones in the war; they lost their enterprises, they lost their pride. . . ."

"Yes, and they're taking it out on the easiest targets," Paul replied. "They're lynching dozens of people every year, and going on killing and burning sprees."

"But they actually lynch criminals, don't they?" Nathan asked.

"They accuse black men of looking at white women."

"People don't have to make accusations," Katharine said. "They can still hang someone right out in the open, with dozens of people watching, and the people who commit the lynchings aren't held accountable."

"Why?' Annette spoke up. "The police don't catch them?"

Paul answered: "They don't bother trying. They justify it by comparing the victims to animals."

A brief silence ensued; Nathan cleared his throat. "But you have a Republican for president now, you must be happy about that."

"I was backing Harrison," Paul agreed, "but everyone knows that the election was a sham. Elections were tampered with in the swing states, and Harrison's campaign organized—"

"Yes, I heard about the buyout," Nathan said impatiently.

"Harrison and a few of his men could easily have gone to prison for election fraud, but the man is in the White House instead."

Nathan shrugged. "Democrats have been committing election fraud for years. If it's the only way to win, it's no wonder the Republicans are following in suit. It's still something to be upbeat about. Change is sweeping over the nations at ever increasing speed. In a few years, industry will replace slavery, and life will be so easy and utterly fascinating that we'll lose interest in killing one another over resources and pride. What do you say, Katharine? Do you see a better future, or are you as pessimistic as your new husband?" He asked the question lightly, returning his attention to his soup bowl.

"I think that we develop our technologies quickly, but we're slow to advance socially."

"I'll bet my soul that the same thing will still be happening a hundred years from now," Paul said. "The twenty-first century will be about to kick in, with an overabundance of new technology; but political parties will still be controlling the vote by blocking marginalized groups from the polls, making up false prison records, tampering with ballots in the swing states, and securing the term of a fraudulent president."

"And our government will still be finding ways to legalize the kidnapping of non-whites and political deviants," Katharine finished.

"You two do sound alike." Nathan nodded to Katharine. "I hope Paul didn't make you that way. I suppose he held some sway, when you met him at Bellevue."

"Katharine has never been to Bellevue in her life," Paul replied crisply, "and she's too smart to let me influence her."

Katharine ignored Nathan's insinuation, speaking carefully. "I'm grateful for some of the progress we're making, but I think I'm stating the obvious when I say that it's easy for us to be grateful. Our gratitude is trivial because we're already privileged. We're sitting in—"

"Ah, that's right." Nathan grinned suddenly, but without pleasure. "You were a speaker for the young Reform movement. I'd forgotten. You still have the bug, do you?"

Katharine stared at him, felt fire and ice flash across her eyes. "The 'bug'?"

"You speak very eloquently," he corrected himself, flushing a little.

"Yes, well, that's my point. We can focus on eloquence and such things, but there are other people living next-door to the devil, knowing he's got his eye on them and can rip their world out from under them at any moment. They've seen him do it before, and they know that when he does it again, people will be too frightened or self-interested to help. People will avert their eyes, pretend nothing's wrong, and defend themselves by looking at you as though you deserve it." She looked steadily at Nathan. "But that's just a guess. Some of us don't have to know what it's like to be scared all the time."

He lowered his eyes.

Suddenly, the entire table went crashing and spinning away. Katharine went numb, her eyes immediately zeroing in on the source of the calamity—a staggering, short-haired man in a white suit—*not Damgaard*. The table cloth had been whipped away from beneath the dishes, sending bowls and glasses tipping and shattering; Katharine's water glass and soup bowl had overturned and splashed their contents onto her clothes. The drunken man in the expensive white suit began

yelling boisterously in French, staggering past the table and flinging the
cloth as he went.

Paul was the first to recover. "Drunk jackass . . . ." He saw
Katharine's splattered clothes and quickly moved to help her. "Are you
all right? Here." He grabbed a stained napkin, used the clean spots to
wipe at Katharine's clothing.

"It's fine," she said shakily.

Waiters were rushing to put the table back in order, cleaning up
shards of glass and mopping up spills. Paul looked on in disbelief as
other restaurant staff politely showed the drunken patron to a table.

"They're letting that idiot stay?"

"They are," Nathan said. "That's J. Gordon Bennett, publisher of the
Herald."

"That's Bennett?" Paul stared at the man incredulously.

"Unfortunately."

"Well that explains a lot. You'd think he'd have learned his lesson
after being run out of Gotham."

Bennett. Katharine had met the man years ago, in 1875, when she was
practically still a child. Her father's business partner—interested in
Bennett's social position, and amused by the fact that they were the same
age and shared the same birthday—had finagled his way into the man's
social circle. Katharine and her father had attended parties and dinners
with him, and she had not forgotten his severe face and manner, or the
mean-spirited tantrums which his friends were prone to pass off as
quixotic ravings. She remembered him with tousled hair, a stern face and
bitter mouth veiled by a heavy triangular moustache, and pale snake-eyes
that seemed determined to penetrate whatever he saw. Now she found
him much the same, but with gray streaked through his short slicked hair,
and with a more severe expression and heavier moustache on his
ridiculously intoxicated face.

Bennett had raked up trouble during a New Year's party-hopping
spree in 1877. Arriving at his fiancé's home fully inebriated, he undid his
trousers and urinated in the crowded parlor, in full view of the guests.
His hosts took great offense. A whipping from the fiancé's brother
followed, and then a duel in which both men fired amiss. Bennett fled to
Paris and resumed his offensive behavior essentially unscathed.

Annette spoke around the wait staff, who were still re-setting the
table. "You've been spared the worst of it. Nathan and I have seen him
stark naked, in full moonlight."

"Yes, and with electric lights to add definition. Bennett streaked nude
through the fairgrounds a few nights ago. And prior to that, I've had the
displeasure of seeing him leaning naked from the door of his carriage

during one of his nightly excursions through town."

Paul shook his head. "And he overturns tables, and still gets the best seat in the house? What's his trick, is he the richest man in Paris?"

"He doesn't overturn them, he just likes to yank the tablecloths," Annette said.

"They let him stay because he writes good reviews, both in the New York *Herald* and the Paris edition, and brings in all kinds of new customers," Nathan explained. "They can't afford to offend him."

Paul's gaze was still fixed on Bennett, his face contorted with disgust. "I think I prefer the way he was handled in Gotham—driven out with Freddy May's whips and bullets flying around his head."

Nathan laughed; Paul stood and addressed a still shaken Katharine.

"Come on, let's get you cleaned up. We can have dinner at the hotel."

Nathan reached down, opening the wallet attached to his belt—but Paul gestured for him to stop. "Don't you dare pay them anything," he demanded.

Annette stood close to Katharine, wiping uselessly at a stain on her dress. "It's strange, isn't it?" she said quietly. "I think that a man of his status could commit a murder, and people would still rush to set his table."

12

QUEENS, NEW YORK: 1883-1888

Katharine's new home was a hundred and sixty miles to the south of
Troy, in the Ridgewood neighborhood of Queens—far from everything
she knew, with perhaps one exception: the Hudson River would remain a
few miles to the west of her home. Her uncle, Will Cropper, was a
surgeon. It was through him that she met Dr. Paul Gardiner.

Paul's focus, when he first began visiting the house, was purely
professional. He gave no attention to Katharine except for occasional
quizzical glances, as if puzzled by her lackluster demeanor. She
sometimes thought she saw a share of the same in him: the occasional
flash of grief in his eyes, a hollow spot somewhere in his being.
Katharine subjected him to the same study that she made of everyone
who visited the house. From a distance she listened to his words and
tone, discreetly examined his face as he listened to case studies and
updates about patients.

Paul showed up perhaps once a month. One night in August he stayed
for dinner, and his attention was caught by Katharine's dispiritedness. He
may have looked on her as a patient in need of treatment. Paul, who
loved to tease, made it his goal to provoke a genuine smile.

He failed. But Katharine could at least respond to his attentions in the
way she would have done in the past—with the same words, but without
energy behind them. Here was a woman who spoke words that seemed to
come from someone of spirit, but who nevertheless looked and sounded
as though she had none. Katharine tolerated Paul's conversation because
she'd seen compassion in him, seen real concern for his patients and
respect for her uncle. Paul was thirty-five at the time—twelve years her
senior, with a receding hairline and care-worn face, and pale blue-gray
eyes that became the main focus of Katharine's studies.

He was a widower, her uncle told her, and a former student at
Bellevue, with a house in neighboring Glendale.

Katharine had not the slightest romantic interest in him. But after

79

some time, she realized that she took some small pleasure in the way he abruptly turned his jovial eyes on her and confronted her with an amusing quip or good-natured bout of teasing.

He arrived at the house one afternoon when Katharine was alone. She showed him into the parlor and almost turned to seek refuge in her own room, but decided to obey the custom of the house: the women were expected to entertain Dr. Cropper's friends until his arrival. Katharine eyed the long, thin book that Paul carried, and after making the obligatory offers of food and drink, said, "If you like, I can leave you alone to review your notes."

"I wouldn't mind some company, actually."

Katharine disguised her disappointment, turning to seat herself just across from Paul. "My uncle shouldn't be long. His research always takes up more time than he anticipates."

"I've noticed." Paul relaxed into a plush chair and rested an ankle over the top of his opposite knee. "It's very tiresome for your aunt, I think—and presumably for the rest of you."

"I just hope he succeeds in finding a proper treatment."

"I don't believe he's formulated a proper diagnosis yet. In the meantime, you should prepare to hear your uncle's patients complaining of the incurable Cropper Syndrome." He cast her an inquisitive glance. "Your name is Cropper, too, isn't it?"

"No, it's Katharine," she deadpanned.

He scrutinized her with mild puzzlement, trying to discern whether she'd misunderstood.

"Mrs. Cropper is my aunt," Katharine explained. "Her name was Eliot."

"Hm." Paul looked down at his notes. "Funny, I assumed it had always been Margaret."

She forced a smile, though Paul wasn't looking at her.

"You haven't been long in this neighborhood, have you?" he asked. "I don't recall seeing you until a few months ago."

"I've been here a few years."

"Really. You must be expert at keeping yourself hidden." He added hastily: "It must be pleasant to have a cousin so close in age. You seem to get on well together."

"Yes, we do."

"I understand Helen just passed her fifteenth birthday. You must be about the same—or younger, perhaps?"

Katharine regarded him with disbelief. "Helen is several years my junior. I'm twenty-three."

"I apologize."

She nodded absently. "I think that a woman is supposed to feel flattered when someone underestimates her age."

"You say that as if you don't agree."

"It seems unfairly condescending. You, for instance, wouldn't feel flattered about being mistaken for a boy."

"I would, since I'm much more likely to be mistaken for an old man. I should have guessed you were older; you speak too eloquently for such a young person. Are you in school?"

"I . . . finished school."

"What did you study?"

She hesitated, then spoke grudgingly: "I went to a women's seminary for a few years, when I lived . . . up north."

"Northern New York? Where, exactly?"

"Well . . . ." She quickly formed an evasion. "Aside from the Seminary, I spent some time in Albany, working to raise money and create awareness of the Red Cross Society. I had friends who wanted to persuade some of the more established doctors and nurses to create a local chapter. My friend Tania had been with the Dansville group. She helped deliver relief items to victims of the great fire in Chicago. You might remember it; the smoke drifted over us and blotted out the sky for some time. It must have been 1881."

"Yes, I remember."

"She helped me get some training as a nurse's aide. I suppose that after I left, she might have succeeded in establishing an Albany chapter, but I haven't kept in touch."

Paul leaned forward, speaking with interest. "I admire the aims of the Red Cross. We could use a chapter here as well. You're close to Bellevue, and surrounded by doctors. You might succeed in garnering some interest—"

"I'm not involved with the nursing community. I had plans to study nursing, but I ended up having to abandon them."

"Oh. So you don't work as a nurse's aide?"

"No."

"That's unfortunate. We could use some good nurses, and more women in our profession in general. You're not thinking of starting up again?"

She hesitated. "No. But . . . ." Katharine didn't finish the thought. She had no desire to discuss her plans, or her lack thereof.

"What turned you away?" he asked.

"Nothing in particular. My studies were interrupted."

Paul opened his mouth, then seemed to be checking himself. "You mean, they were interrupted when you moved here?"

"Yes."

He nodded, studying her intently. Katharine lowered her gaze from his prying eyes.

"It must have been a taxing transition," Paul said. "I suppose your uncle hasn't encouraged you to continue studying. He has traditional views about women's roles."

"He does."

"But you must have something that keeps you occupied, or at least away from the house."

"No, I'm just expert at keeping myself hidden," Katharine replied dryly.

Paul smiled. "I suppose Cropper puts pressure on you to marry. I know that he already has his eye out for a beau for Helen, and has several young doctors in mind."

"Really. Does that include you?"

"Me? God, no. I'm much too old."

Katharine spoke quickly, diverting any other questions he might be formulating. "What about you, Dr. Gardiner? You must be thirty, at least, and probably studying surgery if you're working with my uncle."

"Dr. Cropper is giving me his expertise on various types of closed surgery."

"You must be a Bellevue graduate."

"Yes. 1875."

"And you own a nice-sized house on this side of the river, my uncle says, that you use as a private practice. You must be married. Do you have any children?"

He hesitated. "No, I don't have children."

"But you plan to, in the future?"

"No. I don't have much in the way of plans. I'm really not that interesting."

"Perhaps not. But you've been interviewing me, so I think it's fair that I should put the same questions to you. After all, I'm not one of your patients."

He looked at her with subtle astonishment. Paul was still considering how to reply to her comment when Katharine remembered her uncle's words: *Poor man, his wife died from consumption. He buries himself in his work, I think, to stop himself from grieving . . . .*

"Oh," she said, her face flushing, "I'm sorry—my uncle already told me you're a widower. I had forgotten." She cringed, still feeling the sting of her own words, and hurried to ease them in some way. "My father died recently, and I lost my mother when I was young, so I understand what it's like to lose someone close to you."

"It's all right," he said, with a hint of surprise. "Actually, I'm not accustomed to such heartfelt condolences. You're right, I'm not married. I'm halfway between thirty and forty. And I thought about studying open surgery, but I don't think I'm 'cut out' for it, if you'll pardon the pun."

Katharine's mind raced for a polite response. "I imagine it being very enervating."

"So do I." He smiled; his gray eyes were clear and friendly. "It was easy enough to practice on cadavers, but it's entirely another thing to work on a living person whose body is alive with rhythm and—well, you live with a surgeon. You probably hear more than enough of those stories."

"On the contrary, my uncle doesn't discuss surgery with his family. And most of his colleagues would consider it pointless to discuss medicine with me, even to pass the time."

"You gave me little choice, I think. I have to make up for interrogating you. I hope you'll forgive my prying. It's just that you're normally so quiet, if not entirely invisible."

"You don't need to apologize. I know I'm quiet. I've had a rough couple of years; they've made me quiet. I'm sure you understand."

Something flashed across his eyes—a hint of sentiment, dangerously close to the spark of affection. "I didn't really think you were a fourteen-year-old, by the way, I was just trying to get a rise out of you. I think I enjoy hearing you speak even when you're irritated."

Katharine smiled faintly. "I suppose I'll take that as a compliment." She paused, adding reluctantly: "I've heard you discussing medical phenomena with my uncle, and you seem to put faith in one's attitude in the alleviation of disease. I've heard you say that emotional trauma can make a person vulnerable to physical illness, and you think it's important to lift your patients' spirits without dismissing the seriousness of their maladies. You like to draw them out, so to speak, and shift their focus to better things."

"I do believe that the state of one's spirit has a bearing on physical health—directly, as far as it affects one's interest in maintaining health, and indirectly in the way that one's emotion has a constant bearing on the vital functions of the body. It's theory, but I think the results are perfectly visible."

"I think you're probably quite successful with your aims, even if your patients initially resist them."

"Well, you've never seen me in action."

"Perhaps I have. I meant to imply that you see me as an invalid in need of having my spirits lifted."

He stared at her for some time. "I see. That explains your comment about not being one of my patients."

She shrugged. "Yes, you've caught me."

"Actually, I try not to see even the most dispirited person as an invalid," he said quietly. "I think it negates the transitory nature of disease." He paused. "I hope you won't be annoyed to hear me say it, but if you're ever inclined to go back into nursing, you're in a good position for it. You uncle may not fully support it, and I don't know what your financial circumstances are, but if you've had some training, you could at least offer yourself as a volunteer assistant. There are women doctors who I'm sure would be happy to provide the opportunity. We have a drastic shortage of women in the profession. It's a detriment to the practice of medicine, if not an outright danger—if you don't mind hearing my opinion?"

Katharine paused. "I don't think I've ever heard a doctor excuse himself for voicing his opinion to a woman."

A footfall sounded on the front step. Katharine stood abruptly as the front door swung open. "There's my uncle. Good day, Dr. Gardiner." She addressed her uncle as she passed him: "Dr. Gardiner is here to see you."

She didn't see Paul for another month, when he showed again for dinner; and then not for two months; and each time, although he continued to lightly tease her, he seemed to maintain an understanding of some mutual agreement between them. But a wrench was unexpectedly thrown into that understanding during his dinner visit, when he announced to Dr. Cropper that the psychiatric ward at Bellevue had a peculiar new benefactor.

"Have you met this man?" Paul asked. "He's not a physician. He owns a factory up north, and doesn't seem to have any family or acquaintances at Bellevue or anywhere in the city, but he's taken up quite an interest in our psychiatric ward. He came all the way down here to accost Drs. Wildman and Douglas, and gave a hefty sum of money to the operation of the pavilion."

Katharine felt the color draining from her face. She glanced furtively at her uncle, but he had failed to make the connection.

"I don't believe I've heard of the man," Dr. Cropper murmured. "But I can imagine Wildman's response. He couldn't be less interested in discussing psychiatric care with strangers."

"No, nor Douglas. But they humored him because of the donation, and he's been a presence at the hospital and faculty dinners—and he's quite the character. He gives lengthy speeches on his heartfelt pity for the 'poor souls' whose tragic lives and frail psyches have brought madness upon them, and the next moment he launches into a dissertation on the natural inferiority of the poorer classes who refuse to help themselves and who deserve whatever misery they endure. And the most interesting thing isn't that he contradicts himself in practically the same breath; it's that the other doctors don't seem to notice it. They listen to him and voice their agreement with both opinions. It makes for an interesting study."

"What's his name?"

"John Damgaard."

Katharine felt her insides turning to liquid. Her aunt and uncle's eyes were suddenly riveted on her, and she had only a moment to see their perturbed faces before her vision blurred and she made a trembling attempt to stand from the table.

"Excuse me," she said, and hurried from the dining room.

Katharine reached the commode and rushed to remove her drawers, but she had not moved quickly enough. The mention of Damgaard's name—of his actions, of his proximity—had made her ill. She had always thought that the idea of people messing their pants from fear was an exaggeration. Now, seeing the dark trickle across her white drawers and hearing the splash of diarrhetic voiding, she knew differently. Katharine lowered her forehead into her hands and felt her face burning feverishly.

After some time she retreated to her room. She soaked her soiled garments in a basin and hid them under her bed, then lay down and stared at the ceiling.

Katharine had told her relations little about Damgaard. She had described his behavior at the mill and named him as a suspect in her father's murder, and made it clear that she felt it necessary to hide from him. They knew that Damgaard had acquired Charles' share of the mill. But of Damgaard's aggressions toward Katharine, of her own certainty about his guilt, or of her use of the Bellevue insane pavilion as a ruse to hide from him, they knew nothing. Too much talk about such convoluted events, it seemed, would only become sensational gossip, and eventually leak out to Damgaard.

Winter passed, and as spring began to melt the snow and ice from the landscape, Paul took to riding his bicycle and came to the house more often. Katharine simultaneously found dread and relief in his presence: dread because of his connection to Damgaard, and relief because Paul had seen through him.

He caught Katharine one afternoon on her way out of the house. She was clad in trousers, stained at the knees from kneeling in the garden. Paul looked down at Katharine's pants with a familiar twinkle in his eye. "Hello," he said as he dismounted.

"That's a fine-looking contraption you've got," she replied, before he could get a word in about her pants. "How long have you been riding it?"

"Not long. It's the new model. Want to try it out?"

He wheeled the bicycle closer, and Katharine gave it an intrigued study. In Troy she had never ridden a cycle, but had watched as other adventurers glided by on the old penny-farthings, each rider seated precariously atop the sizeable front wheel. She'd seen a young man fly from his seat and crash headfirst onto the street outside her house, breaking his neck and narrowly escaping paralysis.

Paul's model looked undoubtedly safer, with even-sized wheels and a seat much closer to the ground. But the manageability of the so-called "safety bicycle" was not what concerned her.

Katharine cast an anxious glance down the deserted street. "I couldn't. The neighbors would talk, and my uncle wouldn't like it." She nodded to the cycle, adding: "You know . . . there's a taboo about women on cycles. We can't ride side saddle."

"Hm," Paul said shortly, but with an ever-growing glow of amusement. "You can ride properly if you're dressed for it. Why the trousers?"

"I've been gardening."

"Gardening where?"

"Oh," she said, "there's a pathetic little garden plot behind the house. It doesn't get quite enough sunlight; the house keeps it in shadow until afternoon."

"Really. I didn't know you had a substantial yard back there. Is it large enough to ride across on a bicycle?"

She looked at him with silent reluctance.

"Come on." He began to wheel the bicycle away. "You'll have to show me this pathetic garden of your uncle's. Is Dr. Cropper at home?"

"We expect him soon."

"Even better."

They traversed the narrow wedge between houses and crossed into the rear yard, and Paul turned back with an inviting smile. "Come on, give it a try. You'll probably be the first woman in New York to ride one."

"All right." Katharine took the steering handle, scanning the neighboring windows intensely as she pulled the bicycle close to the house.

"Not so near. You'll crash," Paul warned, but she ignored him and kept to the least visible part of the yard.

Stuck fast in her mind, as always, were the judgmental whisperings that Damgaard had so effortlessly sparked. *People will see, and they will judge, and then Damgaard will have more power.* Fear still clenched its grip in the fibers of her muscles. It had settled in and fed on her energy like a parasite, seeming to fester in her upper back; it extended spider-like legs deep into her shoulders, and upward through her neck, with two thin membranes that stretched to the bottom of her spine. At times, the muscles would spasm so painfully that any attempt to loosen them produced no result aside from a migraine. It was for this reason that Katharine moved slowly; she had to give herself time to relax, lest the tension should crunch her into immobility.

Katharine paused to acknowledge the darknesses that moved within her, and began to pull strength from wherever she could: the quiet peace of the neighborhood, the transformative energy of the springtime air. She turned for a moment to look into Paul's eyes, observed kindness and good nature in them. But even as one voice within her said *Damgaard is in the past; you are safe now*, the other voice insisted that there was no such thing as the past, and she would never be safe.

It was an elaborate struggle for so simple and brief an adventure. After a failed attempt at riding alongside the house, she veered to the right and shot out across the lawn, bumping and weaving her way forward with both feet on the pedals—but she slammed her feet back onto the ground as the front wheel began to transgress on the freshly seeded garden.

"It's harder than it looks," she confessed as she struggled to turn the bicycle around. Katharine rode back toward the house, and slowed as Paul called after her to stop before she flattened her face on the brownstone.

"How do you like it?" he asked, approaching.

Katharine shook with laughter. "I'm stuck," she gasped. "I can't get my leg over the top."

"Here, I'll help you—good Lord, you have a slight figure! Doesn't your uncle feed you?"

"No, wait—the bicycle has my trouser leg. The material is stuck in the gear."

"Oh, I see. Here, I'll get it. Try to move backward a little. There, it's loose." Paul clasped his hands around her waist as she struggled to raise her leg over the top of the bicycle.

"It's okay, I can do it," she insisted. "If my uncle sees me on a bicycle, and you with your arms around me, I'll never hear the end of it."

Paul smiled as Katharine freed herself. "I don't think Dr. Cropper would object to seeing us together. He's been extolling your virtues to me for some time."

"Are you serious?" She appraised him doubtfully. "What virtues?"

"He seems to think you're responsible and obedient."

"Obedient?" Katharine uttered the word with mortification. "Did he say that?"

"I guess he wouldn't think it if he saw you now. Listen: I know that Dr. Cropper is going to Vienna for some months." Paul lowered his eyes, then looked toward the tiny garden plot with feigned interest. "I'm sure the three of you will be fine without any intrusions, but I think Dr. Cropper would appreciate it if I checked in on you every now and then— if that's all right with you?" He met her gaze, but did so with some difficulty, as if bracing himself for rejection.

Katharine thought she understood what he was asking. She looked back at him, still breathless from laughter, and didn't respond.

"I thought I might show you around the other side of the river," he added. "Have you been to Central Park?"

"No."

"Would you like to see it?"

"If you're inviting us, I'm sure we'll all accept."

"You'll love it. I'll take you as soon as the weather allows."

"All right then. I'll expect you." She smiled—a genuine smile, she realized. The realization sparked an unnamed fear, and slowly stole the smile from her face.

Katharine's uncle informed her that Damgaard had returned to Troy in December, without any seeming intention of returning to Bellevue or of maintaining a relationship with its doctors. Katharine reveled in the relief of his departure. She became determined to relax, to connect with the man who was slowly winning her over. Her journal became a slow-paced healing chronicle:

Tuesday, August 7, 1888:
By now it is undeniable that Dr. Gardiner is courting me—and I do not know why. I still look in the mirror and see a ghost of a woman, but perhaps Dr. Gardiner sparks some degree of livelihood in me and that is what attracts him. He mistakes my deadened spirit for placidity and my carefulness for patience, attributes my cautious observations to shrewdness, and deems me fearless. I've come to realize that I no longer have "little fears" because my anxiety is fixed on the incidents surrounding Mr. Damgaard's attacks and the possibility of them reoccurring. Dr. Gardiner seems not to notice all the peculiar mannerisms that I bear, overwhelming to me but perhaps unseen to others. Lately I realized that I always pause just before passing through a doorway, discreetly checking to see whether anyone is on the other side—because Damgaard might be there, or if not him, someone with a

Dr. Gardiner has a way of teasingly hinting at his oncoming proposal, and has such a matter-of-fact way of complimenting me that he can pass off blatant flirtations as objective observations—and then he looks at me with a good-natured sparkle in his eye, and I cannot help smiling in response. That this man can produce a genuine smile from me is a great achievement. Nothing else has been able to do it.

I suspect that Dr. Gardiner is ready to propose now, and is only waiting for the right moment, which I haven't been willing to provide. Lately he has been coming up with the most ridiculous excuses to be alone with me, but can only get a few moments in before Helen interrupts. She adores each of us, and having us both in her company at once is something she will not pass up.

With Dr. Gardiner I have a chance at a future, but every happiness I feel with him is also frightening because I know that it can be violently ripped away. And so I constantly work to accept the present, to accept the safety of the moment, and to simply live—and it feels good to do so. Each week I find myself sacrificing a little less of my happiness.

Paul tolerated her habit of always taking Helen and Margaret along on their outings. In September he brought the three of them back to Central Park, offering to show Katharine the areas they hadn't covered yet and insisting that he had "saved the best grounds for last."

They set up a picnic lunch in the shade of a large tree. Helen attempted to make the spot more hospitable by ripping up a couple of ferns that stood in her way.

"No, don't kill the ferns," Paul admonished her. "Just set the blanket over them. The plants will stand themselves back up after we leave and be none the worse for having been sat upon."

Helen heeded his advice and threw the cloth out across the grass. Paul straightened it and offered Helen his hand. "Here—allow me." He helped the ladies to sit, smiling at his own show of cordiality, and then he stood and looked at Katharine. His face settled into such a look of unsmiling, almost nervous determination that she felt herself blushing.

"Ew!" Helen gasped, scuttling close to Katharine. "Spider! Paul, kill it."

"It's harmless," Katharine said mildly. She offered her fingers to the timid creature, waiting until it dared to crawl onto her flesh before transporting it back to the grass. "See?"

"No, Katharine!" her aunt protested. "Don't let it go. It will come back and crawl up somebody's back."

"I have a solution to that," Paul said. "Katharine, why don't you let me show you around the ramble while your aunt and cousin kill all the insects?" He offered his hand to Katharine before anyone could reply. She took it with a restrained smile.

"We'll be back shortly," Paul said, and nodded to Helen. "Get rid of all the bugs and spiders while we'll gone; Katharine will have them crawling all over you otherwise." He had turned and was walking away, with Katharine following.

They went westward into the forest. Katharine walked in silence as Paul delved into a brief history of the area, not once looking at Katharine as he spoke.

"I used to come here thinking that this part of the landscape had been left untouched," Paul explained as he led her deeper into the woods. "See how the trails weave around the trees and boulders and rivulets? I figured the designers wanted trails cleared in the most practical places, instead of having everything moved and uprooted, and that was why they rambled so aimlessly. I thought it was really lovely, the way the area was made to be intruded upon without being violated. But after a while I learned that everything was done by human design, and the trees and rocks—and even the topsoil—were moved here to create the impression of a natural, rambling woods walk. Here—let me give you a hand." He led her up a rocky incline, toward a massive boulder; but abruptly he stopped, still holding her hand, and looked down at her with a flushed face. "Katharine, I want you to be my wife," he said.

The proclamation, expected as it was, provoked overwhelmingly mixed feelings of dread and relief that nearly drowned her initial sensation of tenderness. Katharine felt herself blanching.

She managed two words: "All right."

"All right? Are you saying yes?"

She nodded.

"You're not going to think it over, or . . . ."

"I don't need to think about it. Of course I'll marry you."

Paul looked pleased, but his smile was laced with something akin to suspicion. "That was easier than I anticipated. You must have . . . I suppose you knew I was going to ask you."

"I suspected, yes." The nausea began to recede as she looked into Paul's eyes. Katharine broke into a faint smile. "I think you couldn't have made it much more obvious."

"So you've thought about it already."

"Yes—I suppose so."

"You suppose so? I want you to be sure. If you change your mind, it'll crush me." His voice lowered a notch. "Can I kiss you?" Paul moved closer, sliding his hands slowly around her waist.

"No, don't kiss me yet." She held up a hand to stop him. "I think I'm going to be sick. It's nothing to do with you," she added quickly, as she saw his look of astonishment. "Just let me sit down."

She lowered herself onto a flat rock, sitting quietly until the sensation passed. "Paul, there's something I need to talk to you about before you agree to marry me."

"What's the matter?" he asked warily, sitting beside her.

"It's just that I haven't said certain things about . . . where I come from, and I think you should be a little more familiar with my background before you engage yourself to me."

"All right. What is it?"

She opened her mouth, but couldn't find the words. Her throat constricted painfully.

"Let me guess: you're a convicted criminal," he said. "I knew it. What'd you do?"

She shook her head.

"You come from a questionable family. That's all right; my parents aren't model citizens either. What is it? You're worried that I'll judge you on some past circumstance?"

"No, that's not what I'm afraid of. Not really."

"What, then?"

"It's . . . Mr. Damgaard."

Again, he was nearly dumbstruck. "Mr. Damgaard? You mean John Damgaard, the so-called philanthropist from—" He hesitated. "Do you know him?"

"He co-owned his steel works with my father. They were partners, and Damgaard murdered him . . . ." Katharine's throat closed up; the teeth locked together.

"Damgaard . . . murdered your father?"

She nodded.

Paul was quiet for a moment, and asked: "Is that why you got sick at dinner when I mentioned him?"

"Yes." Katharine winced at the memory. "I didn't think you'd noticed."

Paul's eyes became clouded. "What happened? He can't have been convicted . . . ."

"No, he wasn't convicted, but I know he did it."

"For what? Money?"

"Damgaard was able to obtain my father's share of the company without paying for it. The money would have gone into my inheritance. But there's more to it than that."

"How certain are you that he did it?"

"I caught him leaving my father's house just before I found . . . ." She choked up, changed track. "They had been arguing about the company. Damgaard made infrastructure changes without permission, started riots . . . lawyers got involved, and things got so bad that my father sent me away from the house. He was worried that Damgaard would . . . *do* something. After I accused Damgaard of murder, he came to the house and threatened me; but when I reported it, everyone accused me of lying to implicate him. And it's not just that. Damgaard somehow managed to persuade everyone that I'm . . . ." She shook her head. "Name it, and he said it. I'm crazy; I'm wicked; I'm a liar; I'm a loose woman; I was trying to have him convicted of murder so I could get all the company profits for myself. It's not just that he said it, but that people believed it and started—"

"Wait," Paul interrupted. Katharine was trembling; he put an arm carefully around her shoulders, as if to steady her. "Are you worried that I'll regret marrying someone who has . . . ." He shrugged, searched for words. "A reputation?"

"Partly."

"All right. I get it, but don't ever worry about that. I have more respect for you than for anyone who could be swayed by Damgaard. What do you mean, partly? What else?"

She hesitated. Relief swirled deep within her being, but she tried not to give in to it. *Not yet; not until I've said everything.* "I don't know how to explain it. It's just that Damgaard spent so much time following me, and taunting me, after my father's death—and I'm sure that the reason he gave that money to Bellevue is because it tied in to his false sympathy for my supposed 'hysteria.' I led him to believe that I had been sent to the insane pavilion. I was trying to cover the fact that I had come here to live with my aunt. I wasn't sure that he fell for it until I heard about his contributions to Bellevue."

Paul's eyes were lit with amazement.

"I know it's . . . it's a lot to take in . . . ." Katharine fumbled for words. "I would understand if you didn't . . . ."

He blinked, cleared the intensity from his gaze. "Sure, it's plausible; you could have gotten into Bellevue easily," he said casually. "Third class insanity: patient files complaints to police and court justices about imaginary persecutions. It isn't unheard of for a patient to skip police proceedings if one is willing to be committed."

"Yes, exactly. I thought that if Mr. Damgaard believed he'd broken my spirit, he'd give up pursuing me. But if he finds out that I simply moved away, and that I'm happy . . . ."

"You're worried he might come after you, even now?"

"I'm afraid of him, Paul. I know that you like to compliment me on my fearlessness, but Damgaard scares me. And it's not just because he killed my father. It's because . . . I don't know how to explain it. It's something about his manner."

He pulled her close. "You don't need to be afraid. If Damgaard ever comes anywhere near you, I'll take care of it."

Katharine resisted his embrace. "It isn't that easy."

"I didn't say I thought it would be easy."

"He might try to cause trouble for you, just because . . . ."

"I see. I think I can deal with that, Katharine; you don't need to take so much upon yourself. I'm very happy that you want to marry me. I was worried that you would say no." His voice was unusually serious; all traces of his sparkling humor were absent, yet he spoke gently. "But since you've accepted, I think it's appropriate that we should spend some time on our own. It would be good for us to sit down and talk more about . . . what happened with Damgaard. And of course we'll have to plan a wedding date, and all of that—unless you change your mind."

Katharine sighed, felt some of the tension easing. "I already know you're a good man, Paul. I would be very happy to be your wife. I'm flattered that you think I would make a good companion. I don't feel like I've been at my best these past months."

He looked genuinely taken aback, but the light-hearted gleam reappeared in his eyes. "Really. I had no idea you thought so little of yourself. I'm more astonished by the idea of you wanting to marry *me*. I'm old. I'm going bald."

Katharine suppressed a smile. "Yes, but you make me laugh."

Their intimacy was interrupted by Helen, who was yelling their names from a nearby trail.

"Damn," Paul muttered. He stood and called to the intruder: "We're here . . . up here. Be careful of those roots. You're better off going the other way around. No, the other way—and without killing everything, please." He pulled Katharine to her feet and wrapped an arm around her waist as Helen approached. "Guess what? I just convinced the most beautiful woman in the world to marry me."

Helen's eyes went wide. "You mean Katharine?"

"No, I mean Margaret. Of course I mean Katharine. Don't tell your mother I said that; she might take it the wrong way. How would you like to be the first one to tell your mother that Katharine is getting married?"

Helen looked questioningly at Katharine. "You don't want to tell her?" she asked, and then her expression became sly. "Oh—of course. You want to be alone." She ran back down the path.

"I like her," Paul said dryly, "but she's a bit slow. I've been trying to get you alone for months, and she's only now realizing it."

13

PARIS: TUESDAY, MAY 21, 1889

Paul and Katharine spent the morning touring the neighborhood with Annette, perusing shops and sampling a French bakery. Annette showed a friendly partiality toward Katharine, often walking arm in arm with her—a welcome relief, Katharine decided, after she'd anticipated a cold reception from Nathan and perhaps the same from his wife.

They sat for tea, and Annette took time to go through the Exposition guide with them—again, responding mostly to Katharine's interests, and merely tolerating Paul's. After they returned to the hotel, she left them to check in at Nathan's office. Paul wasted no time in commenting on the attentions that so far he'd only raised his eyebrows at.

"Annette certainly likes *you*," he said as they ascended the stairs. "I was beginning to feel like I was imposing."

Katharine chuckled. "Be easy on her. She told me she doesn't have any women to talk to."

"I don't know; I'm worried she's going to carry you off as soon as I turn my back. What did she talk you into, aside from the tower and the Wild West show?" He rifled through his pockets, searching for the room key.

"Cairo Street."

"Of course. What's the lure? The infamous donkey rides?"

"Not that." Katharine paused outside the door and studied the guidebook, making a futile attempt at remembering the words Annette had interpreted for her. "If I was a child, I might want to, but who else rides donkeys?"

"The virgin Mary rode one to Bethlehem. You never had a donkey, you wouldn't know if it's any fun."

"I'm not interested in riding side saddle on a donkey."

"Well if you're bold enough to ride full straddle, you're very welcome to ride me when we get inside."

Katharine's mouth opened in astonishment. She looked up to

95

admonish him—but she was distracted by the sudden presence of two women in the hallway.

The younger woman had overheard the comment. She had a pleasant, plain face and warm brown eyes, and she glanced briefly at Katharine as she passed by, giving her a small smile. An older woman—the mother, probably—walked behind with her head lowered, and after her was the porter carrying most of their luggage. Katharine waited until they had passed, then slapped Paul's arm and opened the door.

Paul closed it behind them and waited for Katharine's reaction, cringing. He put a hand to his mouth—a mistake, because his wife suspected that he was smiling with guilt-laced amusement.

"Paul," she said severely. "You promised me . . . ."

"I'm sorry, I thought we were alone."

"Well you can stop talking to me like that when you think we're alone, then." Katharine folded her arms, studying him admonishingly. "You know, this is exactly why women are abused for doing something as innocent as riding a bicycle. Men like you have to make everything into some type of fornication."

"I'm . . . not going to say the first response that popped into my head. I want to make you happy."

She shook her head, unconvinced.

"I'm sorry; you're so beautiful, I can't stop my mind from going in that direction."

"Don't . . . ."

"Can I still kiss you?"

"No. I'm leaving. Annette is taking me to lunch at the Eiffel."

"What, and leave me all alone, when we're supposed to be celebrating our wedding?"

"You haven't had any time alone with Nathan. I thought you might like to catch up with him. I know you don't want to have lunch in the tower."

A knock sounded on the door.

Katharine gave Paul a warning look and whispered: "Behave yourself."

Annette was in the hall, smiling brightly. She greeted Katharine and kissed both of her cheeks. "You're ready?"

"Yes." Katharine smiled back, but turned to Paul with stark austerity. "Have fun with Nathan," she deadpanned. "We'll come and fetch you after lunch."

Charlotte entered her mother's room, number 342, and paused to admire it. "Oh, your room is lovely," she breathed.

The room was much more spacious than her own, and decorated in richer tones. The wallpaper was elegantly embellished with images of dark-tinted roses; plum-colored velvet curtains adorned the windows at the far side of the room, matching the spread on the queen-sized bed. On the far side of the room was a high-backed sofa with white plush cushions, and a mantel holding a single item: an exquisite ormolu clock.

Elizabeth lowered herself onto the bed and removed her hat. "Is it very hot in this room? I feel so tired, I don't even know whether I am feverish or . . . ."

"It is hot. Let me open the window." Charlotte moved to the window, taking a few moments to look outside. The fairgrounds were obscured by surrounding buildings, but she could see a familiar metal protrusion rising above the rest. "We can see the tower from our rooms—but I think the view *inside* your room is more pleasant." Her attention was quickly drawn to the clock on the mantel. "Look, an ormolu—a real one, I think." She leaned in for a closer look, examining the gilded flowers that encompassed the clock face. "Do you remember Uncle Howard talking about his ormolu? He said that all the craftsmen were struck down with a mysterious illness; it was discovered that they were dying from quicksilver poisoning. All of the real ormolu clocks are antiques. People call them death clocks." Charlotte's gazed moved over the figurine that stood atop the base: a slender, blindfolded woman holding a sword and a pair of scales, vanquishing a serpent beneath her foot. "It looks pretty, though, doesn't it?"

She turned to her mother, saw her slumping on the bed. "You do look pale. You should rest."

"Yes, I will." Elizabeth clumsily began to remove her corsage, and her daughter immediately moved to help her.

"There." Charlotte set the garment aside, then helped her mother strip down to her underclothes. "Do you still have a headache?"

"Yes."

"Can I get you something for it?"

"No . . . I think I shall just sleep."

"All right. Sleep as long as you want; and if you're feeling better later, perhaps we can take a tour inside the Eiffel."

"Yes, it's tall," Paul was saying.

Nathan's hotel room was large but modestly decorated. It opened into an office with an expensive-looking teakwood desk and a ridiculously comfortable chair at the front, and behind the desk set were neatly arranged bookshelves with a miniature liquor cabinet tucked away to one side. The cozy chair was obviously reserved for Nathan, so Paul made himself comfortable on a small couch.

"World's tallest man-made structure," Nathan said. He draped his jacket over the back of the overstuffed chair and dropped himself heavily into the seat. "It beat out your Washington Monument."

"Yes, we were pretty proud of our pathetic obelisk for a few minutes," Paul chuckled. "It just opened in October, and now France has already erected a bigger monument, with restaurants and elevators inside of it. A true symbol of the age. And a telling competition."

Nathan looked blank.

"You know. America erects a giant phallus, and now France gets to say 'Oh yeah, well ours is bigger.' Now everyone's in a heated competition to prove that they've got the biggest prick."

"You really can be crass."

"You weren't thinking it, too? The Eiffel isn't even finished yet, and the U.S. has already announced that it's planning to erect an even bigger tower—as if the Eiffel hasn't said it all. It's not enough that we have to cut up the U.S. and the rest of the world with iron lines. At least that has an element of practicality, but now we have to drive an iron road up into the sky, too, and whoever can go the highest gets to crow and strut about it."

"It's an incredible engineering feat."

"It is. Actually, I prefer the tower to the railroads. And I know Eiffel is a railroad man; maybe this is a good diversion for him."

Nathan nodded, but countered: "Don't forget, you came here by train."

"Touché. You see, I do speak a little French."

"It is a good diversion, if you want to call it that. Eiffel treats his workers a hell of a lot better than railroad workers are treated in the states."

"He had better. I'm sure the tower was a much riskier venture."

"It's *still* a risky venture. He still has men up there, trying to finish the highest parts of the tower." Nathan picked up a newspaper from his desk and paged through its contents. "Did you see today's paper?"

"No."

He flashed a paragraph at Paul.

"I can't read French," Paul reminded him.

"The workers have been clumsy of late. A couple days ago, a group of tourists was splashed with paint that one of the workers spilled. Pieces of iron have fallen onto the platform and caused damage. They're lucky no one was hit—and that none of the workers have fallen."

"I see," Paul replied flatly. "I believe our wives are lunching at the tower right now. It's bad enough that they're suspended hundreds of feet

in the air, without the added possibility of being crushed by chunks of
iron and falling men."

Nathan chuckled. "Sorry, I didn't mean to put the scare into you. I
forgot about your fear of heights. You haven't changed—with one
exception, I guess." Nathan pulled a bottle of brandy from a small liquor
cabinet. "Brandy?"

"No, I'm fine. Just one exception?"

"Well, you went through with marrying the Eliot girl. I was surprised
to hear you're already married. I thought the wedding was scheduled for
May."

"We got tired of waiting."

"She hurried you into it, did she?"

Paul caught the faint note of disapproval in Nathan's tone. He paused,
studying his friend for some moments. "It was Katharine who insisted on
not hurrying," he said at last. "By the way, we ran into John Damgaard
on the Pont d'Iena this morning. Did you happen to know he was in
town?"

"Yes, I knew he was here. You don't need to worry. He's here for the
exposition, like everyone else. He's been touring hotels, and he visits the
fair daily."

"You spoke with him?"

"We said hello."

Paul was quiet; heard the ticking of the wind-up clock, measuring the
passing seconds. "Nathan . . . ."

"What, are you going to tell me to ban the man from the hotel? Tell
you what: while you're here, I'll try to avoid contact with him."

"Thanks. I appreciate your genuine concern."

"Damgaard's harmless, Paul."

"Really. What the devil is he doing in Paris? I thought he was busy
dealing with his contract problems back in the states."

"He had an opportunity. What, does your girl think he followed you
here?"

Paul was quiet for a moment, considering. "Katharine isn't a 'girl,'"
he said mildly.

"Very well; your woman, your wife." Nathan poured himself a drink,
then gestured toward Paul with his glass. "Do you know what she told
people?"

"What's that?"

"A few nights after her father died, Katharine told the police that
Damgaard showed up at her parlor window, dancing and waving a bottle
of whiskey, and bragging about how he had murdered her father and
would kill her within the week."

"So?"

"That doesn't sound a little nuts?"

"Of course it does. It doesn't mean Katharine's nuts."

Nathan stared. "But you believe her?"

"Yes."

Nathan frowned, looked disconcerted.

"Really," Paul said, speaking lightly, "if I thought she was a nut, I wouldn't have married her. I'm acquainted with Mr. Damgaard, Nathan. I know his personality."

"And you think he seems like a cold-blooded killer?"

"I think he seems persuasive and opportunistic. And animated and charming, and I know for a fact that he's good at garnering privileges and protection from other people. And as far as his dancing spree at Katharine's window, I don't doubt that it happened. Yes, I heard the story about the whiskey dance. Her contention is that he knew she'd report the incident immediately, so he did something that would make her sound crazy. Katharine told the police that Damgaard was drunk. When they showed up at his house, he was perfectly sober, and claimed he'd come straight home from the police station without stopping anywhere—and that he never drinks whiskey, which, of course, is true. Katharine thinks he just used the whiskey bottle as a prop."

Nathan leaned forward, as if to hear him better. "A prop?"

"To make her sound like a liar, so people would dismiss the rest of what she said. After that, she was afraid to report anything he did, because it would sound like another lie. I'm sure Damgaard expected that, too. He told the police that Katharine was 'obsessed' with him."

Nathan shrugged. "Well . . . ?"

"It seems natural to me to become fixated on someone who kills your only living parent and then stalks you."

"You've only heard Katharine's side of it," Nathan said. He looked on Paul with something like estranged disappointment; the friendly, familiar shine had faded. "The whole thing sounds pretty ridiculous to me."

"I'm sure Damgaard had the foresight to anticipate that."

"Paul, look, I think she's—"

"No, don't say it, whatever you're going to say, just stop. Katharine doesn't even want me talking about this. She's terrified of Damgaard—really *terrified*. She made me promise I wouldn't bring it up, and I'm breaking my promise."

"Really, that's interesting."

"What's interesting—Katharine, or Damgaard? The whole thing makes perfect sense. You commit a crime, you don't want the witness to have credibility, so you destroy it. You cause her to see something that no one else can see, and then you make sure that no one else can see those same details. You accuse her of being delusional, of making things up, and you insinuate that she might even be covering up her own crime by blaming you. She has no credibility and everything to lose, so she backs off. You win, and with very little effort."

"It all sounds a bit complicated for John Damgaard."

"But not too complicated for Katharine? Why are you so defensive of Damgaard?"

"I understand how the murder of a loved one might make a person feel scared. And desperate. I'd want to know that the killer was put away."

"You and I wouldn't risk pinning it on an innocent man. Neither would she. But Damgaard is a different character completely. Do you happen to know the details of his latest contract crisis?"

Nathan sighed. "No."

"Outside contracts for prison labor were outlawed a few years ago, but Damgaard is still milking the industry by sending raw materials to prisons and having the finished products shipped back to the company. That way, it's not technically an outside contract for the prison system, and Damgaard can still take full advantage of cheap, forced labor. The unions are trying to shut him down over it—among other things—but he's hanging on until he can get his next boatload of desperate, starving immigrants into port. This time they're coming from Russia. You know what things are like in western Russia right now? Damgaard is right up there with Joe Brown; he just hasn't seen the same level of profit yet."

Nathan held up his hands. "All right, all right; I know he's a profiteer, I get it. And I said I'd keep him away. Okay?"

"Does he know that Katharine is my wife?"

". . . I did mention the two of you."

"Oh, you did. And he knows we're here? Did you tell him which hotel we're staying at?"

Nathan averted his eyes, pretended to be interested in the newspaper.

"Do me a favor, Nathan, and I'll say this as kindly as possible. The next time Damgaard squeezes you for information on me or my wife, keep your goddamn mouth shut."

"Paul . . . for Christ's sake. I'm not even going to say what I'm thinking."

"Right, I'm exaggerating. He doesn't need to squeeze you; you give the information voluntarily."

A sharp knock sounded at the door. Nathan set down his glass and strode across the room, eager to put the conversation to rest. Arnaud waited in the hallway.

"Doctor Neville," he said, "I have a guest who needs your services."

"Be right there." Nathan grabbed a case from below his desk, looking momentarily at Paul. "Can you entertain yourself for a while?"

"Sure."

The door closed. Paul made himself comfortable at the desk, spreading the newspaper in front of him. After a moment, he shook his head and scoffed at himself. "French," he muttered. "I'm an idiot."

14

Charlotte sat on the bed near her mother, staring down at the pale figure in silent dread. The woman's breath was heavy, as if she was in a deep slumber. It was a slumber from which she couldn't be roused. Her lips were flushed, and her face hot; but her fingers were blue, as if with frost, and they hung limp and unresponsive in Charlotte's hand.

The manager returned with the doctor. Charlotte stood, facing them and clasping her hands. "She is still unconscious."

Nathan spoke with calm reassurance. "Let's have a look."

He stood over Elizabeth, touching her face for an indication of body temperature.

"She has been unwell for a few days," Charlotte told him. "We came by ship from Bombay, and I thought she might have seasickness."

"She has a fever."

Elizabeth had fallen rather haphazardly across the bed. Nathan gently pulled her by the feet, straightening her, and delicately rolled her onto her back. "What were her other symptoms?" he asked, never taking his eyes off the woman. "How was she sick?"

"She felt fatigued for much of the journey, and she said that she felt strange, as if something was . . . *wrong*. She had a headache, but did not complain much—though I think she simply did not want me to worry. When we arrived at the room, she complained about feeling feverish. She undressed, and a minute later she turned pale and collapsed."

"All right. Please, miss, have a seat."

He gestured to the high-backed sofa. Charlotte walked across the room and seated herself anxiously. The doctor lifted Elizabeth's arm, pressing his fingers to her wrist; his eyes shifted away from Elizabeth as he focused on the rhythm.

Just before he set the arm back on the bed, his gaze moved to a spot below Elizabeth's shoulder.

Charlotte saw the flash of fear in his eyes as he dropped her mother's arm. He took a couple steps backward, distancing himself from the bed.

A barely veiled look of panic covered his face.

"Arnaud?" he choked.

Katharine stood at the base of the Eiffel, staring up into a mind-boggling and seemingly endless array of iron networking.

"Good God," she breathed. "I would not have expected it to look so magnificent."

"I knew you would like it. Come, let's get our tickets."

The Eiffel, still in its first week of public accessibility, was run over with crowds that thinned out to trail like ants up and down the narrow, winding stairs. Packed with people from top to bottom, the staircase rattled under their steps, easily creating an inescapable sense of claustrophobia. Katharine had not climbed far when she began to feel a recurrence of the nausea that had plagued her the last several days; but she steeled herself, tightening her grip on the shaky rail as she ascended after the masses. As Katharine neared the final steps, her nerves were rattled by a sudden explosion.

Annette turned to her with a smile. "Don't worry. That's the noon cannon," she said. "If we don't have to wait for a table, we may have some time to walk the fairgrounds."

At last they were free to walk the first platform, and view the sprawling Paris landscape from the heights. At some points they found themselves peering through nets of protective wire; but as they came to face the river, Katharine stepped tentatively toward an unguarded lookout, gazing down on the miniscule figures that moved along the Iena bridge. She chuckled. "Yes, it was a good idea to leave Paul behind," she murmured.

She had never before beheld such a vast perspective of the world below—never looked down upon the domes and towers of a modern city, never seen great expanses of nature reduced to dots and lines. The wind blew more freely here than along the ground, and Katharine found herself leaning over the railing, indulging in the sensation of being a high-flying bird in open air. For a moment she was overcome by a peculiar sense of freedom, such that it that sent a small shiver of excitement through her body.

They chose to dine in the French restaurant, Café Brébant, and settled for one of the inner tables with an obscured view of the jostling fairgrounds. Annette helped Katharine with ordering lunch, then chatted enthusiastically about the upcoming Wild West show.

"I suppose it's less interesting for Americans," she said. "I never saw any red Indians when I was in America, but I was only there a few years. Have you seen them in person?"

"I think that the people traveling with Bill Cody are mostly Sioux. They're from the Midwestern areas."

"And they're friendly with whites?"

Katharine hesitated.

"They must be to some extent, if they're traveling together," Annette added.

"Well . . . the Sioux are still quite at war with the States."

"I see. I suppose they're like our Algerians. But in New York—do you have Indians there?"

"There are some Mohicans and Iroquois in the areas where I've lived. I grew up in eastern New York, near—"

"Oh, yes—in Troy. Near Nathan's family."

"Right." Katharine smiled faintly.

"I've never been there. I didn't know Nathan when I was in America, but he'll take me to meet his family someday. Is that where you attended school?"

"Yes. I was enrolled at the Troy Seminary, a school for young women."

"A finishing school?"

"No . . . not that kind of school. I had courses in advanced mathematics and other subjects that my governesses couldn't teach me, or wouldn't. But I never officially graduated. My studies were . . . interrupted. I had to move to another city."

"Why?"

"My father died. I didn't have any other family, so I went to live with . . . ." Katharine hesitated, eyeing Annette with sudden caution. "Some friends."

Annette was genuinely moved. "I don't have a family either. I used to," she added quickly, "but we've had our struggles in Paris. My sisters died from smallpox, and my parents and brother died during the last war—the war with the Prussians, in my father's case, and then . . . ." She hesitated, collecting her nerves. "We had a difficult time afterward. You've probably heard of it. I'm not sure of the details, but I lost my mother and my brother during the battle between the army and the Communards."

Katharine detected the trembling strain in Annette's voice, moisture collecting on the woman's eyelids just below the pained gaze. "I hadn't thought about that—that you were here during the war."

Paris' recent history had indeed been tumultuous. In 1870, France had suffered massive defeats in the Franco-Prussian War. A new French Republic was formed as Parisians barricaded the city against invasion; they held out for more than a hundred days while German soldiers camped outside the boundaries. Communication wires were cut. Food from outside the city was inaccessible. To stave off starvation, people eventually began to eat carriage horses and rats, and then consumed household pets and the animals at the local zoo. December and January brought a remarkably cold, bitter winter, and Parisians desperately sought ways to keep from freezing to death.

The new French government, housed at the Hôtel de Ville, surrendered when the Prussians began bombing the city in January 1871. The terms of surrender were met, and the German soldiers left. The National Guard took over Paris; government officials had fled to Versailles, and a new party, the Communards, took over, arresting anyone suspected of being in league with the old government. They destroyed Napoleon's column at Place Vendôme and, objecting to the glorification of monarchy and religion, ordered the burning of the Louvre Museum and Notre Dame Cathedral.

Before the latter acts could be accomplished, the French army marched into the city by night. The Communards barricaded themselves at the Place de La Concorde and surrounding streets, and what ensued became the bloodiest battle in the history of Paris. The Communards instantly ordered the execution of dozens of jailed clergymen, and set several parts of the city on fire. Perhaps it was the prolonged starvation and extraordinary cold that drove Parisians to madness; whatever the reason, the most ordinary citizens seemed suddenly capable of the most monstrous, fatal cruelty, which was quickly emulated by the invading soldiers. Human beings set upon one another with unprecedented ferocity. Anyone suspected of belonging to the opposing party, or even of sympathizing with it, risked a merciless death. In their mad rage, human beings literally tore one another to pieces.

Somewhere among the erratic surge of fire and violence, Annette had lost the two remaining members of her family. Katharine looked out past the tower's iron railings at the Paris landscape—a landscape that had been scrubbed meticulously clean of its horrors. Below, peaceful crowds sprawled across the fairgrounds: people from markedly different nations and cultures, even those subject to colonialism, were now gathered peacefully in the clean, sunlit elegance of Paris. For a moment it all seemed too immaculate—as though the constant attempts at cleansing the city was proof that the monster still lurked, unsettled and slimy, beneath the fabricated glamour and had to be kept at bay.

Annette followed her gaze—and her thoughts. "It's hard to believe, isn't it?" she asked. "They've done a lot to clean up the city. We had a World's Fair in '78 to celebrate our recovery from the war, but Paris wasn't quite cleaned up like it is now. The evidence has essentially disappeared except from memorials. I was eight years old when it ended. That's not so long ago, and eight years isn't so very young . . . but I don't remember it well." She paused, and added softly, "People seem to remember it vividly or to have trouble thinking of it at all. I suppose it depends on how you handle what you've seen—whether remembering every detail makes you feel safer, or whether it's easier on your mind to forget."

They sat quietly for a moment. Annette pulled her focus away from the vista. "We displayed pieces of your Lady Liberty statue at the last fair. She's fantastic—better than the tower, I think."

"Yes, I saw her for the first time only recently."

"On your way here?"

"Yes. She's quite a sight . . . our very own Colossus. It was strange to finally visit that area—to walk around lower Manhattan. My father grew up there, and that's where my mother's family first entered America, but I had never been to that part of the borough before. My parents described it so differently."

Annette was regarding Katharine with guarded curiosity. "What happened to your family? Do you mind if I ask?"

"My mother died in childbirth—when I was eight years old. After that I just had my father. But he passed away a few years ago."

"He was sick?"

"No . . . ." Katharine felt the oppressive grip of fear closing around her throat. "He was killed," she admitted, rather grudgingly.

"In an accident?"

"No . . . murdered."

Annette's eyes widened. "By whom?"

Katharine hesitated, searching Annette's eyes. She had an inexplicable urge to tell the truth—to share an honest understanding of Annette's pain, perhaps. After leaving Troy, she had almost never dared admit that she knew who had murdered her father—not even to her aunt and uncle. Only to Paul; and that was because she felt obligated. *If I tell Annette, she will certainly repeat it to Nathan; and then I'll have to worry about Nathan repeating it* . . . . Once again she felt torn: would she make herself safer by telling the truth, or by concealing it? Annette lived across the ocean from the heart of the tragedy; she was removed from it, and yet . . . .

"There was a suspect with strong evidence against him, but his involvement was never proven," she said. "He was after my father's money for some time, and in the end, he was able to confiscate my father's business holdings."

"How terrible. Do you think he did it?"

"Yes."

"And he wasn't convicted? Where is he now?"

Katharine looked away, toward the vast expanse of air that hung over the fairgrounds. "Oh, he's around somewhere," she said vaguely.

In a corner of room 342, near the door, the manager and doctor stood whispering excitedly. Charlotte looked anxiously from them to her mother: the two men speaking in hushed French, words she couldn't understand; and Elizabeth, still unconscious on the bed, her breathing increasingly heavy and ragged.

Charlotte's voice was choked with nervousness. "Excuse me, doctor, could you please enlighten me as to my mother's condition? Is she seriously ill?"

The doctor finally approached her, standing an arm's length from the sofa. "Miss Morgan," he said, clasping and unclasping his hands as he spoke, "your mother has an infection, and she needs a special kind of medicine. There's some available at a local pharmacy, but I'll need you to go and fetch it."

"*Me*?" she asked in disbelief.

"We'll send you in my personal carriage. I have to stay here and observe your mother. The driver will take you directly to the pharmacy." He took a pen and a small pad of paper from his pocket, quickly scribbling a note.

"Can you not send someone else?" Charlotte looked anxiously at her mother. "I would prefer to stay. . . ."

Arnaud spoke up: "I am sorry, miss, but we cannot spare anyone. We are overburdened because of the fair."

The doctor handed her the note, then stood abruptly. "You'll be fine, and I'll be here watching over your mother." He nodded to the slip of paper in her hand. "That's the name of the medicine she needs. Give the note to the pharmacist, and she'll find it for you. The driver will wait and bring you back."

"Very well," Charlotte said weakly. "Do you think she will . . . recover?"

"Probably, but she needs medicine."

Probably. Surely there was some hope in that word.

Arnaud was beckoning her. "This way, miss. I will escort you to the carriage."

He opened the door, covering the knob with a cloth as he did. Charlotte barely noticed; she gazed worriedly at her mother as she left the room, trying to stave off the terrible fear that threatened to overwhelm her.

Arnaud left her in the lobby while he fetched the driver. Several minutes passed; Charlotte stared at the clock, growing increasingly anxious and fidgety. "Hurry," she whispered as the tenth minute approached. *What the devil is taking so long?*

She fixed her gaze on the ceiling, in the direction of her mother's room, as precious time slipped through her helpless grasp.

A young boy brandished a spear at the entrance to the Village Nègre, thrusting it into the air as he greeted passing tourists. Beyond the gate, a wide path cut through the sprawling encampment of small huts and thatched roofs. Katharine paused at the threshold; her gaze met those of several Congolese women and men who sat in the foreground and watched the arriving tourists. Young children milled closer to the walkway, sporting tattered European garments, while their elders wore colorful skirts tucked neatly at the sides.

Katharine immediately found herself cringing at the spectacle of white, over-dressed Europeans looking on at the ebony-skinned villagers. Though Katharine had never seen them in person, similar "human zoos" had come to New York in the seventies; audiences flocked to see displays of authentic Native tribes, then of African and Asian savages. Katharine's schoolmates had organized their own human exhibit in response. They rented fencing from a local factory and set up a "cage" on the lawn of a local church; advertisements for the event read: *SEE! Rituals of the native upper classes of Troy—on exhibit for one day only! Tribal dance—authentic handicrafts and costume—communal games— and more!* Katharine had quickly volunteered to be one of the subjects, and spent a Saturday afternoon on display: having her hair done up in plaits by a "maidservant," gambling at cards, embroidering, and performing competitive dances before an increasingly rowdy audience. Outside the fence, students passed out literature on the phenomenon of human zoos.

The organizers' concerns that the event would be ignored proved unwarranted. While a few passerby hooted at the spectacle (especially at the dancing), some in the wealthier spectrums reacted with shocked offense. Editorials in the *Troy Daily Times* and the *Evening Standard* complained of the "shameful exhibition of society's esteemed customs in the presence of drunkards and ruffians" and "the outrageous spectacle of innocent children being provoked to dance—and then being rewarded with biscuits, which were passed through the fence as one might feed animals at a zoo."

Looking at the village that now sprawled in front of her, Katharine imagined the reverse: a few hundred Congolese looking on with detached amusement while ruffled women and men in top hats played bridge and danced "The German."

Annette, seeing Katharine's smile, said: "If you like this, you should see the exhibit at the children's zoo. We had Hottentots on exhibit last summer."

"Hottentots?"

"Yes—savages from South Africa."

Katharine's smile vanished. "Savage what? Animals, or people?"

"People."

"At the zoo? That's mad," Katharine said. "Is it part of the fair?"

"No, the children's zoo has had human exhibitions for years," Annette replied. "They show savage tribes from all over the world. The anthropological exhibit gets twice as many visitors as the animal zoo did. Oh, you should have seen it a few years ago! They had a Ceylonese village, full of people and all kinds of Indian animals, even giant elephants; and they had snake charmers, and native games and all kinds of exotic things. And before that they showed red Indians—real ones from America—but I didn't get to see them because I was living in America at the time."

"How ironic," Katharine murmured.

Annette glanced down, distracted by a sudden jostling at her side. A baby carriage had strayed from its owner and bumped against her. Inside, a toddler in a matching dress and bonnet looked precociously at the women, and with merrily shining eyes said "Bonjour."

"Bonjour," Annette replied, and flashed an amused look at Katharine. "A baby has found us. That's good luck, I hope." She delicately rolled the carriage back to the mother's side; the woman was staring intently into the exhibit, speaking in excited tones. "Nathan and I have been trying for a baby," Annette continued discreetly, "but . . . nothing so far. What about you and Paul?"

But Katharine was suddenly oblivious, caught up by a spectacle within the fabricated village. Somewhere ahead of her, two boys had begun to play on a pair of drums, while others gathered to dance. Several tourists had stopped to watch. One of them was John Damgaard.

The music seemed to slide to a stop. Katharine heard only a dull roaring, a far-away ocean, something just above silence. Her body tensed with sudden fear.

There in the center of her focus, Damgaard was diverting his attention from the village scene, turning toward Katharine as though he sensed her looking on. Even before he caught sight of her, she saw a flash of yellowed teeth as a grin began to spread across his face.

Dr. Neville's carriage plodded through the Paris streets while Charlotte looked on in helpless agony, her face darkened by anger as yet another hansom passed by at a quicker pace. She leaned forward, calling to the driver: "Can you go any faster?"

He sat stiff-necked, giving no indication of hearing her.

"Excuse me," she said in a near shout. "Is something wrong with the horse? Why are we going so slow?"

Her pleas elicited no response. Charlotte's body began to ache with tension as the carriage crawled along and her frustration surged. After some time, she looked on with disbelief at her surroundings; her face was drawn with new concern as the carriage proceeded down a familiar-looking street. She leaned forward, raising her voice.

"Driver." Charlotte rapped on the front of the carriage with her hand, and was immediately disappointed by the weak sound it produced. She leaned forward, rising from the seat. "Did we not pass through this area already?"

The driver glanced briefly over his shoulder, but didn't respond.

"How long before we arrive at the doctor's office?" she shouted.

Again, a brief glance. "No English," he fumbled.

Charlotte leaned back into the seat with a thud and gave her surroundings another frustrated once-over; then she stared down at the incomprehensible scrap of paper in her hand.

Remembering Katharine's desire to see Cairo Street, Annette suggested touring the opposite side of the fairgrounds—much to Katharine's relief.

Sprawled around the tower were exhibits of varying nations and cultures, and as Katharine scanned the streets, she found herself overwhelmed by the confusion of styles, colors, and languages. The women boarded a small train to spare themselves the walk. "Cairo Street is just beside the *Palais de Industries*," Annette explained. "My favorite exhibit is there; we must see that, too. I promise you won't regret it."

The Palace of Various Industries was an imposing structure of iron and glass, so thronged with fairgoers that Katharine felt herself sweltering—but Annette was enchanted by the warm sunlight streaming through glass ceilings, especially when she came upon her most beloved display: the crystal exhibit, which reflected that light from countless dazzling displays of candelabras, vases, and jewels.

"It's lovely," Katharine said tonelessly. The shimmering obscured her vision as she glanced around the room.

"Look there—the Tiffany Company is showcasing there, as part of the American exhibit. Theirs is supposed to be the greatest exhibition of jewelry anywhere in the States. They recently purchased our French Crown Jewels. Of course, that was another affront to Britain and the monarchy."

"Of course."

"It really is unfortunate that they have snubbed the fair. They have some exhibitors here, but think of the effect they might've had with their full support. The British Empire has amassed all the diamond mines in South Africa, and could have added such glamor. Just think: thousands of African crystals shining here in the sunlight, among all these other beauties."

In Cairo Street, the women stepped out of the flow of tourists and stood admiring the ornate facades and arches of the high buildings. Annette pointed to various embellishments and doorways, explaining that the designers had salvaged a number of architectural pieces from destroyed buildings in Cairo; other items were replicas made in Paris, including the ornate minaret that rolled and spiked above the other buildings. "The house with the minaret is supposed to look like a mosque," she said, "but if you go inside, it's actually a coffee shop with dancers and music."

The curving architecture of the arches seemed to spill out into the street, part of a connecting movement between the shops and booths. Musicians looped in and out of repetitive melodies that drifted dreamily from the cafés, accompanied by the tinkering of craftsmen who molded their wares and vendors who loudly touted their worth. Fairgoers weaved and turned in wave-like patterns as if they couldn't decide which way to go or which sight to rest their eyes upon. Katharine watched as a man led a slow-moving donkey past her. On the animal's back, a little boy chortled with laughter.

At last the carriage came to a halt. The driver pointed to a building, indicating Nathan's office. Charlotte leapt from the carriage and raced away.

Inside, she found a vacant front desk.

"Hello?" She scanned the area wildly, projected her voice toward a narrow hall leading into a back room. "Hello?"

Moments passed. Sounds of shuffling came from the back.

"Hello?" Charlotte's voice was cracked and raw. "I need help, please."

A woman with gray plastered hair and a tentative, lined face came slowly into the front room.

"Hello. I speak no French, but Doctor Neville sent me. Doctor Neville?" Charlotte held out the paper, hoping for an acknowledgement;

but the woman stood quietly on the opposite side of the desk, her face blank.

"He gave me this note," Charlotte tried again. "I need medicine."

The woman took the paper—slowly—and looked it over.

"Do you speak English?" Charlotte asked weakly.

A shake of the head. "No . . . no."

"Can you hurry, please, with the medicine. Fast. Pronto."

The crowd sat in heavy silence as a small, stout woman raised a rifle and pointed it steadily at the man standing opposite her. He tossed a playing card in the air, and Annie Oakley began to fire. The card was split in two with the first crack of the gun. She shot the halves several more times before they finished their erratic, fluttering ascent the ground. Bill Cody picked up the tattered remains and displayed them to the thrilled audience.

Buffalo Bill's Wild West was in mid-performance, in a stadium packed with fifteen thousand people. Annette and Katharine sat among the back rows, barely having made it into the stands before they filled to capacity. They had missed Paul at the hotel. The desk clerk had stopped them in the lobby, relaying the message that Paul and Nathan were unavailable and that the women should continue on without them. Katharine's heart sank at the news. Her second exposure to Damgaard had bestowed her with a new sensation of vulnerability, and she desired the comfort of Paul's presence. Over and over again, her gaze diverted from the Wild West spectacle, nervously scanning the crowds in search of dark curling hair and a top hat.

Annette gripped Katharine's arm excitedly. "She's the most amazing woman, and the best shot in the show. I read that she supported her family by hunting wild game, starting when she was six years old, and she did so well that she paid off her family's farm before she turned sixteen. Don't you wish you could shoot a gun like that?"

Katharine looked again at the crowd. "Sometimes."

She found herself unable to enjoy the show, or even to focus on it much beyond what was necessary to keep up a pretense of interest. "Buffalo Bill" Cody's cavalry finished off the performance by subduing a band of rowdy Sioux and rescuing a wagon full of settlers. The crowd burst into applause, and over the din Katharine conveyed to Annette her pressing desire to return to the hotel and see if she couldn't locate her husband.

Annette accompanied her as far as the Clément's front doors, and went on to do some shopping down the street. Katharine paused in the entryway to survey the lobby; then hurried, in a hunched-over sort of way, through the colossal room. Felt her body tightening, uncomfortably, in all the wrong places. *Relax . . . relax,* she prompted herself. She slowed, straightened, felt a shudder coursing through her body.

"Mrs. Gardiner?"

Katharine turned, saw the desk clerk raising a hand as if to halt her. "Yes?"

"Your husband asked me to pass another message to you. He would like you to wait for him here in the lobby."

"Here? Why, where is he?"

"He should be here momentarily."

She looked around, vaguely bewildered; then moved to a wall near the desk. Katharine stood with her back to it, staring steadily at the front doors.

Charlotte sat with her head in her hands.

Across from her, the front desk was vacant. The back room, into which the receptionist had disappeared, had scraped and slithered with occasional sound, and now ebbed into silence. Charlotte clutched at her skull, white-knuckled, fighting off an urge to call out. *If I interrupt her again, she'll come back out empty-handed . . . .*

The nervous woman appeared suddenly, miraculously, with a small bottle in one hand. Charlotte leapt to her feet and lurched toward the desk, and the woman held back for a moment, drawing the bottle close to her chest; but Charlotte, placing one palm on the desk, vaulted toward the woman and snatched the medicine from her hand.

"This is it?" she asked, only pausing to glance at the label. *French.* More than ever, she felt like a fool for not having studied the language; but the notion passed quickly, having dissipated along with every other trivial concern by the time she jumped back into the carriage.

15

Katharine had just opened her mouth to greet her husband when she noticed what was following just behind him: all of their luggage, toted along by the dutiful young porter.

She stared. "What's going on?"

Paul's voice and expression were muted. "There was a problem with the room," he said. He took her arm, his focus locked on the front doors. "We're staying at Nathan and Annette's house until Arnaud finds us a room at another hotel."

"What kind of problem?"

"Come on." He led her resolutely toward the doors. "They double booked the room. Some other guests were supposed to check into it today, so I agreed to give it up."

"You gave it up, just like that?" She looked anxiously at the luggage. "Are you sure you packed all my things?"

"I'm sure. Everything's here."

They stood near the busy street, waiting for the bellhop to secure a carriage.

"It's a lucky coincidence, actually," Katharine said. "I found out from Annette that Mr. Damgaard is staying here, at the same hotel."

"At the Clément?"

"Yes."

Paul glanced back at the hotel. His already-clouded eyes became distinctly more troubled. "Does Nathan know that?"

"I assumed so."

"Well, never mind now."

The porter was loading their luggage onto a hansom, and Paul escorted her in that direction, not wasting a moment. "Let's go and get settled," he said without enthusiasm.

Charlotte spotted Arnaud the moment she entered the lobby; he stood behind the front desk, speaking with the clerk in hushed French.

She hurried toward them, the bottle gripped tightly in her fingers. "Sir?"

Arnaud looked up calmly, and made no move to meet her.

"I brought the medicine," she said anxiously. "How is my mother? Is the doctor with her?"

He looked at the medicine, then at Charlotte, with an air of puzzlement. "To whom do you refer, mademoiselle?"

Charlotte balked. She could only stare into Arnaud's face, perplexed by his seemingly genuine ignorance, for some time before recovering. "My mother, Elizabeth Morgan, in room 342. I left her with you and the doctor. Is he still with her?"

"I beg your pardon, miss. She is in a room at this hotel?"

Again, she stared. She opened her mouth to address him, but thought better of it and hurried toward the staircase instead. She ran the steps, down the hall toward the room where she'd left her mother.

The door to room 342 was locked.

She pounded on the door. "Mamma?"

Charlotte was met with silence.

"Mamma?" She slammed her knuckles again and again, harder this time. "Mamma?"

Nothing. She raced back downstairs, found Arnaud still at the desk, and accosted him.

"Sir, is my mother still in her room?" she demanded in an angry, unsteady tone. "Her door is locked."

"I am sorry, miss; I do not know to whom you refer, but I will help you as best I can."

"She was with the doctor. I left her with the two of you." She shook the bottle in his face. "Your doctor sent me to his office to fetch this medicine."

"Please, which room is your mother staying in?"

"Room 342." Charlotte looked at the clerk in exasperation. "Does he have a poor memory?"

The clerk glanced nervously at Arnaud.

"I assure you I do not, miss," Arnaud said gently as he opened the register. "When did your mother check in?"

"Today. We checked in today."

He paused, reading over the register; then he turned it around and displayed it to Charlotte. "Are you one of the Broussard family?"

Charlotte looked at the listing with silent confusion. Her own signature was scrawled on the register, assigned to room 344; but directly above her signature, room 342 was signed out to Remy Broussard. She scanned the register, flipped through other pages, then stared at her own signature again.

"This is my signature here," she said hesitantly. "My mother and I have separate rooms: I am in 344, she is in 342. When we checked in, she signed her name here, above mine."

The manager looked doubtfully at the register. "Did your mother sign the name Remy Broussard?"

"No, she signed the name Elizabeth Morgan," Charlotte replied impatiently. "Where is the other clerk who was here earlier? We checked in five hours ago. A woman checked us in. Where is the doctor? I want to see the hotel doctor."

"Our doctor is likely in his room. I can have him fetched if you wish."

"Have him fetched right—"

Charlotte broke off as she caught sight of Doctor Neville hurrying from the stairs into the lobby.

"There he is," she said with a twinge of relief.

She fled toward the doctor, meeting his eyes; and when he looked back at her, it was clear from the momentary look of fear on his face that he recognized her. But he quickly wiped the look away and turned his gaze toward the front doors of the hotel, walking in that direction.

"Doctor?" Charlotte pressed him, disheartened by the strange look that had come across his face. "I brought the medicine you asked for."

She held up the bottle for him to see. The doctor halted, glancing at the medicine and then looking at Charlotte with confusion.

"I'm sorry?" he said.

She stared at him for several moments, still holding up the medicine. "Do you not remember me?" She spoke softly, but with accusation.

"No, I'm sorry, have we met?"

Charlotte was quiet, staring into his eyes. She lowered the medicine. "Doctor . . . I didn't get your name."

He was silent. His brow glistened with sudden perspiration.

"Doctor?" Her tone was icy. "Could you tell me your name, please?"

"Neville, I'm Doctor Neville. If you'll excuse me—"

"And the hotel manager, there at the desk. What is his name?"

"That would be Mr. Arnaud." The doctor's voice was tight and dry, strained by an effort to sound casual. His eyes flitted back and forth, unable to fix on hers for more than a second at a time. "Are you a guest here at the hotel?"

"Dr. Neville, this medicine came from your office, did it not?"

Nathan Neville suffered a moment of fully exposed anxiety. Panic lit in his eyes. Then, catching himself, he shook his head and reached for the medicine, as if to study it more closely—but Charlotte snatched it away from his grasp and turned away. She stalked toward the front desk, where Arnaud and the receptionist were watching her intently.

Nathan took the opportunity to leave the hotel.

"I want you to let me into room 342, please," Charlotte told Arnaud.

"I'm sorry, that room is let to a—"

"That room is let to my mother." She raised the bottle again, but kept it safely away from Arnaud's grasp. "Doctor Neville sent me to his office, in his personal carriage, to fetch this medicine for my mother who is ill in room 342. I am not interested in what the register says. I find it impossible to believe that both you and Dr. Neville have already forgotten her, and if you don't let me see her room, I will go to the police and have them investigate. And I will go to the press, and have them compose a story about how my mother was treated during her stay at the famous Hotel Clément. Shall I go, or will you let me see the room?"

Arnaud paused, exchanging a look with the clerk before answering. "Miss Morgan, I am very sorry to see you so upset, but I cannot help you. If you have become separated from your mother and feel you must go to the police or to your embassy, I will be happy to give you directions."

She studied him, waiting for any kind of slip—any twitch of fear or uncertainty. But there was none. "I will call them. Does your telephone line run to the police station?"

Arnaud hesitated.

"The phone, please. I know you have one. You must have an emergency line."

"I will contact the police myself. Just a moment, Miss Morgan." Smooth; his tone was utter smoothness.

Minutes ticked by as Charlotte waited for an officer to arrive, and each second was agony. With each second, her mother was lying sick somewhere, gravely ill, without treatment, getting closer to the danger of losing her life. *Or worse.* Charlotte couldn't bear to think of the reasons behind Arnaud's farce. If her mother was only ill, why would he pretend not to remember her? Did he really mean to pretend that she had never existed there—that she would thus not be found? *No, don't think it; it isn't possible! Do not think it . . . .*

She stared at the manager with wild anger in her eyes, anger mutating into vile hatred. The fact that he maintained a steady calm, and even courteousness, only made her hate him more voraciously. Arnaud had done her the favor of requesting an English-speaking officer "so that you may make your concerns as clear as possible."

The officer arrived, and Charlotte quickly led him upstairs. Arnaud trailed along, using his deep, rich voice to talk over Charlotte, drowning out her explanations of the afternoon's events. Charlotte turned a pair of raging eyes on him.

"Let me finish," she said in a near scream.

Arnaud pressed his lips together.

"The room is a good size—larger than mine, and more richly decorated." She spoke evenly as they reached the top of the stairs. "There is an ormolu clock on a mantel at the far wall, with gilded flowers and a Lady Justice figure below the timepiece. The wallpaper is decorated with roses, accented with a plum color, and the curtains and bedspread are the same shade of plum. I left my mother lying on the bed when I left. If I had never been in that room, I could not remember it in so much detail."

"I have no objection to letting the officer look into the room," Arnaud explained to her, "yet, we must respect the privacy of our guest." They had reached the door; he knocked on it, and listened.

Arnaud was holding the room key in one hand. Charlotte's gaze was fixed on it as she waited for him to unlock the door; then, in a desperate frenzy, she grabbed it from him and shoved it into the key hole. Arnaud and the officer protested and moved to stop her, but she twisted forcefully from their grasp—and after a moment, the door was flung open, and she was lunging into the room.

And then came to a dead halt.

The room had changed. The bedding and curtains were gold, not plum. The wallpaper was gold and white. Where the ormolu clock had been, there was now a red and gold vase. Two ornate mahogany chairs stood in place of the sofa. The satinwood table was gone. A few suitcases and small trunks were scattered throughout the room, and a man's jacket had been draped over the back of a chair.

Arnaud had recovered the key. He and the officer held Charlotte's arms, pulling her back into the hall. She stumbled weakly in their grasp.

"Miss Morgan, I cannot let you go any farther," Arnaud said, a note of anger impeding on his tone for the first time. "You can see that a family is staying here."

She stepped behind the door and looked at the room number, making sure. *Was it 342?* She walked to her own room, put the key in the door. Looked inside. *My room; my belongings.*

She stood back, looking from her own room to room 342, trying to figure out what had happened.

The officer had fixed a disapproving gaze on her. "Miss, you say you and your mother checked in together?" he asked stolidly.

Charlotte slowly returned, staring at the number on the door. "Her room was right here. They must have changed it."

Arnaud frowned. "Miss Morgan . . . ."

"No, they changed it," she insisted, fully aware of how unbelievable she must sound. "I am certain that this is the same suite. This room is arranged just as before. See, it is larger than mine, as I said. The bed was there, and the sofa sat where those chairs sit now. That is why everyone took such a long time to help me. I was away for four hours. They have changed it."

"Miss, I have no reason to continue harassing Mr. Arnaud over this matter," the officer said. "Your mother is not signed into this hotel, she is not here, and her belongings are not where you claimed they would be. Now, if—"

"But she *was* here," Charlotte insisted. "I can prove it. We came here by carriage. If I can find the driver who brought us here—and people saw us together. Other guests at the hotel saw us arrive. The guests on this side of my mother's room—in number 340—they saw us just as we arrived. I swear it. Could you speak to them, please?"

"I'm sorry," Arnaud cut in, "but the occupants of room 340 checked out of the hotel earlier today."

"What were their names? You could—"

"I'm sorry, Miss Morgan," the officer cut in impatiently, "but if you want to pursue this further, you will have to file a formal report with the police or with the British Embassy. I can take you there myself if you wish."

She ignored him, turning angrily on Arnaud. "No, I refuse to leave until you tell me what has been done with her."

The officer stepped between them. "Miss Morgan, we can't have you causing trouble in Mr. Arnaud's hotel."

"I want you to talk to Doctor Neville," she pleaded.

"If you want to file a report, you will have to come to the police station."

"They changed the room. Peel away part of the wallpaper, and I swear you will find the rose paper beneath. That smell—wallpaper paste! Did you not detect it? If I leave now, they will have it scraped and re-papered by morning, and you will never see the old paper. But it is there, I swear it."

The officer shook his head. "We won't be going into another person's private room to ruin Mr. Arnaud's wallpaper. That's enough now."

"I swear it to you!" she cried. "If you just peel back a small piece, then you will have to listen to me. He is lying. If you will just look at the paper, I will leave without making a scene."

"Miss Morgan, if you don't stop harassing Mr. Arnaud immediately, it is in my power to arrest you."

She hesitated, staring at Arnaud. The man was unmovable.

"No, I will speak to someone else," she said evenly.

As she retreated toward the staircase, Arnaud called after her. "Do you mean to check out of your room?"

"No."

16

Nathan's office was nestled on a crowded city block in the eleventh arrondissement, with a reception and pharmacy that faced the street. Behind the office rooms, tucked into a rear corner, was a tiny kitchen; upstairs were the other living quarters, including a spare room with a bed barely large enough for two people. Annette apologized for the inconvenience but seemed to delight in having guests, and was eager to showcase the local sights.

"You probably rode in on Boulevard Voltaire. If you had followed it southeast, you would have come to the Place de la Nation. It has a fantastic sculpture by Jules Dalou that was just finished, to commemorate the Revolution; we can walk there later, if you feel like going out. Otherwise, the cross street Rue de la Roquette leads to the Bastille, if you follow it south. You really should visit the Bastille grounds before you leave. We can all go together, at least to see the July column."

"What's that?" Katharine asked.

"Just what it sounds like—a large stone column, commemorating the Revolution."

Katharine smiled at Paul. "What do you think, Paul," she teased him softly. "Want to see another of the tall pillars you're so fond of?"

"Sure," he muttered—tonelessly, absently.

Annette went on with an ultra-condensed history of the area, describing how Boulevard Voltaire had served as a main route for gun runners; how the revolution had inspired the re-naming of countless French streets after various social luminaries and artists; how the Bastille prison, just down the road, had been overcome and destroyed a hundred years ago, in a symbolic effort of the masses against the monarch Louis XVI, who would later be arrested and guillotined on the fairgrounds (here she added a rather graphic account of how Governor Bernard-Rene de Launay—who had actually been born within the Bastille—was captured and decapitated by the mob, his head gored through with a pike and paraded through the local streets).

Annette bustled around the kitchen as she spoke, heating water for tea and trying to plan a light dinner for the three of them. Nathan, she said, would be working late, and they were not to expect him.

Katharine repeatedly made offers of help, but Annette seemed to revel in serving them. "Oh! No! Make yourselves comfortable, I can manage it." She lifted a whining kettle from the stove. "Would you like tea?"

"I'd love some," Katharine replied.

Annette fairly beamed as she filled the cup. Katharine was disarmed by the woman's pleasantness; she tried to be enthusiastic in return, though she shied from matching Annette's exuberance.

"I have to spend time using the kitchen while I still can," Annette said. "Nathan plans to stay on as the hotel doctor, so we're going to sell the house as soon as the fair is over. It's going to be a big project, to sell things off and settle into the hotel suite, and we don't have the time to do it right now; the hotel is always fully booked and Nathan is always so busy . . . not that I mind. He's paid well. And the fair has done wonders for the city, even before it opened."

"I imagine it will bring in quite a lot of money," Katharine replied.

"It will, but it has done more than that. We've had terrible social conflicts for such a long time. We were on the verge of another uprising, and . . . ." She cast Katharine a strained, nervous look. "I've had enough of war. Truthfully, the fair has kept us from slaughtering one another. And if the fair restores confidence in France, and continues to feed our economy and our camaraderie, we will see better times."

Paul feigned interest in Annette's vignettes, and not very convincingly. He sat with distant eyes, abstracted and mute, and didn't eat or drink. After a few minutes he complained of a headache and went to lie down in the guest room.

Katharine finished her tea and slipped away to check on him, and found him lying on his back, fully awake. He sat up when she entered. She halted, taken aback by a strange dullness in his slightly bloodshot eyes.

"You're not feeling well?" she asked, drawing near.

"It's just a headache."

"You look terrible."

"Thank you. Sorry I missed the show today. How was the fair?"

"Annie Oakley was incredible. We'll have to go back together. The fair is extraordinary, but . . . ."

Katharine stared down into his gray eyes, wondering at the absence of light there. Paul's gaze was murky, and his skin had a strange pallor. "I'm going to lie down for a while," she told him, surveying the bed. "If there's room enough for both of us."

"Are you feeling all right?"

"I've had a bit of a sour stomach. Seeing Damgaard makes me feel ill." She shook her head disbelievingly. "Mr. Damgaard, who is everywhere I want to be. He's at my school; he's at my friends' social functions. He's at my house. I cross the ocean and there he is. We're in a crowded city, yet I run into him every day."

"Come here." Paul pulled Katharine onto his lap, held her close. "Are you sure that's all? You're not feeling . . . ."

"I'm all right. All the travel was a bit much for me. Our adventure across the ocean made me nauseous, seeing Damgaard made me infinitely more nauseous, and I can't say that parts of the fair didn't make me nauseous."

He kissed her cheek and neck.

"You really should see it for yourself," she continued. "The fair, I mean. There's a human history exhibit with three categories: pre-historic and historic, and one called 'primitive contemporaries,' full of people whose cultures and land we've been colonizing. And they've turned one of the local zoos into an exhibition of human 'savages' from around the world—not just for the fair, but as a permanent exhibit. Annette said they've been bringing in different groups for more than a decade. The Wild West show was more of the same. The exhibitors really know how to stick to a theme."

Paul didn't reply, but quietly placed a hand on her forehead.

"Checking for a fever?" she asked.

"Do you feel feverish?"

"Not yet, but I might in a few minutes. I have a feeling you're going to offer to 'examine' me."

He smiled faintly.

"What about you? That's the first time you've smiled since we left the hotel. And you look so pale." She put a hand to his face; it seemed unusually cool.

The hint of a smile faded. He averted his eyes. "I'm just tired."

"Did something happen?"

"No . . . ."

"You're sure? You didn't get into an argument with Nathan?"

"No. We talked for a few minutes, and then I had to deal with giving up the room."

"Really. You just talked for a few minutes? We were gone for hours."

"I thought you were going to lie down."

"I was, but you've taken me prisoner on your lap. Are you going to lie down with me?"

"What about that exam?" He slid a hand along her back, began to undo her dress. "I really think I should take a look at you, just to make sure . . . ."

"You're so predictable," she whispered.

"Yes, but that's what you like about me."

"Don't get too carried away. I told Annette I'd walk the neighborhood with her before it gets too late. Do you feel like walking a bit?"

"No." Paul was occupied with the removal of her clothing; he moved quickly, expertly, and soon had her stripped down to her undergarments.

"I suppose I can skip the walk, if you'd like to stay in bed," Katharine suggested and slipped her arms around him. "And I don't feel much like dinner, for that matter. Would you like to . . . ."

"No. Not tonight."

"No?" she asked, surprised.

"No. Just lie back."

Katharine relaxed in his arms as he ever so carefully rolled her back across the bed. The bones in her neck cracked, drawing her focus to the tension that writhed there; the tendons felt dry and parched, the muscles knotted in spasms of fear—a fear that had crept in, inhabited her body, so stealthily that she was only now becoming aware of its intensity. Her head fell gently back, but beneath her skin the sinews groaned and crackled, struggling to accommodate her shifting form. Her neck ached and shoulders burned; the fire raged down either side of her back. But the bedspread and pillow were soft and cool against her flesh. She tried to adopt their sensations, willed the muscles to release their crunching, roiling misery.

"I'm worried about Damgaard," she sighed. "Annette asked me about my father's death, and I mentioned that he was killed and that the main suspect took his business holdings. We ran into Damgaard an hour later, and as I was dragging Annette away, she recognized him and started talking about how he was a friend of Nathan's and a guest at the hotel . . . ."

"Don't worry about that," Paul said quietly. "Nathan won't tell her who you meant."

"But if she says it in front of Damgaard . . . he saw me with Annette, and I'm worried that he's going to start—"

Paul kissed her, and said in the same quiet tone: "I know what you're afraid of. It won't happen like that. I made Nathan promise to avoid Damgaard. Okay?"

"How comforting," Katharine said dryly.

Paul drew back and stared at her for a moment, as if deciding what to do with her. "Now, about that exam: I want to start by testing your reflexes. If you're any less sensitive than usual, I'll know something's really wrong."

He lifted her arm, and she immediately tried to draw it away; but he gripped her wrist with one hand and tickled her side vigorously with the other.

"Don't," she laughed, struggling against him.

"That side seems normal. Let's check the other."

She fought him until he at last gave up and embraced her, kissing her along the curve of her neck. "You're so lovely," he whispered against her skin. "I didn't say it enough when we were married, but you're so incredibly lovely. I don't deserve you."

He kissed her again, but Katharine drew away and looked into his face, inexplicably startled—not by his professions of love, or his claim of being undeserving. Paul teased her that way out of habit, but there was something amiss in his tone now. She stared into his eyes and tried to read him. Something was there—something he was concealing, something she couldn't decipher. It crept through voice, and muddled his gaze, but remained formless and elusive.

Paul didn't look back at her. His skin was warm now, his face flushed rather than pale.

"You deserve me," she whispered. She ran her hands up and around the back of his neck, smoothed the thin hair on his head. "What's the matter, Paul?"

"Nothing."

"No, there's something. You should tell me."

Something like fear flickered across his eyes, then vanished. "I'm just worried . . . ."

He left the sentence hanging.

"About?" Katharine prodded him.

"I don't know." His tone imparted uncharacteristic helplessness. "About you."

"Me?" she asked with genuine surprise. "You mean . . . because of Mr. Damgaard."

"No. No, it's not that." He sat up, and Katharine followed in suit.

"I'm . . . ." Paul seemed to struggle for words; he stared vacantly at the floor, unable to look at her. "I don't know." He paused, and said in a strangely empty tone: "I'm not that good of a husband."

Katharine looked on him with silent astonishment.

"I never told you about Clara—how I went to see her at the sanatorium."

Clara, his first wife. She had died from tuberculosis in 1879, when they'd been married not two years. Paul had spoken of her only a little.

Most of what Katharine knew of her had been conveyed by Paul's mother. *Other men could visit their wives, but Paul had to wait outside the sanatorium with the little children . . . .*

Paul's father and two sisters had also died from tuberculosis, and he was considered susceptible to the disease. Clara had thus refused to allow him to visit her at the sanatorium; he could only go so far as the outer gates, and call to her if she happened to come out onto the balcony, which she did only in the first few weeks. After that she seemed to vanish within the institution. The separation added another element of pain to an already grievous suffering.

"I wasn't supposed to go inside, but one of the guards snuck me in," Paul said. "He brought me to her room. She was going to . . . to pass on, and I wanted to see her, at least once, before she went."

Another silence. Katharine kept quiet, but slid an arm around him. Waited.

"I don't know what I thought," he continued. "I had seen it—consumption—of course, so I braced myself for what I was familiar with. He opened the door, and I saw a thin, bald, crooked, ghastly white person lying in the bed, asleep, with her mouth sunken in, and breathing with such terrible noises—gurgling and squealing . . . ."

Katharine nearly shuddered, but fought off the impulse, fought the vague feeling of horror brought on by his narrative. His tone, too, haunted her; he spoke without feeling, not from any lack of emotion, but rather with the weight of exhaustion, as though his emotions had been taxed beyond their limit.

"I saw her and I couldn't move. The guard saw how shocked I was; he pulled me back outside and closed the door, and he started explaining that they had shaved off her hair because of lice, and they had pulled out her teeth to prevent infection. I don't know what else they did to her—if it was the treatment, or some other condition, but she had become hunched and crooked somehow. And skeletal—white and skeletal." His voice became whispery, dry with scraping slivers of fear and grief. "Nobody told me. They concealed it from me, to spare me the grief. But the point is, when I saw her . . . ."

Katharine saw the tears finally brimming in his eyes. She put her arms around him, resting her chin on his shoulder. He had some distance this way—still close, still being held, yet no longer being stared at and studied. "You got scared?" she suggested softly.

"Yes. No . . . well, yes, but it wasn't that kind of fear. I stood there crying. Finally the guard said he couldn't let me stand there, and he took me back outside. And I never saw her again. She died a few days later, and I never saw her. You understand what I'm saying?"

"Yes, but Paul, you're just human. You can't scold yourself for grieving."

"If it had been me, she would have come to me. She was . . . ." He trailed off. Katharine heard the soft spattering of a tear that fell onto his trousers.

"Perhaps, but I think that's easier said than done," she said softly.

"You're always very fair." Paul's voice was strangely dry, almost accusatory—but Katharine could hear the weighty self-condemnation that dominated his tone.

She kissed his neck and drew away. "If it was me, and I wasn't able to see you—if it was too hard for me—you would understand. Even if you were disappointed, you would understand."

"No, I don't think I would." He rubbed his eyes, sighed deeply. "I'm a coward," he mumbled. He lay back on the bed. One arm was draped across his face, covering his eyes. "And an idiot. I don't know what I'm doing."

Katharine shook her head, disturbed by the mood that had come over him. This revelation about Clara—this sudden, inexplicable confession—couldn't be all that was troubling him. Something had brought it on. The only idea she had was that Paul was afraid of being unable to protect her from Mr. Damgaard.

She lay next to him—a delicate operation, as she had only the narrowest space—and made herself comfortable, resting her head on his chest. Felt his heartbeat, surprisingly slow and muted. "Fine," she said, "but *I* understand, and I think Clara would have understood. She didn't want you in there anyway. I think she would have been upset to see you risking your own health. And I hope you don't mind if I speak for her, but if she was the way everyone describes her, I know she would have understood in any case."

Paul was quiet for some time. When he uncovered his face, Katharine lifted her head to look at him, and once again was startled by the starkness of his expression, the flat emptiness in his gray eyes. He stared at her, not moving. She was about to speak when something shifted in his gaze—as though he'd made a decision.

"Katharine," he began, but didn't finish. He was thoughtful, then absent. The faint light was once again extinguished from him.

"What is it?" she asked.

"Nothing," he said, and closed his eyes.

"You can talk to me, Paul. I'm not going to judge you." Katharine waited, then kissed his cheek and lowered her head again onto his chest. "I love you."

"You shouldn't," he replied.

17

PARIS: WEDNESDAY, MAY 22, 1889

The ambassador's house was fit for royalty. Indeed, in 1855—during the last World's Fair in Paris—Queen Victoria had enjoyed her own throne room within the stately mansion. The property on rue de Fauborg Saint-Honoré was widely known as the most beautiful of all the British embassies; it had been luxuriously decorated, mostly by Napoleon's sister, the princess Pauline Borghese, before being sold off to the first Duke of Wellington in 1814. The room on the ground floor shone with clean, perfectly kept hues of royal blue and gold, and boasted all the embellishments, extravagance, and amenity that one would demand for society's elite. The manicured grounds reached far to the southwest, all the way to the Champs-Élysées; and the street was lined with other stately buildings, the Presidential Palace among them.

Charlotte felt dwarfed by the prestige of the area. She went to the window, averting her eyes from the palatial décor with a downcast heart. Charlotte was a commonplace citizen—not any kind of Lady, or even an artist, or anyone with a claim in society. *I am nothing, and no one will help me.*

The ambassador himself was no less grand. He was the Earl of Lytton, also known by the pen name Owen Meredith. At home, Charlotte had a little green and gold book full of his poems, worn out from repeated readings. Normally she would have been thrilled to meet a man whose lovely and clever way with words had so inspired her; but as she stood at the front windows, gazing out at a city so far from home, she felt only the creeping irony of her situation. The narrator of Lytton's "The Wanderer (in Paris)," for whatever reason, seemed to have ended up at the same place and mood as Charlotte. The introduction read: *But I must to the palace go; the ambassador's tomorrow; here's little time for thought, I know, and little more for sorrow.*

She could not help thinking of the poem, though it was a detriment to her composure. The wanderer dreamed of a lost love; he held and

129

whispered to the corpse of the woman he so desperately missed and mourned. Mingled with his tender words were acknowledgements of a grave, grotesque reality: *There's a small stinging worm which the grave ever breeds from the folds of the shroud that around us is spread: There's a blind little maggot that revels and feeds on the life of the living, the sleep of the dead. . . .*

The wanderer awoke from his morbid dream to a sunny, bustling Paris, reveling in the comfort that one finds in the acknowledgement of a mere nightmare. *Whate'er the strange beings that visit us nightly, When Paris awakes, from her smile they retreat*—but only for a little while, and never completely.

The vignette embittered Charlotte. At one time she had admired it, but now it rang of superficiality. It separated her from Lytton as much as his status and extravagant mansion—*because people who have lost their most precious loved ones don't honor them with sensationalist odes about maggots and worms.*

Presently, Lytton arrived. He was a thin man with an elongated face, exaggerated by the length of his gray beard. His demeanor was serene, yet he retained a keen and robust energy. He greeted Charlotte with an appropriate mixture of pleasantness and concern.

Charlotte had been to the residence the previous evening, and made an appointment to see Lytton. She had spoken to his secretary, a Mr. Austin Lee, and other embassy staff, but to no avail. Now, she once again explained the situation in full. Lytton's eyes moved to her trembling knees and tightly clasped hands, and she saw the flash of pity in his eyes; but for all his attentiveness, the Earl of Lytton found her story implausible. He said so in his most polite way, suggesting that a mistake had been made. Charlotte could not convince him otherwise.

He assured her that he would do everything in his power to cooperate with the police, to support an investigation into Elizabeth's disappearance. That much he believed: that a woman had disappeared. As for the rest of the story, he took it no more seriously than anyone else had—the police, the local press, his own staff. And then Lytton asked the questions Charlotte had dreaded hearing: *How was your relationship with your mother? It isn't usual for her to disappear for some time? Might you have become confused by the unfamiliarity of Paris? And— excuse me, but I have to ask—did your mother indulge in any habits that might have caused her to stray? Do you suppose that her illness might have caused her to wander? As for yourself, have you no history of becoming confused?*

Lytton made notes and promised to check in on her. Then he led Charlotte back to the front door, assuring her that she was welcome at any time, and could ask for any help in finding shelter and getting back to London. Then, to clarify, he introduced himself more precisely as Robert Bulwer-Lytton, who could be found here at this residence, and who could be approached at any time regarding such a grave matter— and then he seemed to regret his use of the word "grave," and winced.

"I know who you are," Charlotte said dispiritedly. "I was fond of your poetry . . . but I can take no interest in such things at present." She told him that she planned to stay at the Clément until her time ran out—that she would not return to London, or even check out of the hotel, without her mother.

She left the place with a heavy heart. As she passed through the doorway, she instantly felt the oppressive entrapment of the street. Grand stone buildings towered over her in all directions, as if to affirm her insignificance. Charlotte paused numbly on the sidewalk and gazed up at the cold, immobile giants, her mind at a loss for what to try next.

A man with a short moustache and bowler hat was approaching the residence. He met her gaze, stopped short at the sight of her soulless eyes.

"Bonjour, mademoiselle," he nodded.

She ignored him at first—but after he had passed, she turned and studied him. Something was amiss, yet familiar, in his accent.

"Pardon me—are you British?" she asked.

He stopped. "I am."

"Are you employed at the embassy?"

"No, I'm a reporter."

Hope stirred in her soul. "A British journalist? Do you think you could help me? My mother went missing from the Hotel Clément yesterday . . . ."

Once more she unleashed the painful narrative. It was becoming easier now; the choking, crushing grip of grief gave less interference.

The reporter's eyes were bright with interest. After a couple minutes, he interrupted: "If you will wait, we can speak after my appointment here. There's a café a few blocks away where we can meet."

He introduced himself as Albert Dawes and gave Charlotte the name of his hotel, in case he missed her at the café.

"I will wait there," Charlotte assured him. "I have no reason to be anywhere else."

Not more than an hour passed before he caught up with her at the small café on Rue Penthièvre. He escorted her inside, and she sat wringing her hands as he busied himself at the counter. Charlotte found herself staring at the man intently, as though watching his every maneuver could give her insight as to whether he would come through for her.

"Thank you," she said, as the journalist offered her a cup of tea. He seated himself across from her with his own cup, quickly abandoning it and taking out a notepad and pencil. Again they went over the details she'd divulged to him outside the embassy.

"I thought of something else," she said, "but I'm not certain I can prove it. Mr. Arnaud and Doctor Neville both claimed to have never met me, but I recognized both of them when I returned to the hotel. The clerk saw that I recognized the doctor. And I do still have the medicine from the pharmacy."

"What about Neville's office? Do you remember how to get there?"

"No. The driver traveled in circles. It took four full hours to get there and back. We moved so slowly that every other driver passed us." She paused. "If you were to find out where Dr. Neville's office is, and take me past it, I would recognize it. I could point it out to you."

"What was nearby? Do you remember other buildings?"

"There were buildings on either side, but I didn't see what they were. I was in quite a hurry to get the medicine—but I would recognize Doctor Neville's office upon seeing it."

The reporter sat immobile, with his eyes lowered and a troubled brow, as if reluctant to meet Charlotte's gaze.

"Mr. Dawes, I can repeat every word that was said in that room, and describe every movement," she insisted.

He nodded. "All right, go ahead. What happened after Doctor Neville entered the room?"

Her eyes were fixed on Dawes' hand as he scribbled notes. She started nervously, telling him of the doctor's visit and of her own report to him.

Dawes looked up at her for a moment before resuming his note taking. "That's what you told Dr. Neville?"

"Yes, I told him those things and he asked me to sit on the sofa—a high-backed sofa with white cushions. I was standing near the doctor and Mr. Arnaud, watching the doctor examine my mother. After I sat down . . . ." She paused. "The doctor checked her pulse, I think. He held her arm up, with his fingers on her wrist. Then he dropped her arm and stepped back, as though something had startled him. He told Mr. Arnaud to look at her, and he stepped forward and lifted her arm again—but this time, he took a white cloth out of his pocket and lifted her arm with it, as though he was afraid to touch her skin."

"The doctor did this, or Arnaud?"

"The doctor. Arnaud simply looked on. The doctor left the cloth on the bed beside my mother, and then they both went into the far corner of the room and started whispering in French."

"The doctor lifted her arm, to show Mr. Arnaud something?"

"I believe so. They whispered for some time, and . . . I do not know French, so I understood none of what they said. Oh, that's important, too: before they began whispering, Mr. Arnaud looked at me and said, 'Mademoiselle, your mother may need medical care. Do you speak any French?' I said no, and they began to whisper. And I know that they both speak fluent English. The doctor sounds American. They whispered for several minutes, and then the doctor came to me and . . . I was sitting on one side of the couch, and he stood some distance away while we spoke—and I thought it was strange that he would not sit with me, since he spoke to me for some time. He seemed afraid that I might be ill as well. He asked several questions about the ship we took from Bombay."

"What exactly did he ask?"

"He asked if anyone else was sick like my mother." Charlotte's voice was steady, her nerves settled and determined. "He pressed me for details about cargo and other passengers—whether my mother had exposed herself to a cargo area, or visited other rooms. He wanted to know when she first showed signs of illness and what specifically I had noticed, and what she complained of. My mother did not feel unwell until a day or two before we arrived at Marseille. I told the doctor that while we were on the ship, we spent time with a family from . . . ." She frowned. "I am unsure of the city; it began with an 'L.' I spent a lot of time with the daughter who was about my age."

"Was someone in the family sick?"

"Yes, the parents—the mother especially. Both were tired and felt ill, and the mother had a fever. But they left us at the port, so I know nothing of how they fared afterward. Doctor Neville asked many questions about the family, and when I told him they spoke Cantonese, he returned to—"

Dawes stopped writing and looked at her sharply. "The family spoke Cantonese?"

"Yes. They came from . . . Liyang, or Lijang . . . ."

"In China?"

"Yes. Somewhere in southern China."

"And Doctor Neville was interested in that particular fact?"

"Yes."

He paused, regarding her with intense seriousness. "Do you have any idea why?"

"No. But the father was a merchant, and the doctor asked me several questions about that."

"Did he have cargo on the ship?"

"Some, yes." Charlotte studied the reporter's face intently. "Doctor

Neville asked me that same question. Is that important?"

The reporter gave her a brief once-over, looking mildly disturbed. "Charlotte, you haven't been feeling ill, have you?"

She hesitated; felt a quivering in her lips, and restrained it. "Not in the sense that you mean. Why?"

"Did you notice anything else about your mother—any other changes besides the lethargy and headache?"

"She had a fever by the time we reached the hotel."

"Anything else? Anything different about her skin, or . . . ."

"Not really. Before she collapsed, she turned white. Her face was hot, but her hands were clammy—and her fingers were starting to turn blue. That's when I went to get the doctor."

"They started to turn blue when she collapsed?"

"I believe so. She was wearing gloves until she undressed."

"They were dark blue, or just slightly blue?"

"Rather dark. Yes, dark, especially at the fingertips."

He was silent for several moments, looking searchingly into her eyes. "Charlotte . . . ."

He looked away, evidently troubled. After a moment, he ripped a blank sheet from his notepad and began to write. "I want to investigate this."

"You don't believe that I've imagined things?"

His look was inscrutable. "No. Quite the contrary." Dawes slid the paper across the table. "This is the hotel where I'm staying. It's not far from here. Any hackney driver can help you find it. Will you meet me there tonight at eight o'clock?"

Charlotte looked disconcerted.

"What's the matter?"

She pressed her lips together, considering her words, and spoke carefully. "I appreciate that you want to help me, Mr. Dawes. You are the only person who has offered thus far. But . . . I'm a bit shaken up about other people right now, and I don't feel that I know you well enough to come alone to your room."

"Right. Meet me outside the hotel; I'll wait for you on the steps. One more thing: What was the name of the ship that you took to Marseille?"

She thought for a moment, desperately. "It was . . . I want to say 'Sikh,' but it was something else. It was a place name. No, it was 'Sindh,' I think. S-I-N-D-H."

Dawes wrote it down. Charlotte watched him, wrought with anxiety, but relieved to be heard by someone who had clout and who exuded confidence and sharpness of mind.

"Since the police are uninterested in pursuing your story, I will try to find some of the witnesses you mentioned," he said. "Are you still staying at Arnaud's hotel?"

"For the next two nights," she said, "unless I get thrown out."

"The hotels are well packed, but you should look into getting a room somewhere else. Do you have money to book a different room?"

She said nothing. Her eyes began to tear up; she looked away painfully.

"I only have my clothes," she said finally, her voice trembling. "I spent what I had to get around the city. My mother had most of our money, and all of her things are missing."

Dawes slowly sat back down. "You have no money for anything? Not even for food?"

Charlotte shook her head, still choking back tears. "I have enough to take the omnibus back to the hotel."

"All right." The man seemed genuinely upset. His face seemed to harden with sudden agitation, even anger, as he reached into his pockets. He put a few francs on the table in front of Charlotte. "Use that to buy yourself some dinner." He watched her for a moment, thinking over her situation. "How will you get back to London? Did your mother pay the ship fare?"

"My uncle did, I suppose. But I don't know which ship, or what time, or how to get to the port. My mother knew, but I never asked. I just assumed she would be here." Charlotte was crying openly now, wiping tears from her face.

"What about the British Embassy, are they offering to help you?" Dawes asked gently.

"They said they would help me get home. They're contacting my uncle in India. But . . . ." Charlotte felt a momentary stab of dread at the thought of her uncle's family, of the trouble over Mr. Asher—but the memory was quickly eclipsed by newer troubles.

"What is it?"

"I am afraid to talk to them. None of the embassy staff believed anything I said. The secretary suggested that I submit to a psychological evaluation, and . . . they asked me about my relationship with my mother, if we had been fighting, if my mother was prone to going off with men, if my mother drank alcohol, if I drank . . . they refused to listen to what I said about the hotel. They think I'm mad, or that I have crafted a story to cover up something else that happened. They are much the same as the police."

"All right, listen. You should refrain from speaking to anyone else for the time being. Wait a little while, until I come up with some solid evidence." Dawes studied Charlotte seriously, adding, "This is about to become very ugly."

Charlotte looks up at him with helpless resignation. "It is already very ugly for me."

He nodded quietly.

Dawes saw her to the omnibus, made sure she was headed in the right direction. As he was leaving, she suddenly called back to him: "Beaumarchais."

He turned, looked inquisitive.

"Dr. Neville's office—it's near a street called Beaumarchais, like the author of the Figaro plays. That was the last major avenue we were on. Dr. Neville's office is in the same district as that street, I am certain of it; and if I was to go back there, I could find my way to the office, and point it out to you."

18

Katharine heard peculiar crunchings and cracklings in her body as she ascended steps of Hotel Clément. Parts of her anatomy seemed to be petrifying. She had slept little during the night, and had trouble waking; Paul had mumbled something about having to go out, and was absent when she finally rose. It was later, as Katharine was readying for the day, that she rifted through her luggage and finally realized what was missing: her personal journal. Paul had neglected to pack it.

The journal was relatively fresh. She'd only started it within the past couple of months, and hadn't recorded anything since leaving the ship; there were no notes about Mr. Damgaard, only the intimate impressions of a newlywed in love. Katharine might have flushed with embarrassment at the idea of having such writings intruded upon, if not for a more overpowering impression of anxiety.

She wasted no time in going back for the book, leaving Annette to fix breakfast while she caught the omnibus back to the sixteenth arrondissement; but as she drew ever nearer to the Clément, Katharine struggled against herself, trying not to indulge in her old habits. Seeing Damgaard in Paris had renewed the paranoid suspicion that he had some supernatural connection to her—some way of putting himself in her path, of knowing where to find her. She approached the steps and found herself praying silently: *Please, God, don't let me run into him; please don't let him see me.* A desperate impulse. Her neck cracked as she looked up at the lobby doors. She let out a strained sigh and tried to relax.

The desk clerk answered her request immediately. Yes, a book had been found in room 346; it was in a back office; he would fetch it for her. As he withdrew, Katharine's attention drifted toward the gilded staircase, where Mr. Arnaud stood in conversation with a British man in a bowler hat. Arnaud's eyes met hers momentarily. She detected from the look on his face, from his stiff pose and the hushed and strained tone of voice, that he didn't appreciate an eavesdropper at the moment—a fact that piqued her curiosity and made her listen more closely.

"I am rather in a hurry. I just have a couple more questions," the other man was saying. "This room that the girl describes—the room with rose wallpaper, with plum-colored curtains and bedding—does it resemble any room you have at the hotel?"

Arnaud's eyes darkened with irritation, but his face remained impassive. "No."

"Are you certain? You have no suites with that same decorative motif?"

The rephrasing of the question seemed to rattle Arnaud. Katharine saw him avert his eyes and inhale deeply.

"No," he said after a breath, and continued in his leisurely way. "We may have wallpaper of that style, or curtains of that color—in some of the rooms. But the description, it does not match any of our suites. If you have questions, Mr. Dawes, I will gladly allow you to interview me in my office."

"Sorry, one more thing. The clerk stated that all of the suites contain ormolu clocks. Is that correct?"

Arnaud took a moment to answer, all stiffness and discomfort. "Many suites do. But ormolu clocks, they are no longer made. It is not possible to have them in every suite. If that is all, Mr. Dawes . . . ."

"Certainly. Thank you."

"Thank you," Katharine said simultaneously, as the clerk arrived with her journal. She took the book and hurried back through the vast lobby, and had taken to the sidewalk when she heard a voice calling after her.

The man with the bowler was jogging down the steps, waving as she turned in his direction. "Excuse me—*mademoiselle—sil vous plait*—"

Katharine smiled at his garbled attempts. His pronunciation was no better than hers. "I speak English," she assured him.

"Ah, good. Do you have a moment?"

"Yes," she said, trying to mask her reluctance.

"My name is Albert Dawes. I work as a reporter for London's *Daily Telegraph*, but I am here on rather different business." He gestured toward the hotel. "Are you a guest here?"

"Not at the moment. My husband and I stayed here earlier."

"Could I trouble you with a few questions? A nineteen-year-old girl claims that her mother has been missing from this hotel since yesterday."

"Oh—certainly. I hadn't heard of it."

"She says her mother checked into room 342, but the hotel register shows that the girl checked in by herself. The police are trying to figure out what happened to the mother."

"That's close to the room I was in. We were in room 340."

The gentleman regarded her with abrupt interest. "You were in 340? When did you check out?"

"Yesterday."

"Did you happen to see who was staying in the rooms next to you, numbers 342 and 344?"

Katharine thought for a moment, flipping through memories. "No. We didn't stay very long. We were only at the hotel for a couple of days."

"What time did you check out? Was it before noon?"

"No, it was a few hours later. I went to the three o'clock Wild West show at Neuilly Park, and we checked out shortly after I returned to the hotel."

"Do you—I am sorry, what is your name?"

She replied hesitantly, with the slightest notion of distrust and impending trouble. "Mrs. Gardiner," she said.

"Mrs. Gardiner, do you happen to remember walking into room 340 with your husband around eleven o'clock yesterday?"

She averted her gaze, thinking back.

"This girl, Charlotte Morgan, says that she and her mother walked past you as you were going into your room. She said that you would remember her because as she was walking past, your husband made a vulgar comment, and you looked embarrassed because she overheard it."

A look of recognition spread across Katharine's face.

"Does that sound familiar?"

"Yes, I remember that." The girl with soft brown eyes and the lovely little smile.

"Was the girl alone?"

"No, there were definitely two women—a younger one, and another woman following behind her. And the porter was behind them with their luggage."

Dawes paused as he digested the information. A strange spasm crossed his face—as if he didn't know whether to feel relieved or disturbed. "Can you describe what the woman looked like?"

"She . . . she was thin, pale-skinned . . . well-dressed, but not overly fanciful. She was wearing a wide-brimmed hat."

"Do you remember what color the dress was?"

"I'm not sure. It was a light color. The hat was white, I think."

"Hair color? Eye color?"

"I didn't really see her face. She had her head bowed and didn't look up when she passed."

"Would you be willing to tell the police what you saw? None of the other guests have come forward to say that they saw this woman inside the hotel. Miss Morgan is accusing the manager and the hotel doctor of covering up her mother's disappearance. The police are investigating, but they are trying to persuade the daughter that she is suffering from delusions."

His words seemed to slam against Katharine's soul. The man couldn't possibly have guessed that so many elements of his statement would cause such a disturbance in her, but he noticed that she suddenly went pale, that her eyes glazed over with the burden of her own conflicting emotions.

"She's accusing Mr. Arnaud, and Doctor Neville?" she asked.

Dawes frowned, seemed reluctant to answer. "Yes. Do you know them?"

Katharine's mind was whirling, rapidly reviewing the previous day's events. "I've met them both. Mr. Arnaud seemed very uncomfortable just now. Were you asking him about the interior of the woman's room?"

"I was. Miss Morgan was able to describe the suite her mother was staying in, but when the police checked room 342, they found quite another room than the one she described—so we have quite the puzzle to put together."

"What time was her mother reported missing?"

"The initial report to the police was at a quarter to five."

"My husband was at the hotel while I was at Neuilly. I'll speak to him and see if he knows anything," she said steadily. "I will certainly speak to the police—and as for you, where can I find you?"

"At the Hotel Véronique." He tore a sheet of paper from his note pad and scrawled quickly. "Room 112. If I am out, please leave a message for me and tell me where I might meet you. Can you do that?" He handed her the note.

"Yes."

"And you, where are you staying?"

Katharine hesitated. "We're . . . transitioning to another hotel, but I'm not sure of the name. I promise you, though, I will come and meet you."

"I am on my way to see the girl now. Is it all right if I mention you to her?"

"Yes. Please do." She felt a pressure behind her eyes, felt a deep empathy for the girl that pushed her toward tears. "Am I her only witness?" she asked.

"No, as it happens, you're not."

19

Just down the street from the Clément, Albert Dawes stood frowning as Charlotte fumbled in her purse. "What are you doing?" he demanded. He put out a hand to stop her. "Allow me to pay. What would you like?"

Charlotte's eyes moved over the bakery case. "I was just going to buy a roll."

"The least expensive item? Please, eat whatever you like."

"I don't care much for pastries."

"What did you have for dinner last night?"

She hesitated. "I wasn't very hungry."

"I see. Forget the rolls. We can finish our tea, and then I'll take you to breakfast. There—have a seat."

Charlotte moved to a table, and momentarily he joined her. He took a brief look around the bakery before speaking. The room was nearly empty, save for the cashier and an elderly gentleman at a corner table. Dawes spoke in a low voice: "You remember the couple you mentioned, who were staying in room 340?"

"Yes," she said, and dared not hope.

"I found the woman." He looked at Charlotte with sudden seriousness. "She saw you with your mother, but she was unable to remember exactly what your mother looks like—the color of her hair and dress, those details. But she can still serve as a witness that a woman was with you at the hotel, and that the porter was carting your luggage toward your rooms."

"That is something," Charlotte said breathlessly. "Where is she?"

"Nearby, I presume. She promised to get back in touch after she speaks to her husband."

Charlotte's heart sank. "But you didn't find out where she is staying?"

"She'll be back," Dawes assured her. "And I have her name. I will talk to her again, and we can figure out the best way to handle things— but you must not meet with her or any other witnesses until they have

had a chance to describe your mother to the police. If you meet before
that, the police will think they got the description from you."

"All right," Charlotte conceded.

"Can you tell me anything else that might be helpful? A description
of the train car you were in, and who was sitting near you? It would
benefit you to have character witnesses—people who can verify that the
two of you weren't fighting."

"We were *not* fighting," Charlotte insisted. "We never fight. We
disagree about things sometimes, but that is all. Here . . . ." She dug into
her purse again, withdrawing a slender book. "I cannot tell you which car
we were on or who was nearby. But I have this: a journal I have kept
since January. Anyone can discern my character and my relationship
with my mother by reading it. I have written about our journey to India
and Paris, and about what has happened since my mother—" She
abruptly choked up.

"Can I take it?" Dawes asked.

Charlotte handed him the book. "It's private, but I don't care about
that now. You can read all you like and show it to anyone."

In the solitary peace of the guest room, Katharine dreamed of the
monster.

Charles Eliot's murder had swept through Troy with a fatally sharp
blade. Katharine and Dawes tracked the killer's patterns, and finally
found justice: the monster appeared, its body a dripping mass of pasty-
white sludge. Dawes aimed a pistol and shot it three times.

Katharine watched the monster slump lifelessly to the floor. "I think
we've finally got it," she said, turning to Dawes.

But the detective was lying there dead, his face white, eyes and mouth
gaping in an expression of terror.

The monster lifted its face to look at Katharine. "I love teasing you,"
it said.

Katharine's fear faded into exhaustion as the creature rose from the
ground. It stood before her, regarding her with its all-too-familiar stare—
wily, malicious. "I make myself from people's ugly parts," the thing
said. It pinched its arm, removing a lump of doughy flesh, and in that
small expanse Katharine could see a flash of a vision: Nathan and Mr.
Arnaud, hurriedly dumping a woman's body into a box and slamming it
shut. In yet another clump of cells Katharine saw Mr. Damgaard,
reaching around to cut her father's throat.

She averted her eyes, unwilling to watch the scene play out. She
became resolved to stand there and let the monster kill her. Surely, death
was preferable to spending out her livelihood in this manner: a futile

attempt at escaping this seemingly immortal terror.

But the monster didn't attack. It stared into her eyes, searching for something it could not yet see. It described all the things it would do to her before she died. Katharine saw a flash of frustration in the monster's eyes, and she knew that it was trying to scare her. That it *had* to scare her. A monster made of fear would consume the fear that it created in others; and if she refused to fear it, it could not feed on her.

Katharine stood in the face of its threats, looked into its malicious eyes, and said: "I'm not afraid of you."

A door flew open. Katharine was jolted awake.

Paul was standing across the room, opening his suitcase. Katharine oriented herself. Paris. The missing woman. Damgaard at the World's Fair.

Paul glanced at her over his shoulder. "Did I wake you?"

Katharine sat up and lowered her head into her hands. She rubbed her forehead, pressed the fingers into her temples, rubbed her face. She'd been dreaming, again, of a way to defeat the monster; her mind still struggled for some method of permanently subduing her fears. Each and every resolution made perfect sense in the dream world—but upon waking, the tactics always seemed to lose their power.

"I was having a nightmare," she said.

He looked again at her, his expression indicating that he knew the theme of her unpleasant dream.

"Is Annette still here?" she asked.

"No, she must have gone out."

"Were you with Nathan?"

Paul hesitated. "Yes."

"I was having a nightmare about him."

He regarded her with surprise. "About Nathan?"

"And Arnaud."

Paul's movements seemed to slow, but he didn't look at her. Katharine observed him for a few moments before speaking again. "What are you doing?"

"Getting my things together. Arnaud found us another hotel room . . . but I thought, with the way our trip is turning out, that it might be a good idea to spend our time somewhere besides Paris. What do you think? It would get us away from Damgaard."

She paused for some time, noting the weak, hollow tone in which her husband spoke. She felt her throat constrict, but responded anyway. "I'm not so sure that Mr. Damgaard is what I'm afraid of right now. Was it Nathan's idea for us to leave? Or Arnaud's?"

He turned toward her now, with a piercing look. "Mine. I can understand why you're upset with Nathan, but what've you got against Arnaud?"

"I'm not sure." She paused, considering. "What's to have against someone so affluent and personable . . . and persuasive?"

He stared at her. The contents of his suitcase were forgotten.

"Mr. Arnaud . . . he's a slick liar, but he hasn't perfected the art of it," she continued.

"What's that supposed to mean?"

She slid her feet onto the floor, looking him fully in the eye. "I was at the Clément earlier, watching Arnaud lie to a journalist."

Paul was clearly rattled by the remark. His voice was strained. "You were at the Clément? Today?"

She picked up her journal from the bedside table. "When you were fleeing the hotel, you left this behind." She closely watched his reaction. He turned his back.

"Sorry about that," he mumbled.

Katharine watched as he fumbled with a shirt—folding it haphazardly into a jumbled mess, then folding it again.

"I went back to get it just as Arnaud was being questioned about a woman who went missing from his hotel. I watched Arnaud's face. He has this very particular thing that he does when he lies."

Paul glanced back, spoke with an anxious edge. "Really, what's that?"

"He tries to make eye contact, but whenever he's about to tell a lie, he takes a really deep breath, as though his heartbeat has just accelerated and he's gasping for air"—she put a hand on her chest, taking an exaggerated deep breath—"and his eyes move off to the right." Katharine moved her index finger to indicate her own focus moving off to her right side. "Every time."

"How astute of you."

"Am I wrong? You know, I've just told you that a woman was reported missing from the Clément, and you're not asking me any questions about it. So I assume you already know the details."

"I found out this morning." Paul spoke with a note of genuine sorrow. He paused, and added grudgingly: "About the daughter. She's accusing Nathan and Arnaud of covering up . . . a disappearance."

"Are they?"

He ignored her, continued his futile attempt at packing.

"You should know. You were there." Katharine waited for a response, but got none, and continued. "Arnaud lied about some pretty peculiar details. From what I remember, he lied about . . . . ." She began counting on her fingers. "The rose wallpaper; the plum curtains; the ormolu clock—"

"You should get your things together," he interrupted.

"Did Nathan have to kill the woman, or was she already dead?"

Paul stopped; looked stricken; turned to face her. "What are you talking about?"

"You know what I'm talking about," she said softly, calmly. "You were with Nathan, you hurried me out of the hotel, and you certainly look like you know. Was she dead already? Or did someone have to kill her?"

He made a sound of disbelief. "You're—" He cut himself off abruptly, looked away.

"I'm what?" Katharine asked sharply, but Paul was quiet. "I know that the daughter is telling the truth. Paul, I saw both of those women walking past us in the hallway, when you made that comment about me riding on top of you. I'm sure you haven't forgotten that."

He turned to confront her, moved closer. "Katharine, please do not involve yourself in this."

"You must know what they're doing to this girl. People are trying to convince her that she's crazy."

Paul looked mildly pained.

"You know how I'm going to feel about that. The girl just lost her mother. I spoke to the journalist, Mr. Dawes, and—"

"You did *what*?"

"And he told me that the girl has no other family, aside from aunts and uncles."

"What did you tell him?

"Nothing, I was asking questions."

"You told him nothing?" Paul's eyes were strangely feverish.

"I told him I wasn't there."

"Katharine, trust me: whatever happened, it isn't the same as what happened with you. Please don't meddle in this. We're supposed to be celebrating our wedding, and—"

"Yes, we're married now," she interrupted. "You remember what you promised me? We share our burdens, deal with each other honestly . . . ."

He stared at her, then turned away.

"Mr. Dawes told me that after Nathan examined the woman, Elizabeth Morgan, he asked her daughter where they'd come from," Katharine continued. "The girl told Nathan that she and her mother had just traveled by ship from India to France, and that they spent time with a family who was carrying cargo from Southern China. The parents in that family were sick. Probably with the same illness that Mrs. Morgan had." She waited, got no response. "But I guess you already know that."

Paul leaned against a cabinet door and looked at her stonily.

"The Black Death is spreading through southern China," she continued. "Especially along trade routes, and through cargo deliveries. Dawes suspects that Mrs. Morgan contracted it, and that Arnaud and Nathan covered it up to prevent a quarantine of the hotel. Arnaud would have lost a fortune if that had happened. And Nathan, and all the other hotel staff, and possibly the whole country of France, that invested so much money in the Exposition and was expecting such a huge return . . . ."

"It doesn't take a doctor to know that the Black Death isn't something that one person carries around without infecting anyone else." Paul spoke flatly, but with a faint note of doubt. "I'm going to pack your things." His voice was cold, as though he was talking to a stranger. Again, Katharine felt the weight of disappointment closing around her heart.

She watched as he collected her belongings. But when he approached the bedside table to pick up her journal, Katharine abruptly reached out and seized his index finger. "Sit down and talk to me." Inside, she was pushing through the heavy, lethargic swell of heartbreak. She searched for something more assertive, more severe.

"Katharine . . . ."

"I'm not letting go of you until you tell me the truth." She stared into Paul's closed-up gaze, trying desperately to connect with her own anger—with that rage that had once threatened to overwhelm her, to sabotage her attempts at a new life. She made a quiet inventory of Paul's promises, his ready stream of soothing words. *All lies. All lies now . . . see, he's no more sincere than the rest of them. He'll lie and call me crazy just to cover his own fears. He'll push me down to save himself, and he will let that girl rot.* The anger quickened, and she let it rise, fed it with judgments. She needed that anger. She needed confrontation. The heartbreak was not enough; it would weaken her, distance her from Paul, and swallow her up.

"Quit behaving like a child," Paul said icily, trying to pull away; but Katharine fiercely gripped his other fingers.

"Who's behaving like a child?" she demanded, her voice rising. "Sit down and tell me—"

"I'm done talking. Let go, you're going to break my goddamn fingers."

She took hold of his arm. "I am not leaving Paris."

"Fine, stay, but let go. You—"

Katharine was wrestling him now, pulling him violently onto the bed, struggling to climb on top of him. Paul's face contorted with perturbed amazement as he freed himself. He stood a few paces from the bed. "Are you insane?"

"*You're* insane." Katharine's face blazed with anger, with a fierceness he had never seen in her; and her voice, though kept at a controlled volume, was raw and resonant with the power of emotion. "Who do you think you're fooling?" she hissed. "I don't even need you to admit the truth, because you've already done it without saying a damn thing." She paused, as if to steady herself, and continued in a calmer tone. "You know, when I was talking to Dawes, I worried for a few moments that you might have contracted the plague, because you seemed sick and fatigued; but then I thought about the way you behaved that evening, and all day yesterday, and I realized that you felt sick because of something you'd seen. You rushed me out of the hotel, wouldn't even let me go upstairs, came back here and then what? Paul Gardiner, probably for the first time ever, doesn't want to make love, but makes jokes about wanting to examine me." Her voice rose again, scathing and accusatory. "You were checking me for sores."

Paul leaned against the wall, felt his energy waning as his fears materialized before him.

"You looked under my arms, probably just like Nathan did with Elizabeth Morgan. I felt sick and you were seeing if I had symptoms. You could at least explain what was going through your head. I want to know why you dragged me away from that place so suddenly. Was it because you knew there would be an investigation? Or was it because of the plague?" She waited, and added, "If it's the plague, I appreciate your consideration for my well-being; but I don't consider that girl's well-being, or that of every person sitting in that hotel right now, to be any less important than mine."

Paul had covered his face, the flesh slowly paling behind his fingers. "Katharine," he said at last, "that's quite enough." With an effort, he met her eyes. After a moment he added tonelessly, "You've said more than enough, and very eloquently, I might add. But I suppose it's easy to be an idealist from your position."

The anger seeped from her face; her expression softened, overcome by sadness. "No, it isn't."

They passed some time in silence, unable to meet each other's gaze. Finally, Katharine added: "It's not just that. It's the way you were talking about . . . Clara."

Paul stared at the floor expressionlessly. He felt a furious grief stirring deep within him, threatening to ascend, to come barreling to the surface; but he kept it at bay. Such a thing couldn't be endured.

"Paul, you need to talk to me about this, because I know some things that you don't. Dawes has confirmation that the mother and daughter arrived in France from India three days ago. They took the train from Marseille to Paris, and they left the train together as well. Dawes told me that he spoke to the carriage driver who brought the woman and her daughter to the Hotel Clément. The driver claims that he dropped them off together in front of the building, and that the porter took their luggage, and they walked together toward the front door. The girl can identify Nathan, and she knows where his office is. She still has the medicine that she fetched from this very house." She paused, and added weakly: "And I can serve as witness that both women checked into their rooms."

Paul stood immobile.

"They're going to get caught," Katharine insisted. "Whatever Nathan and Mr. Arnaud thought up was clever, but it isn't going to work. There are too many witnesses who saw what happened, and this journalist isn't going to stop investigating. He'll find out the truth, and he's going to the police with everything he finds. And if you know what happened, that makes you an accomplice—and it will be better for you to come out with the truth before that happens. You could go to prison for conspiring in this. For covering up the fact that the *Black Death* came to Paris. It infected people on the ship, and this woman carried it all the way across France, on a crowded train. If it spread to other people . . . ." She shook her head. Paul was staring at her now, but was still and silent. "You're a doctor, Paul. And like you said, it's unlikely that it hasn't spread. Please tell the truth. I'll stand by you."

At last, he raised an eyebrow. "Stand by me? You can't. You won't be able to."

She regarded him with cautious puzzlement.

"Fine, Katharine; you notice things; you're trying to help. But you don't have the faintest idea what happened. Yes, there was a sick woman. And yes, it was Mr. Arnaud who was giving directions. But he's a smart, shrewd businessman, and I'm not. Arnaud is smarter than me, and he's smarter than Nathan."

She sat quietly, digesting his words. "What's that supposed to mean?"

But he only stared at her, growing visibly more upset.

"Paul . . . ."

Again he lowered his eyes. "I'm afraid to tell you what happened," he said in a near whisper. "Please do us both a favor, and let this one go. Let's go home before . . . ."

A look of dread had crept over Katharine's face. "What did you do?" she asked, almost in a whisper.

He stood, still and silent, and miserable.

"What did you do?" she asked again.

20

Paul was perusing the miniature library when Nathan burst into the office. Urgency rang in his voice: "Paul, I need your help."

"All right," Paul said, bewildered. "What's the matter?"

"I need your opinion on a patient." Nathan led him up the stairs and entered the suite just beyond Paul's room. Paul, with no warning of the patient's condition, was startled by the sight that greeted him: a woman sprawled unconscious and half-dressed across the bed, her mouth open, with skin the color of corpse flesh. Paul felt sudden horror rising in him as he stepped closer.

The woman's fingers were black. Her arm was angled away from the body, revealing the large, bruise-colored bubo that swelled within her flesh.

"Nathan this woman has the Black Death." The words rushed from him; Paul moved and spoke automatically, his feet deftly backing him toward the door. "How long has she been here?" His eyes moved to the right-hand wall—the wall that adjoined his own room.

"She had it," Paul told Katharine. His voice trembled. "Right in front of our faces, she had the Black Death. Her hands were turning black, and she had the sores under her arms. We wrapped her up right away; we wanted to get her contained as fast as possible."

"Wrapped her up in what?"

He hesitated, not wanting to answer. "In the bed sheets, and the curtains."

It was Nathan who took the plum-colored velvet curtains from the windows. "She checked in by herself less than an hour ago," he said, sliding the sofa across the floor and easing it beneath the window. "She must have expired just after she arrived."

"Just after?"

"Cover her up, Paul, would you? With the bed sheets—I'll get more

149

material to wrap her in." Nathan climbed atop the high-backed sofa, grasped at a curtain. "Quickly, please. If there's any contagion on her body, we can't let it spread."

Horrors swirled in Paul's mind. At Nathan's words he abruptly surged forward and yanked the edge of the bedspread over the woman's body— but she was too close to the edge. The spread slipped back off.

Paul grabbed it again and pulled upward, intending to roll the woman toward the middle of the bed; but as the body began to shift, the eyes opened. The woman's breath came in a slight, frail gasp. In the sickly, tormented face and slight squeal of air through the drying, blackening lips, Paul became suddenly haunted. He saw someone else in that face. A specter from his past.

"Paul," Nathan prodded him.

The eyes closed.

"This woman isn't dead," Paul choked.

"If she's not, she'll be there in a minute," Nathan said. "The woman has the plague, Paul. Look at her, for God's sake. She's dead. Cover her quickly before it spreads."

The woman was still, her breathing no longer evident. Paul slowly covered her face.

"Get the body wrapped," Nathan was saying. He laid the curtains along the floor, next to the bed. "We'll lift it onto the curtains and wrap it again. Quickly . . . ."

Paul finished wrapping the blankets. The two men lifted the heavy bundle, Paul at the head and Nathan at the feet, and laid it on the curtains.

"Would you roll that, please. I have to tend to some other things . . . ." Nathan moved quickly around the room, collecting random objects.

Paul hardly noticed the strangeness of his friend's actions. He threw the edges of the curtains over the bundle on the floor, then froze as he heard the faintest wheeze, a tortured gasp, from within the heap of fabric.

"Nathan?"

He jumped as a sharp knock sounded at the door. His eyes were suddenly wild with panic; it occurred to him now that they were doing something wrong—something that must not be intruded upon.

Nathan opened the door, and in rolled the laundry cart, pushed by a workman. Paul could hardly make sense of the sight: the workman unloaded long rolls of paper from the top of the cart and set them across the bed, then withdrew a number of tools.

Nathan stopped him with a command: "Go and fetch Mr. Arnaud, please."

The workman left. As soon as the door closed, Nathan began tossing his collection into the bottom of the cart. Paul looked up in time to see him carelessly drop an ormolu clock onto the pile.

"Help me load the bundle inside, would you?" Nathan said.

Again, Paul took the head of the bundle. *Get it away. Get the plague away from our room, away from my wife . . . .* Lowered it into the cart. Stepped back and stared. Not a sound, not the smallest movement came from the blankets.

"I'm going to wash up," Paul said numbly.

In his own room, he spent several minutes rinsing his flesh in the water basin, sensing a uselessness in his actions; but he knew not what else to do. At length he sat on one of the ornately carved chairs and stared motionlessly at the wall—the one that adjoined room 342.

A knock sounded at the door. Nathan would surely be there, with more bizarre requests. *Could you wrap the body, please? Put it in the laundry cart, would you?*

He opened and saw Nathan pale-faced and fidgeting in the hall. "Paul, we need to talk."

Paul regarded him mutely.

"You should leave the hotel," Nathan continued after he'd closed the door. "Mr. Arnaud will find you a room at another hotel, and in the meantime, you can stay at my house. I have a place across town. Pack up your things and Katharine's things, and bring them to my office. You can wait there until Katharine gets back. And, Paul?"

"What?"

"Keep a tight lip about this, please. There are some complications . . . ." He hesitated. "The woman may not have been dead, for one thing. If she was seen alive and then pronounced dead so quickly, it may seem peculiar . . . ."

Paul was shaking his head. "What are you talking about?"

"We're trying to avoid a panic at the hotel, and . . . well . . . there's the added complication of the woman's death. I'm afraid we panicked, and . . . I suppose we reacted with rather drastic measures. I mean, it isn't protocol to wrap a live woman's body and have her carted away. It might be best for you not to mention your involvement . . . ."

Paul stared.

"It's just that you may have killed her," Nathan said.

"Nathan was incredibly methodical," Paul told Katharine. "I didn't even notice it until later. But Arnaud was the one giving all the directions."

"How do you know?"

"Most tellingly, he wasn't there," Paul's voice was flat, empty. "He

had me and Nathan doing all the dirty work. But later on he brought
Nathan into the office, and he gave us a talking-to about how to handle
things. And he was much smoother than Nathan."

"What about the furniture?" Katharine asked. "What did they do with
it?"

"They moved it into our room. And they had the workman re-cover
the walls, and then they took our furniture and moved it into room 342."

Katharine started. "So the evidence is in our room."

He shook his head. "It was. But I doubt it's still there."

"It must be. They couldn't move it very far without people noticing.
How could they even have moved it one room down without someone
seeing?"

"Easily. Everyone was out at the fair, and there were only a few
pieces to move. They could have brought the sofa and table into our
room in two minutes' time. Then they just had to move our two chairs
and the little decorative embellishments, and the drapes and bedding.
And even if people had been in their rooms, no one would have heard the
scraping around and the re-papering, because our room and the
daughter's room were on either side."

"Mr. Dawes said that a Frenchman and his family were signed into
room 342. Some of their belongings were in the room. Do you know
anything about that?"

"I'm not sure of the details. I got the impression that the man whose
name is listed is a friend of Arnaud's; but I doubt that he or anyone in his
family was staying at the hotel. Arnaud rounded up some trunks and
clothing to make it look like the room was occupied."

"What did they do with Elizabeth's body?"

Paul blanched. "I don't know. I think they . . . ." His voice broke; he
lowered his head, rubbed his eyes. "They brought it into a cellar or
something, and then, I don't know . . . ."

Katharine's mind was organizing details, calculating figures. "How
many people know what happened? The workman, Mr. Arnaud, Nathan,
you—who else?"

"One of the receptionists might know. Other than that . . . I'm not
certain who knows what."

"Five people involved."

"At least. There's also Nathan's driver. And the pharmacist at his
office. They may not know the details, but they know enough to arouse
suspicion." He paused. "I don't think the workman even realized that we
had a body wrapped up in the laundry. Nathan sent him away before we
put it inside the cart." He looked at Katharine bleakly. "I'm sorry . . . ."

"I know."

"Arnaud gave a very concise speech about how we couldn't start a plague scare in Paris because it would drive everyone away from the fair and plunge France back into famine and civil war. That much is probably true; he had me convinced of it. But he was still afraid I would go to the police, and so he kept using the word 'murder'—as though I would be charged with killing this woman if we were found out."

"That's ridiculous."

"Perhaps, but I was in such a panic that I couldn't think straight. Ever since I saw the woman . . . I didn't even see her. I saw the plague, and all I could think about was the fact that it was right next-door to where you'd been sleeping. I saw this woman's face and I remembered how Clara looked just before . . . ." He was overcome once again by a sickly pallor, and his eyes bore glimmerings of dispirited fear.

"I know, Paul."

"I thought the same thing would happen to you—that I would lose you. But . . . ." He shook his head. "I'm going to lose you anyway."

"No, Paul, you have me," she said softly. "Don't ever think otherwise. I would be afraid to get out of bed in the morning if you weren't lying next to me." Katharine put an arm around him, laid her head on his shoulder.

"Then you should expect to be afraid every morning for a long time to come," he said flatly.

"I think it's perfectly understandable that you panicked."

"It may be understandable, but it's also punishable—especially considering how long I've gone without reporting it. I found about the daughter this morning. Nathan had convinced me that the woman was alone, and this morning he announced that she has a teenaged daughter, wandering Paris alone and looking for her mother. And even then . . . I had decided not to tell you. Or the police."

"But now you've told me."

"Yes, and only because you forced me." Paul dipped his head; his voice wavered. "I'll do whatever you want. You seem clear-headed; I still can't think straight. Just say the word and I'll do it."

"Please don't put the burden on me. I'm afraid you'll end up resenting me."

"For what? You haven't done anything, except marry a man who's afraid of his own shadow."

"I'm just as scared as you are," she said softly. "I was afraid that something like this would happen—except I thought that it would be Mr. Damgaard's doing. Not Mr. Arnaud."

"I'm sorry, Katharine."

She kissed his cheek. "I know you're a good man."

Paul closed his eyes, shook his head with inconsonant fervor. "Please don't call me that. I'm not a good man. I'm just a man." He was quiet for some time; then he looked at her with clouded eyes. "I'll go to the police and tell them everything," he said. "But you have to be prepared for what's going to happen."

"Nathan and Arnaud were using you. Surely most of the burden will fall on them. What could you have possibly had to gain from all this? It's their hotel, their jobs, their decisions . . . ."

"Yes, but Katharine, even if I don't end up in prison, it'll be all over the papers. I won't be able to practice medicine. And you of all people should understand how the justice system works in favor of people like Arnaud. I was the one committing all the incriminating actions. I'm a doctor, I knew this woman had the plague, I packed her into a laundry cart while she was still alive, I kept it secret. Even if I can prove she was there, Arnaud will slip around it. He'll lie, and Nathan will . . . ."

"I have an idea," Katharine said. "I told Mr. Dawes I'd come and see him after I talked to you. I can go to him and find out what else he's learned. It might be the case that we won't need you as a witness, and that Arnaud and Nathan will be exposed without our help. They'll probably never admit to their involvement, so they'll have no reason for exposing you; but if there are enough outside witnesses, they still may be able to prove that Elizabeth's daughter is telling the truth."

"Katharine . . . ."

"Just let me talk to him first, please, and I'll see what I can find out."

Paul sighed quietly. "Fine, do that; but first, let's get the hell out of Nathan's house. He's taking leave from the hotel, and I don't want to be here when he comes back."

21

THURSDAY, MAY 23, 1889

Every minute—every *second*—that Katharine was gone was maddening. She had insisted on seeing Dawes alone, to avoid—as she put it—the "confession or blatant deception" that Paul's presence would demand.

So he was left to fester alone in wild and dire possibilities. Paul sat alone in the new hotel room—a rather small and plain room compared to the other, a little nook that offered nothing to distract him. On the bureau was a heavy-looking ormolu clock with an angel figurine and gilded flowers. It reminded him of the clock that Nathan had tossed into the laundry bin. He stared at it, conquered by the fog of fear: the kind of numbing, claustrophobic dread a man knows when he has to wait for an outcome that may change the course of his whole life, and incur the deepest losses, the loss of all that is dear and beloved to his mortal life.

Over and over again, he worked through the moments that had brought him to this unforeseen wreckage. His mind was slowly turned from despair by his growing anger at Nathan. Not just at him; at Arnaud, at Damgaard. Especially Damgaard—but then, especially Nathan, who'd been casually chumming with a cold-blooded murderer—who had lured Paul into ruin, and who, as a friend of many years, had so taken advantage of his intimate knowledge of Paul's fears and weaknesses.

He could no longer endure the wait. In a fit Paul fled the room. He jumped into an omnibus and rode back to the eleventh district, his passions stirred by the accusatory notions that were forming potent and ever more organized in his mind.

Along Boulevard Voltaire, he disembarked and tried to orient himself, then tried to gather courage.

Near the corner was a little café with tables outside, and Paul seated himself, needing time and focus to gather his energies. *And drink. I need a drink.*

As soon as he sat, a man hurried toward him from off the street. Paul gave him a warning look, spewing mute unfriendliness; but the man responded with a smile, and with a knowing directness about his gaze. He placed a card on Paul's table and walked on.

Seconds later, a finely dressed woman passed by and did the same: with a discreetly elegant maneuver of her arm she slipped a heavily perfumed card onto the table, so stealthily that he barely noticed the gesture. She eyed him from beneath a thick, dark sweep of piled-up hair and smiled demurely before walking on.

Paul stared and didn't smile back.

A waiter appeared—stocky and weathered, with an impenetrably relaxed manner. He addressed Paul inquisitively.

"Sorry, I don't speak French. I need a drink." Paul pantomimed drinking from a glass. "Por favor. Anything."

The waiter looked him over, then spoke slowly. "Not a good day, yes? You are American?"

"Yes."

"'Por favor' is Spanish. We would say *s'il vous plait*."

Paul pronounced the words clumsily. "S'il vous plait, can I get a drink."

"What do you like?"

"I don't know. Something with rum." He picked up the perfumed card, studied it. "What's this?"

The waiter chuckled. "That is a beautiful young lady's address. You go to the address, you see the lady, and . . . ." He shrugged. "You receive any type of service you desire. I can assist you with directions."

Paul tossed the card back onto the table. "I'm married."

The waiter shrugged. "Yes, but sometimes, a man becomes—"

"What, there aren't enough ways for a man to lose his wife?" Paul snapped. The waiter stepped back, and Paul tried to steady himself. "Just the drink, please."

"If you want something not too strong, we can give you a little punch. You know it, *Ti'Punch*?"

"No, but please bring it."

The stocky waiter left. Paul released a strained breath and lowered his head into his hands.

He downed one drink, then another; then drifted to another café and drank again, still unable to face up to a confrontation with Nathan, or even to be certain of what to accost him with.

When he felt sufficiently "relaxed," he wound back toward Nathan's cottage, silently dodging the wandering merchants and cleaning crews who swept the streets. He veered onto Rue de la Roquette, remembered

Annette's stories: something about a church hospital in a field of rocket-flowers.

Presently he became aware of an ominous, unkempt mass of stone and mortar that rose to his right. He stopped and stared; turned around; stood immobile. He had gotten lost. Muttering to himself, he approached a small crowd that had gathered in a nearby square. A gray-haired gentleman stood at attention at the edge of the group. Paul tapped him on the shoulder, praying that he spoke English. "Excuse me . . . ."

The man turned and shushed him. Paul interpreted the sound perfectly. The crowd was fixed on something ahead—something of intense interest—and was not about to be distracted. Paul heard a voice speaking loudly beyond them, as if addressing the crowd, and he raised his bleary eyes into the yard just in time to see a white-faced, wild-eyed man being rolled into a guillotine. His body was tightly bound face-down to a platform, and Paul only had time to take in the helplessness of the man's position before the event reached its climax. As the man strained to look toward the crowd—as if for help—ropes were cut, and the blade came hurtling down, cleanly slicing the head from the body, spattering blood across the basket and onto the ground.

Paul turned away and vomited into his hands.

The gentleman next to him made a sound of displeasure, then dispersed with a few others; but most of the group looked on, some quiet, one weeping, others chattering in eager tones of shock and disgust. That Paul didn't understand the language only aggravated his addled brain. He observed a group of strange creatures before him, gross caricatures of human beings, outlandish and alien, watching the butchering of a man the way one might look with detached interest on the flaying of a strange insect.

He bolted then, down the street—back the way he'd come, until he wound toward the branch of Parmentier Avenue and could place himself at last. He stumbled along, hands drying with flaked vomit.

Nathan opened the door, saw Paul's clothes flecked and discolored. "Are you all right?"

"I could use some water," Paul rasped.

He followed Nathan into the house. Kept his temper while he washed his hands and wiped at his clothes.

"What happened?" Nathan pressed him.

"Oh, nothing. I might have vomited a little after watching a man's head get cut off."

"Oh." Nathan sounded sheepish. "On Roquette Square, by the prisons? There was an execution today—"

"You don't say."

"Don't worry about it. He murdered an old woman. The man was—"

"Yes, thank you, Nathan, I figured as much, I don't need you to explain every goddamn thing to me."

Nathan was silent.

"I would like you to confirm one thing for me, though, on that same subject." Paul shook the moisture from his hands, turned on Nathan with fire kindling in his eyes. "It was your idea to threaten me with the woman's murder, wasn't it? Not Arnaud's?"

Nathan was ashen. "Paul," he whispered.

"What's the matter—are you afraid your sweet, unsuspecting wife will find out what you did?"

Nathan's eyes swam with horror. He struggled to collect his nerves, then spoke with difficulty. "Annette is out," he said, looking anxiously around the kitchen. "But . . . what is this? What are you accusing me of?"

"You know perfectly well what I'm saying. You told me the woman was dead."

Nathan shook his head, asked feebly: "When?"

"*When*? When you asked me to wrap her body up and have it carted down to Arnaud's makeshift morgue."

"She looked dead. She was barely alive."

"Well you didn't tell me she was barely alive, you told me she was *expired*. That means *dead*, Doctor Neville."

"We thought she was dead."

"Oh, you're a doctor and you're telling me you couldn't tell the difference? You involved me because you needed my hotel room, and then you made threats so I'd keep my mouth shut. One minute it's 'oh, Paul, she's a dead woman, she's here by herself and no one will miss her, you have to wrap the body to avoid contagion,' and the next it's 'oh, there's a complication, you see, you may have killed her'—*you may have killed her*. What was your role in all of that? And then there was Arnaud, throwing around the word 'murder.' Don't you dare deny it."

"It wasn't like that. I panicked. We both did, Arnaud and I, we were both panicking."

"Really? No forethought?"

"I called for you because you were right there, down the hall. You're a doctor."

"*You're* a doctor," Paul fumed. He was becoming wild with avowed anger, felt spittle flying from his raging lips. "You don't need another doctor to wrap a body. Whose idea was it to rearrange the room and make the girl seem crazy? Was it you or Arnaud?"

"It didn't happen like that."

"You got that idea from *me*." Paul lunged at him; stopped short; but his voice intensified provocatively. "I told you that Damgaard covered up a murder by making my wife look crazy, and you got the idea from me."

"Paul, I didn't plan it—"

"You had the *whole damned thing* planned in advance."

Nathan was shrinking away, toward the edge of the room, but Paul pounced and wrenched his arm with fervor.

"Paul, get off of me!"

"Didn't you? Answer me, Nathan."

"Let go." Nathan struggled, helpless against Paul's rage; but Paul abruptly released him.

"I'm going to the police and telling them everything." He walked by and strode toward the door.

"Paul, you don't want to do that," Nathan called after him. "Arnaud has too many connections in this town, and you're a nobody here. The proof is gone. No one else has fallen sick, and no one would want this to see the light of day. You against Arnaud would be like Katharine against Damgaard."

Paul slowed. He turned, studying Nathan for some time before speaking. "You know that Damgaard murdered Katharine's father. Don't you?"

Nathan lowered his eyes. "I don't know," he said tiredly. "I guess he could have done it. I don't know anything."

"What'd he do for you? Did he have business with you, or offer to introduce you to some glamorous acquaintance of his? Was it just that he flattered you? Or you simply thought it would be easier to be on his good side? What was it?"

Nathan looked back at him in exhausted silence.

"This may astonish you, Nathan, but a murder in the middle of a crowd isn't this easy to cover up. Your police friends may not be taking this case, but there's a journalist collecting witnesses who can place that woman at Arnaud's hotel. We're not the only people who saw her there. We're going to be found out; and even if Arnaud can somehow get it swept under the rug, and even if you can point your finger at me, people are going to know you're a liar." He shook his head and walked away.

"Paul," Nathan said, his tone suddenly sharp.

As Paul strode from the house, he heard Nathan following him; but he walked away without looking back.

"Paul!" Nathan cried from the doorstep, to no avail. "Paul, please, as your friend," he started, and then hurried back inside and slammed the door.

Katharine stood in the lobby of the Hotel Véronique, trying to determine the direction of Dawes' room. Each end of the room led to an unmarked staircase. She started for one, but was stopped by the desk clerk, who took notice of her uncertainty and addressed her in French. Katharine shook her head apologetically and displayed Dawes' note.

"I have a friend who's staying here. He's in room 112," she explained carefully. "Could you tell me which way to go?"

The clerk smiled and pointed to the right-hand stairway. "Upstairs. Go left at the second floor."

"Thank you."

Katharine found the room easily. She knocked at the door and waited; then tried once more, knocking and calling the reporter's name. "Mr. Dawes?"

Still nothing. Katharine was about to turn away, but some inexplicable impulse stopped her.

Something was wrong. She stood and listened to the quiet, far-off noises of the hotel, stared at the wood grain of the door, and tried to determine what had triggered her sudden sense of alarm. Her mind flashed back to the night she'd stood at the threshold of her own house and opened the door to find her life turned upside down—her father dead, bathed in blood.

She suppressed a sigh. *Damgaard has me scared of everything.*

Yet she couldn't leave. Every nerve in her body throbbed with the impulse that something was wrong—that Dawes was in trouble, needed help. Or that help had already come too late.

Katharine's eyes moved down, slowly fixing on the tiny space just under the door. And she realized what had caught her attention: the coppery scent of blood, rising from the place where it was congealing at the edge of the hallway. She could see a little sliver of it, barely peeking out from the threshold of Dawes' room.

She was kneeling slowly, not wanting to look closer, but automatically reaching out and placing her fingers into the stain. She brought her hand up; felt her fingertips coated; slowly turned the hand over and stared at the deep red streaked across her skin.

Numbness enveloped her. Katharine walked back down to the desk in a haze, went automatically, felt nothing. When she reached the desk, she held her fingers up to the clerk.

"There's blood coming from under my friend's door?" She said it like a question, her voice trembling.

The clerk looked concerned, then disturbed. She asked questions that Katharine's brain couldn't interpret. A key was fetched; the woman hurried up the stairs, with Katharine trailing numbly behind her.

And then she had to live it all over again: the door opening slowly, gradually revealing the pool of blood spilled across the floor. With every inch that was exposed, Katharine felt the increasing weight of horror, helplessness, and—most pressingly—despair.

Dawes was crumpled on the floor, face-down, with no visible wound—but the amount of spilled blood gave no hope that he was alive. The clerk cried out and covered her face, then grabbed Katharine's arm in a terrified spasm. The woman made some exclamation and fled back down the stairs.

Katharine put a hand over her mouth and nose, as if to keep the ugliness from seeping into her. *Don't get sick, Katharine, not now.* She stepped around the thickening pool of blood, bracing herself against the wall. She couldn't look directly at Dawes, but from the corner of her gaze, she spied a crimson stain on his throat.

She whispered: "I am sorry for what has happened to you, you brave, wonderful man." Katharine shuddered with renewed grief; tears spilled from her eyes.

She turned away, tried to survey the room through blurred eyes, then studied Dawes' body. He could not have been dead long. Blood still moved in little rivulets between the floorboards. It seemed to darken with the shadow of the murderer, a shadow that slithered beneath the pool, stealthily toward her feet . . . .

Not now, Katharine. You can't afford to feel frightened now. She kept the monster at bay and made an attempt at searching Dawes' pockets. They were empty. No wallet, no note pad, no pencil—nothing.

She searched the room, hurrying now, beginning to collect her senses. A suitcase was open on the bed; she rifled through it, found nothing of interest. Next the shelves, then the bureau turned up nothing; but as she moved to exit the room, she caught sight of a small book corner protruding ever so slightly from beneath Dawes' body.

Without thinking, she fished it out. The cover was blank. She opened it and scanned the pages, expecting to find Dawes' notes, but the contents puzzled her.

. . . along with its supposedly unclean food, was delightfully overwhelming. Mamma would only try the sweet banana fritters, but I was enthralled by everything in the paratha lane. The vendors tossed and poured with such animated precision, lending a sort of livelihood to the foods they prepared, and I sampled perhaps more than I should. Nikhil warned me that I was eating "too much new food" and that I would come away with a stomach ache, and as usual his prediction was accurate.

I found the mausoleums, too, to be quite stunning, with many intricate little decorations pursuing the rolling lines of the domes and stretching along the minarets. The color is also quite nice—organic, earthy colors that make the structures look like giant fruits sprung from the soil of the earth. It is a shame that my presence in Delhi is so uncomfortable, both on my family's account . . . .

"Charlotte," Katharine whispered.

The clerk was returning. Katharine could hear the woman's wailing, sobbing voice drifting up from the lobby, coming ever closer to the stairs.

She slammed the book shut and was suddenly aware of blood soaking much of the back cover. "Damn," she whispered, fighting off another fit of revulsion. Blood had smeared the length of her fingers. Katharine stared at the book for a moment. Then, moving at a desperate speed, she yanked a shirt from Dawes' suitcase and deftly wrapped the stained journal—then leapt to the edge of the room and made her way back outside.

The hall was empty. Katharine hurried away from the stairs, away from the encroaching sound of the wailing clerk, trying to pace herself—*don't look like you're running away, don't attract attention, but hurry.* She reached the opposite staircase and descended slowly and unsteadily, listening carefully to the moaning of the clerk. She was descending just as the clerk was ascending the opposite stair; she kept time carefully, avoided being seen.

She found the lobby empty and moved through the exit with a determined pace. Katharine only faltered once, there on the front step, when she found herself looking into a familiar pair of sly eyes.

John Damgaard stood close enough that she could see every detail of his face. He was chatting cordially with two women. The women never looked up, but Damgaard noticed Katharine immediately. Their gazes locked, and his lips stretched into the all-too-familiar grin: the one that was nearly all bravado, as if he couldn't help swelling with tenacious pride whenever he came across this victim of his own easy duplicity; a grin that maintained a hint of defiance, as though he felt sure of having some justification for his crimes.

With a vague motion of one hand, Damgaard slipped something into his pocket: a note pad. *Dawes' note pad?* Katharine watched the movement, and stared hard into the yellow-flecked eyes, as if to let Damgaard know that she knew; and then she slipped quietly away, leaving the entire grotesque scene behind her.

Damgaard had stood in the way of her desired route. Now she

retreated to avoid him, circling back around the block and straying another street over before heading toward her own hotel. She moved through the world with a fragmented focus, clutching Dawes' shirt and the solid bulk of the journal within it. Katharine was just crossing into a street when a familiar blend of form and color soaked up the breadth of her focus: first the curl of dark hair beneath the brim of a top hat, and then the rest of the all-too-recognizable form of John Damgaard, who strode along the block just ahead of her.

Abruptly Katharine backed out of the street. She felt a sudden sickness—her insides beginning to shift, her body slumping. But the fear was checked by a sudden surge of determination. *Not now, Katharine; you mustn't get sick now.* She grasped Charlotte's journal more firmly. She was carrying the Morgan girl's voice; she had salvaged it, could protect it, had to get it to a safe place.

Katharine stared after Damgaard for a moment, waiting for him to turn and see her—but why would he? He walked determinedly, with a destination in mind, while Katharine remained out of sight behind him. She collected her nerves by remembering nightmares: *I'm not afraid of you.* And the real nightmares: Damgaard at the window, taunting her. *The predator has the advantage . . . the prey's only choice is to run, never knowing the best retreat . . . .*

Katharine began to trail after him. There was something necessary in the gesture—necessary to her livelihood, this temporary relief from the feeling of being stalked. For some time she felt safe in the notion that it was Damgaard who was being preyed on, Damgaard who was oblivious to the eye that watched him from the shadows.

They passed through a few more blocks in that manner, and then Katharine had to speed up after losing sight of him. He had turned right and disappeared behind the mass of tall gray buildings; he was taking Katharine's own route, and as she caught him in her sights again, she felt a vague discomfort as Damgaard began to pass by her own hotel—and was startled when he suddenly turned and walked through the lobby doors.

She stood helplessly on the walkway. Had he come here to stalk her? *He could have found out where I am. Nathan could have told him . . . .*

She hurried then, almost running, but slowed near the entrance. The glass doors offered an obscured view of the interior: the desk clerk sat writing, but otherwise the modest room appeared vacant. Katharine slipped through the doors and felt her heart begin to race. *Calmly, Katharine; calmly . . . .*

She was moving quietly, listening for the sound of steps against the tiled floors. The desk clerk looked up and greeted her: "Bonjour,

Madame."

Katharine smiled; nodded; whispered an almost inaudible "Bonjour" in response. She hurried to follow the fading echo of footfalls in the right-hand hallway, keeping her own steps as light as possible. As the length of the hall came into view, she slowed and proceeded cautiously, watching as a man in a black top hat and suit disappeared around the far corner. In the hall she stopped to lean against the wall and slip her shoes off; then walked briskly onward.

Damgaard stopped partway down the adjacent hall. Katharine waited, listening intently, recognizing the soft shuffling of garments and the mechanical clinking of a key moving within a lock. She held her breath at the sound of a door opening.

Wait for it . . . not yet . . . . She stood and listened for the footfalls to resume, struggled to hear over the pounding of her own heartbeat. Katharine stuck her head around the corner in time to see the closing of a door. She wasted not a moment in walking to it and checking the number.

Another left-hand turn led her to her own room at the back of the hotel. She entered it tentatively. The room was vacant; Paul was gone. Katharine buried the journal under the contents of her own suitcase, and then sat on the bed and stared.

22

At some point the dam broke. Katharine sat on the bed, where she and Paul clutched each other like frightened children, and began to sob.

Paul did his best to comfort her: tenderly caressed her hair, whispered reassurances, waited patiently. But Katharine knew that he was just as scared as she was.

"What is John Damgaard doing here?" she asked at last. "Annette said he was staying at the Clément. It's like he's following us."

"Nathan said he was making a tour of the Paris hotels."

"But *this* one? It's far beneath his standards. It has no amenities, no leisure rooms—"

"He probably didn't know that when he booked it. I doubt that he could have followed us here; it's nearly impossible to get a room that hasn't been secured in advance. It's a small miracle that Arnaud ended up finding this one. We only got it because—" Paul stopped short.

"Damgaard could manage it," Katharine muttered. After a moment she added: "Why *did* we get this room?"

"Well . . . the gentleman who was staying here died—from exhaustion, apparently. He had the room booked until Wednesday."

"Wonderful," Katharine muttered.

"Why don't we pack up and go back to Le Havre?" Paul asked gently. "You can talk to the police, and tell them about Dawes and the witnesses he found; and then we can—"

"I can't talk to the police."

"Why not?"

She shook her head. "I don't even know. I need to think. So many things have happened."

"You could just tell them that Dawes was investigating the Morgan woman's disappearance when he was killed."

"Yes, and then they'd want to interview you as well. We're both witnesses. What would you tell them?"

Paul was silent.

165

"I'm sure it was Damgaard who killed Mr. Dawes. He gave me such a look . . . ."

"He would have given you that look anyway. I don't think it's likely, even if Damgaard is a killer, that he would get tangled up in Arnaud's affairs."

"I can see how he would. Nathan knows that Damgaard is a murderer. He needed the reporter out of the way just as badly as Arnaud did. He might have made a suggestion."

"No, I don't think—" Paul checked himself. "I really don't know what to think anymore." He kissed the crown of Katharine's head and stood with a sigh. "I need to do something normal. Are you hungry?"

"No."

"I have to get out of this room for a while." Paul rose, looking around the small bedroom and tapping his fingers impatiently against his sides. He turned to Katharine with a sudden expression of alarm. "I can't leave you here alone—not with Damgaard down the hall."

"I'll be fine. I'm going to lie down for a while."

"But . . . ."

"If anyone knocks, I won't answer."

"That's not good enough." Paul climbed into the bed beside her, and clutched her tightly.

He lasted only twenty minutes before the room became unbearable. Katharine was about to complain about his incessant tossing about in the bed when he suddenly demanded: "I have to go out. Come with me."

"Go on," she replied. "I'll be fine."

"This is too much; it's insane." He paused. "I want you away from Damgaard. We should leave—if not for the port, at least for some other city."

"I can't," she said. Her eyes moved, automatically, to a suitcase propped up against the closet. She hadn't had a chance to look through Charlotte's journal; she had a pressing need to see it before she left. *I need to know what I am leaving.* "I need some time to think. Let me sleep on it."

"Sleep on what?"

"We're not the only ones who are in danger," she reminded him gently. "There's the Morgan girl. She's here alone, and Mr. Dawes isn't around to look out for her now."

"Katharine . . . ."

"Go and get something to eat. We'll talk when you get back."

"Fine. I'll be back soon." Paul stopped beside the bureau; his eyes were suddenly riveted on the top drawer. He pulled it open with an air of hesitation.

Katharine knew what he was looking at. His razor was lying there, sharp and potentially lethal.

"Don't, Paul," she said softly.

He closed the drawer. "I'm sorry. Just . . . don't open the door for anyone." He kissed his wife, and stood looking at her for some time before moving to leave.

"I'll be fine," she repeated.

Katharine waited some minutes after he left before slipping Charlotte's journal from its hiding place. She sat reading the past week's entries, and what she saw affected her deeply. Within minutes she was hunched over in grief, tears sliding in an inexhaustible torrent down her cheeks. She held the book aloft to keep from staining the pages.

I interviewed again with the police. They speak in French so that I cannot understand, and cast disdainful looks when they address me. None of them show any care. Their questions are abrupt and suspicious. They focus on my behavior rather than my mother's whereabouts. It is made clear to me that I am a nuisance; I am causing trouble, I am making a scene.

Today they asked many repetitive questions, but phrased differently and with details altered. Subsequently I gave different answers. They demanded to know why I could not be consistent, and accused me of fabrications and falsehoods. I do not have words for how I felt—such magnitude of helplessness and despair. I feel as though the world has gone mad. I went back to my room, curled up in the corner and cried for my Mamma. . . .

Among the narratives were hastily scribbled notes—details that Charlotte wished to keep track of—and a number of addresses: Dawes' hotel room, the London Metro Police Department, Paris' Prefecture of Police, the British embassy, Hotel Clément, and a certain Howard Morgan in Delhi. Katharine browsed some of the earlier entries before once more concealing the book. She didn't want Paul to know she had taken it—didn't want him to see the ugly stain of Dawes' slain life on the back cover, didn't want to increase the sense of risk and danger. Paul was already stressed close to his limit, and Katharine needed time to think. She sat with her chin resting on her palm, eyes closed, her mind carefully organizing and rearranging details. Faces, events, objects shifted in orderly geometric patterns, one arrangement after another. And none produced a solution.

The patterns disintegrated as Katharine became increasingly concerned about the length of Paul's absence, which had just hit the two-hour mark. She stared tensely at the ormolu. *Why so long?* A sudden pang of fear stabbed at her heart. *Damgaard. What if . . . .*

A light commotion outside the door interrupted her thoughts. Paul entered a moment later; Katharine breathed a sigh of relief, then rose to greet him and caught the telltale scent of rum on his breath.

"I had to get a couple of drinks," he said apologetically. His eyes were red and puffed at the lids, as though he'd been crying. "I'm not coping very well with . . . ."

"You don't need to explain."

"I haven't come up with a damn thing. What about you?"

"Nothing that would work," she said softly.

"Do you want to get out for a while?"

"No."

"I'm going to get ready for bed." He rummaged through some items on the bureau. "You're sure you're not hungry?"

Katharine studied him. "You didn't eat?"

He cast her a sheepish look. "No. I had a couple drinks and wandered around for a while, and then I had another drink, and then I got some coffee. Where's the powder?"

"What powder?"

"The dental powder."

"You used it up."

"Did I use it up?" His voice regained a hint of its old lightheartedness. "I imagine we both contributed to that."

"You use far too much at a time. It was supposed to last us the whole trip." Katharine addressed him gently. "I'll ask the desk clerk where we can get more."

Paul slipped his arms around her waist. "You don't use enough; you'll end up with rotten teeth. Trust me . . . ."

Trust me—I'm a doctor. One of his oft-used lines, now with a bitter ring to it. Paul let the words trail off and released Katharine from his grasp. "Forget it. If we have to go about in the morning with foul breath, it will be the least of our problems."

"No, I'll ask. Forget about bed for now; let's find something to eat. I haven't had anything since breakfast. We may as well try to keep our strength up."

The rum had done little to sooth Paul's nerves. In the lobby, he stood in a half-daze while Katharine spoke to the clerk; his eyes roved aimlessly around the pretty room, occasionally darting from one hall to another. He had seen the way Katharine hesitated at every corner: pausing at the doorway, listening at the staircase, hovering at a point just out of view of the lobby before she would enter. *Looking for Damgaard.* That John Damgaard was a free man, staying just down the hall from the daughter of a man he'd murdered, was a perverse injustice—one that

Paul felt completely helpless against. He suddenly wished he could do away with the man himself. *And spend the rest of my life in prison. That's brilliant; that's the solution, yes.* He thought for a few moments, wondering. *But if it turns out that I'll end up in prison anyway . . . .*

Paul shook himself. He tried to think reasonable thoughts. *I am keeping it together for Katharine's sake, and she's keeping it together for the Morgan girl's sake. Thank God the two of us can find a reason not to lose it.* He knew now that Katharine composed herself with great effort. For months he had listened and watched as she purged strains of grief and terror, as she carried on in their shadow—and Paul was a large part of what helped her carry on. Katharine had told him as much. He had missed all of that before they wedded, too caught up in his own feelings. Katharine had captivated him; she had a startlingly penetrating gaze, one that often made a quiet study of him. To be looked at by Katharine was to have his soul laid bare. Paul felt exposed and vulnerable before that gaze, and when he caught her looking at him with him affection, he couldn't help feeling flattered. To be truly seen, and loved—that flattery quickly became yearning.

Marriage had profoundly changed her manner. In the public sphere she remained fiercely determined to behave with propriety, but in private her reserved manner dropped away. She spoke without censorship, clung to Paul with unexpected passion. He enjoyed the sudden transformation, and developed ways of teasing her about it. In public he would pull her close, insisting "Don't worry, no one's looking" while Katharine inevitably squirmed away; she maintained a certain distance from him, but would look at him with such pleasure and love that it made his heart race, and left him yearning for the time when they would be alone again. He loved watching her face melt in a genuine smile; he loved the warm flash in her eyes when she looked at him. He loved watching her resist, and then yielding so easily in his arms once they were alone. *And now this.* Since the first sighting of Damgaard in Paris, Katharine's eyes had become increasingly dull, her face ever more strained.

Paul turned toward the desk, fixing a concerned gaze on his wife— and found her staring at him with a peculiar expression. She returned to his side, holding out a small box. "Dental powder. They keep extra toiletries for guests."

He kept his voice low. "Is something the matter?"

"No," she replied. After a moment she added: "Aside from the obvious."

"You're sure?" He gave her a quick hug.

"I'm sure." But there was something far-off in her eyes, as if some new dilemma had occurred to her, something she was turning over in her mind.

23

The Prefecture of Police was situated between Notre Dame Cathedral and the Palace of Justice on the *Île de la Cité*, a natural island in the Seine River, some distance east of the fairgrounds. In London, Charlotte had taken an interest in both dwellings, whose history spanned hundreds of years. At the northeast face of the Palace was the Conciergerie, which had served as both a royal dwelling and a prison; once a Merovingian palace, it was overhauled by French kings beginning in the tenth century, and to the day it evinced all the gloom and grandeur of an imposing medieval castle. During the Revolution, it housed hundreds of prisoners on their way to execution. Among its many doomed captives were Marie Antionette and—ironically—Robespierre, who was guillotined for his lavish use of the guillotine on alleged enemies of the new Republic.

The cathedral was no less compelling. It rose from the island in a complex mass of intricate Gothic beauty, ever more dazzling as one approached and discerned its details. Elegantly carved stone and stained glass sheltered what remained of the holy relics borne into France by Louis IX, among them the thorn of crowns purportedly worn by Christ. At the exterior, newly added stone chimeras feigned to ward off evil, gifting the cathedral with an element of fantasy. Open-mouthed gargoyles occasionally spouted rainwater from gaping maws. The Revolution had marked this place, too; statues had been beheaded, the Virgin Mary replaced by Lady Liberty, Catholicism shoved aside in favor of the Cult of Reason, before the Cathedral was restored to its original themes. Elizabeth had promised a visit to these places, and to the nearby Sainte-Chapelle: a dazzling thirteenth-century chapel hidden within the labyrinthine Palace, famous for the towering stained-glass windows that stretched to its high vaulted ceilings.

Now, of course, Charlotte retained no interest in the cathedral, in gargoyles or architecture or Paris history. The towering Gothic structures, instead of compelling her with their strange beauty, seemed to resound only with the morbid scenes that had paraded through them—the stuff of nightmares.

The prefecture, too, looked enough like a miniature castle to make Charlotte feel small and powerless. But the exterior, hard and domineering as it was, didn't do enough to impress upon her the nightmare that she would face inside.

Dawes was dead. The hotel clerk had gently informed Charlotte of the murder when she came to call on the reporter. The news had stunned, then horrified her. She couldn't reject the reality of it when the clerk insisted that, yes, the man whose throat had been fatally cut was Albert Dawes, a British journalist; the crime scene had been checked over and the body removed; and no, the incident hadn't been in the newspapers yet, and thus she had no other details to spare. The woman directed Charlotte to the police precinct and encouraged her to share any clues she might have.

Charlotte immediately suspected that the crime was related to Dawes' investigation of her mother's disappearance. The suspicion quickly became conviction, and she went straight away to the Prefecture to report her involvement with Dawes—but the interview with the police took a fast and unexpected turn. An English-speaking detective dismissed her concerns about the slain journalist and confronted her with various complaints that had been put to him by Marcel Arnaud.

Charlotte was accused of harassing a night guard at the Clément; of harassing guests; of attempting to damage property.

She had been sitting for long hours with her ear pressed close against the wall that bordered room 342. Thus far she hadn't heard a sound: no one was in the room. In the late night and early morning hours she'd snuck into the hallway and attempted to pick the lock, but the night guard continually prowled the area. He had caught her outside room 342 three separate times. Charlotte had heard him on the steps at first, and fled back to her room before he could catch her tampering with the lock; but he simply crept more quietly. It became a sort of contest between them to see who could move most quietly. Upon finally catching her in the act, the guard had confiscated the hair pin she was using, and threatened to have her arrested if he saw her near the doorway again.

As for her harassment of the guests, she'd reported the disappearance of her mother to anyone she happened to pass by, hoping that someone had seen her. But Charlotte's questioning had no effect except to give Arnaud the ammunition he needed. Now she was sitting in a cramped room on the first floor of the Prefecture, unable to absorb most of what the detective was telling her.

"Do you understand what I am saying, Miss Morgan?" he asked. He had a long, thin nose and a straight moustache below needling brown eyes. Charlotte could only look at his face and think of badminton battledore, played by invisible creatures standing atop the moustache, hitting an invisible shuttlecock over the top of the hooked nose.

"Miss Morgan?" he prodded.

She shook her head absently. "My mother is missing. I was trying to discover whether anyone had seen her."

The detective eyed her piercingly. "You must understand that you will not be allowed to return to the hotel. From this day on, if you attempt to re-enter the property, you will be promptly arrested and put into a cell."

She still shook her head, protesting weakly. "If I can just collect my things . . . how is it that Mr. Arnaud can arrest me?" She dragged her eyes away from the moustache, dared to look into the cold brown eyes, forced herself to focus. "I have done nothing wrong. My mother is missing."

"Miss Morgan, everything has been explained to you in a most clear manner, and your situation is not a matter of debate. You are never to return to Hotel Clément or to make inquiries to other guests there."

"I see . . . . if I could just collect my things, I will . . . ." She trailed off helplessly.

"Mr. Arnaud is having your luggage collected. We have sent an officer to assist him."

Charlotte started. "Mr. *Arnaud*? But you—he has no right to go through my things." She leaned forward anxiously, on the verge of jumping to her feet. The detective smoothly stepped in front of the door, blocking it in case Charlotte should try to flee.

"We have considered the circumstances and determined that we have every right," he said coolly. "Once your belongings arrive, we will have them sent with you to the hospital."

"What hospital?" Charlotte's head ached; her brain seemed to expand, pressing hard against the walls of her skull, blurring her vision, making her weave in her chair. "Has . . . is my mother there? Has she been found?"

He frowned deeply. "No, she has not been found."

"Is it Mr. Dawes, then? Is he alive?"

"Miss Morgan, I cannot make it clearer. It is not your mother or Mr. Dawes, but you. And you are lucky that it is the hospital, and not a jail cell, where we have decided to detain you."

"But I am not unwell," Charlotte protested. "You can see I am perfectly healthy."

He thrust his face toward her, as if to eye her more intensely. "Miss Morgan, we are actively investigating your mother's disappearance.

Perhaps the doctors can help you properly recollect the circumstances in which she first vanished, or at least persuade you to reveal the details you do recollect. We have been unable to establish any evidence of Mrs. Morgan's whereabouts through other sources, and so the weight must be borne on your shoulders."

Charlotte listened numbly to the rest of the detective's monologue. It was only after he stepped out of the room, leaving her alone, that his words began to sink in.

He wasn't implying that she had caught her mother's illness. Charlotte was being sent to a psychiatric hospital, to be evaluated for a psychiatric illness. She would be "treated" and questioned until her uncle arrived to take her . . . *but where to? To London—without Mamma? To India? And then what?*

She thought of Blythe's pale, smooth face, the blue eyes glittering with spite; of Minnie's face drawn with suspicion; of her aunt's quiet disapproval. She remembered the collective resentment of the neighbors. It seemed certain that there would be no help, no understanding from them. *Nikhil, surely, is my only friend, but I shall never see him again.* Tears rolled down Charlotte's cheeks as she thought of him sitting beside her, reciting Zafar's misery in his stolid voice. *Not the light of anyone's eye am I, not the solace of anyone's heart am I; of no use to anyone, a mere clump of dust am I.*

"I am not the song that gives life," she whispered numbly. "No one would wish to hear me. . . ."

Two younger officers stepped into the room. They largely ignored Charlotte, murmuring to each other in French, stealing occasional glances at their dazed captive. She recognized them from previous visits. The taller one, a Scotsman, she'd come to know as the prefect bully; there was something punishing in his manner, as though he was not content to simply disbelieve her, but wished to hold her accountable with his barely veiled insults. The other, a Parisian, seemed kinder; even now, Charlotte could see a humane effort in his eyes when he dared look her way. He had sympathy, compassion. She could see it just as clearly as she saw the snide contempt in the other officer's gaze. *And why is the reverse not true?* Charlotte wondered. *Anyone who looks at me, looks in my eyes and hears my voice, should know that I'm telling the truth. How is it that I can see all of these men so clearly, and none of them can see me?*

At length, the Parisian was called away, and the Scot sat near Charlotte along the adjoining wall. Charlotte felt her heart sinking lower, deep into a bottomless void.

"When your luggage arrives," he said abruptly, "the wagon will take you to the Salpêtrière." He spoke with a thick accent; Charlotte couldn't understand the tail end of what he said. She eyed him warily, zeroing in on the bristles of his golden moustache. *Shuttlecock battledore.*

Exhaustion was taking its toll. The stress of the ordeal was threatening to break her.

"There's a hospital just down the street," he continued, "but it doesn't specialize in derangement." He cracked a grin—mean-spirited, proud. Charlotte averted her eyes.

Just down the street was the Hôtel-Dieu, the seventh-century hospital sprawled near Notre Dame Cathedral. Within the last three hundred years it had gained a reputation as a holding prison for the poor and sick—a dumping ground, a method by which the elite could avoid sharing society with the diseased of the lesser classes. Only within the past century had it become a place of attempted healing.

Charlotte's mind flashed with sudden insight. *I never checked any of the hospitals. My mother might be there; they might have dumped her off.*

She weighed the possibilities, but the more she considered the idea, the more unlikely it seemed. And it wasn't logic that made her stomach sink with despondence; she was simply being overpowered by despair. *Surely, I am waging a futile battle against the worst possible outcome. . .*

.

Sleep deprivation was beginning to meld reality with dreams; Charlotte had a sudden vision of her mother slumping toward her down a long corridor, stiff-limbed and vacant, wandering alone through the Hôtel-Dieu: a ghost hospital where the spirits of a few Augustinian nuns looked on in helpless sorrow.

A back window blasted the corridor with sudden light. The scene grew hazy. Charlotte leaned forward, looking into the blotched face and empty gaze of the woman who so resembled a half-dead version of Elizabeth Morgan; then caught herself as she lurched forward.

The Scottish officer reached out to steady her—and again he grinned, where any reasonable human being would have expressed concern. Charlotte shook him off and sat straight in the chair. Once again she was caught in the bare, stuffy Prefecture office. Its stark white floors and walls glared at her somberly.

"You'll be better off at the Salpêtrière," the officer was saying. "It has both men and women patients, but it's known more for its treatment of troubled women." His eyes flashed with a hint of amusement.

"Stop speaking to me like that," Charlotte whispered.

He leaned closer. "Say again?"

She stared at him silently, but with raging bitterness. In the man's eyes she read the helpless irony of her situation: They were trying to wear her out, to make her seem unstable. Sending her to the psychiatric hospital would add weight to their claims. She would be treated like an invalid, and she would wither there among other invalids. She would slowly go mad; and when she was lost, they would win.

As Charlotte listened to the deliberate malice in the officer's words, anger began to crawl from somewhere below her heart, heating her insides, compressing organs.

"You wouldn't want them to send you to a hospital anywhere else." The officer eyed her with growing condescension, the grin sneaking more boldly onto his face. "There are some frightening things happening in psychiatry these days. In Switzerland, there's a doctor who treats delusional patients by scrambling their brains—not the whole brain, but see, what he does is he takes out a piece of your skull and gets into the brain, and cuts certain connections. It's supposed to make the delusions of the brain become less intrusive. And it's just in Switzerland for now, but the idea is spreading to other areas. If you're lucky, it won't spread to a place like London."

Hatred coiled in Charlotte's being, found its center in her heart and compacted the anger, drawing inward and gaining energy, like a perturbed serpent curling tightly into itself. "Stop talking, you . . . ."

"Me, stop? I'm just saying—"

"I know what you are about," she hissed.

He feigned befuddlement, but the proud gleam still shone in his eyes. "What, what am I about?"

"You cannot frighten me," she said before he could finish. Her voice was rising, the serpent ever tightening, venom surging, almost ready to strike. "I know what happened, I am not crazy, and no matter where you send me, you will never get me to keep quiet about this, and you will answer in hell for the part you played. Do you hear me?" She shouted the words—not just at him. At all of them. "You think that you are so clever and that you will get away with it, but you will answer for it in hell."

Other men were coming into the room now, restraining her unnecessarily, then pulling her away. Charlotte's eyes were still fixed on the young man with his resentfully self-satisfied expression; she dared it, challenged it, condemned it the only way she knew how: "*You will answer in hell for what you did!*"

Katharine checked the ormolu. "Ten-twenty. I'd say it's a reasonably late hour. Should we go to bed?"

"I hate that damned clock." Paul threw himself on the mattress and covered his eyes. "Do me a favor, and put it somewhere out of sight."

Katharine picked it up; hesitated; seemed to weigh it in her hand, let it hang loosely in her grip. "It's an odd shape for a clock," she said. The ormolu was oblong, with a narrow base that tapered into a bronzed angel figurine at the top. Katharine held it by the figurine—just the right size for a secure grip of the hand. "It's heavy."

"Put it in the bureau drawer."

She didn't move, but stood examining the clock. "A gilder that hath his brains perished with quicksilver," she murmured.

"What?"

"It's from Webster's *The White Devil*. Did you ever read it?"

"Never."

"The ormolu craftsmen went mad from quicksilver poisoning. Webster made a reference to it in his play." Katharine paused. "I have been thinking of that story. The Duke of Brachiano has two people murdered so that he can marry Vittoria Accoramboni, and then he claims that Vittoria's grace and beauty blinded him from the evil of such an act—that he could not see it because he 'beheld the devil in crystal.' Webster used his stories to point out that evil often wears the appearance of elegance, success . . . even purity, and we are more easily tempted because of it." She turned to Paul, letting the ormolu hang heavily at her side. "Do you know . . . when Mr. Damgaard looks at me, he has this way of turning his chin up with a look of defiance, as though . . . as though he thinks he is justified in killing my father. As though he truly believes it was necessary, and is daring me to judge him."

"I doubt that Damgaard cares whether it was justifiable."

"Maybe he doesn't. But there are murderous colonists and slavers who believe that God is on their side—and I'm sure that some are opportunists who simply don't care, but others *really believe* it. They claim purity and superiority. Why not Damgaard?" She hesitated again. "There *are* degrees of evil in the world. And what if a crime did have some seemingly justifiable purpose? I mean . . . Nathan lives here, and perhaps he *was* trying to save the whole of France with his actions. Or . . . let's say you're Vittoria, and your murderous brother has promised to kill you and your maid, so you try to kill him in self-defense. What if it only *looks* right, and you believe that you can protect yourself and still adhere to a higher moral principle, when in fact it's just another evil?"

"Katharine, I can't manage that kind of moral debate right not. Please put that thing away before I throw it out the window."

"All right." She tucked the ormolu beside the bureau, on the floor, instead. "I . . . I forgot to ask the clerk something. I'll be right back."

Paul abruptly sat up.

"It's fine," she said, stopping him with a gesture. "I'll just be a minute."

She returned several minutes later, her face pale, her brow furrowed, eyes glittering.

"What is it, Katharine?" Paul asked, studying her. "Did you see him?"

"No."

"What, then? Tell me what's on your mind."

For the smallest fraction of a second, Katharine looked guilty; but she quickly shook it off. "I'm just trying to figure things out," she said.

She had, in fact, figured out a couple of things—things that she would not yet share with Paul. One of them involved Mr. Damgaard.

In the night, as Paul lay sleeping, Katharine rolled herself delicately to the edge of the bed, sliding her feet to the floor and creeping toward the corner closet. It was a large oak structure, a single piece of furniture rather than a built-in unit, and on one side was a row of small brass hooks for hanging coats.

She turned to look at her sleeping husband. Paul snored softly. Katharine stopped to listen to the familiar pattern, the funny little cycle that he sometimes went through during bouts of deep sleep. He would start out breathing heavily, the air occasionally catching in his throat, and work himself into a faint snore; the sounds gradually intensified until he was snorting wildly, spewing a multi-layered cacophony that ultimately sent him sprawling into a more agreeable position.

When Paul's snoring was loud enough, Katharine carefully tore the cover from the *Guide Bleu du Figaro*. Then she unscrewed one of the brass hooks and held it carefully in her palm.

Katharine slid the window open and grabbed the ormolu clock from beside the bureau. She stopped again to watch her husband. He was settling, still unconscious, into easier breathing, almost through with the routine. Now he would finish with a funny little moaning sound—a sort of "hmm," always uttered in a serious tone, as if he was acknowledging the fact that he'd been snoring. Katharine had often lain awake, listening and breaking into a smile every time she heard that final utterance. Paul had warned her that she would soon find his snoring fits maddening rather than adorable; but now she responded to the sounds with such tender, pained affection that she felt as if her heart might burst.

The cool night air penetrated her dressing gown—a welcome sensation that eased the feverishness coming upon her. Katharine stuck her head momentarily through the window, then slipped her right leg over the sill, bending to fit her upper body through the opening.

She felt her feet, clad only in stockings, touch the grass. She was at the rear of the hotel; she needed only to venture around the corner, careful to avoid being seen. She crept close to the wall, eyes constantly moving, as she made her way around and toward the street. At the front corner she turned and went back, counting windows: *One. Two. Three* . . . .

At the ninth window she stopped, scanning her surroundings intently. The building alongside the hotel was a multi-level shop, without balconies; its windows were dark. No one could be seen in any direction. Katharine had set the clock down and was working quickly, screwing the point of the hook into the wooden window frame until it was secure. She slid the guidebook cover between the windows, pulling it upward until it reached the latch. Slowly, she eased the latch up from its place.

The latch came free easily. Katharine guided it forward, away from the panes, and eased it down until it hung loose.

After only a moment's hesitation, Katharine pulled on the hook. Nothing happened. She tried again, pulling harder, fingers trembling.

The window began to slide open. At the first significant sound—a faint sighing of wood against wood—Katharine froze and listened.

Within the room, a man snored loudly.

Katharine released a relieved, inaudible sigh. Her hands shook as she opened the window. She hesitated again; listened to the steady snore; opened the other window. Katharine stuck her head slowly through the opening, straining to see the room in what little light was cast there. After a few moments she could make out the silhouettes of a bureau, a closet, a bed with a sleeping figure, a cushioned chair. The room was set up the same as her own—an advantage for which she was immediately grateful. At last, fate seemed to be on her side. At any upscale hotel, she would not have had this opportunity; the better hotels didn't have private rooms on the ground floors, but were filled with studies, restaurants, and lounges. *But we happened to be here at the same time; I happened to see him going into his room; and now* . . . .

She moved methodically, reaching a leg up and through the opening, gathering the loose draping of her nightgown, pausing to listen at the right moments. At last she had maneuvered her way into the room and had a clear view of its occupant; at last she found herself standing at the bedside of the monster who had killed her father. *Not a man; a monster. You mustn't think of him as a man.* She had learned from life that people were easier to discard if one could only find a way to dehumanize them.

Damgaard's features became ever more visible in the faintly lit night, slowly clarifying for Katharine as her eyes adjusted to the dark room. The man—*no, not the man, the monster*—slept on its back, its head just slightly turned aside, the mouth half open. *So vulnerable.* Damgaard did not have supernatural powers of detection and predation, after all. He snored obliviously as Katharine brought the heavy ormolu near his temple; she lifted it high and lowered it again, slowly, carefully, taking a precise aim before she committed the lethal act.

You're not committed yet. You could still go back, and no one would ever know you had been here. The covert venture had been relatively simple until now. There had been nothing final about it, nothing truly severe; but Katharine was about to take the most severe action of her life. *If only it was as easy for me as it is for Damgaard.* But it wasn't. Her arms felt unable to hit hard enough; her will to inflict such violence was simply too weak. Katharine stared down at Damgaard's face, so boyish and peaceful in the soft light, and filled her mind with the ugly images he'd bestowed on her. Her father's violent death; the cruel, mad jig outside the window; Dawes' blood congealing around him.

Now, Katharine. Before he wakes. Smash down hard as you can, as though you're smashing it all the way through the floor—as though you're smashing him down into hell itself.

Katharine tightened her grip on the angel figurine. She took a deep, quiet breath, inhaling until her lungs seemed about to burst, and lifted the ormolu with trembling arms.

24

FRIDAY, MAY 24, 1889

Katharine woke to the sensation of a tender embrace. Paul's arms
were around her. She heard him moan softly. "You awake?" he asked.

"I am now."

"Did you sleep?"

"A little."

He pressed his lips against the back of her neck, released a warm
breath against her flesh. Katharine pulled his arms, squeezed them more
tightly around her and basked in the comfort of his presence—a presence
she might soon lose, through what means she had no way of knowing.
There were so many possibilities now. Prison; murder; random accident.
The future seemed so uncertain and unfair. She thought of their wedding,
of promises she'd made—spoken and unspoken, the secret ones being
the most heartfelt. She had married this man, promised to spend out the
rest of her life as his partner, ready to walk by his side, bear his children;
she had allowed herself to love him deeply. All this she'd done with the
resigned knowledge that she could not guarantee the longevity of their
time together. And yet this sudden tragedy seemed so heartrendingly
cruel—as though the cosmos had somehow conspired to give her
happiness and immediately rip it from her.

Katharine gave way to the grief that swelled up inside her, felt warm
tears pouring down her face. She wept for some time in silence, and then
gave herself away by sniffling.

Paul stiffened; he propped himself up to look at her face, and turned
her over gently. "Katharine," he whispered, seeing her tears. He sighed
and pressed her close. "I'm sorry . . . ."

"You don't need to keep apologizing," she said.

"I can't think of anything else to say."

"It's not your fault. I'm not just upset over what might happen to us.

It's . . . ."

He drew away. "I know. You're worried about the Morgan girl."

"I am; but it's not just that. I don't want you to think that I care more about her than I do about you. I love you . . . ." Her throat swelled and ached, cutting off words. Paul sighed and squeezed her again.

"Lie with me for a while," he said. "I still can't think straight. Let's just lie here a while longer."

"Okay," she replied.

Paul sat at the edge of the bed, half-dressed, his shirt buttoned up the wrong way; he had abandoned the task with an air of helplessness, and Katharine moved to fix it for him. "I know you want to help this girl," he said, "but things have become so . . . malevolent. And with Damgaard here at the hotel . . . ."

"Let's not worry about Damgaard now. He probably doesn't even know we're here." She paused, and added, "He may have checked out already."

They spent the morning in the room, discussing their options, but the presence of Charlotte Morgan seemed to prevent any reasonable solution. Katharine's concerns for the young woman had intensified upon reading the last pages of her diary. Charlotte had made a detailed record of events following her mother's disappearance, and it was clear from her writings that she was very much alone, even opposed to some extent by the local authorities. Katharine had thought of finding Charlotte and returning the blood-stained journal to her, but quickly discarded the idea. All of Dawes' research had surely been lost, leaving only the details that Charlotte had written in her journal. If something happened to Charlotte—if she was arrested, or otherwise overpowered—the record would likely vanish, the same way Dawes' notes had vanished.

"She's here without any money," Katharine explained. "It disappeared along with her mother's luggage."

Paul lowered his eyes, looked pained.

"And she doesn't speak any French. Her uncle is coming from London to get her, but I've no idea when. It may have taken some time to notify him, and he may not have been able to leave right away."

"The British embassy must be helping her," Paul said.

"I don't think she'll go back to them. They were suspicious of her, and I think she's afraid of being taken into custody."

"All right, listen. I'll go back to the Clément and see if I can find her. I'll give her enough money to set her up for the week, or whatever I can afford—I'll do whatever keeps her safe until her uncle comes. If she doesn't turn up, I'll head to the embassy and see if she's in touch with them."

"What are you going to tell them?"

"Nothing. I'll tell them she's been trying to get in touch with me."

"I don't think it's a good idea to go there. If they ask questions . . . ."

"Fine; I'll try the hotel first."

"What if Arnaud sees you?"

"I'll handle that."

"Please be careful about what you say to people. And remember: we're not supposed to know that Mr. Dawes is dead."

"Right."

"I really should come with you."

"Please don't. If there's trouble, I don't want you involved. I'll handle it," Paul assured her. He turned to the bureau—and paused, his face registering mild puzzlement. "What's all this?"

Katharine's gaze moved to follow his. The ormolu clock was back on the bureau. Beside it was the brass hook she'd removed from the closet and the guidebook cover.

"I . . . borrowed the hook," she mumbled vaguely, and moved to replace it.

"What for?"

She sighed, trying to find an answer. She hated the idea of lying to Paul, but—

A knock sounded at the door. Katharine jumped. She checked the time, and said with quiet relief: "It's Annette. I told her we weren't feeling well and wouldn't go out today, but she said she'd stop by at eleven to see if we changed our minds. She wants to take us to the fair."

"Both of us, or just you?" Paul forced a wry grin. "Go ahead; you should go."

"I don't feel much like . . . ."

"Well you can't stay here," he insisted in a low voice. "You'll be safer with Annette, and you'll have something to do besides sit and worry."

"What time will you be back?"

"I don't know."

Katharine checked the clock again. "Meet me here by five o'clock. Six hours should be enough—and no later, so I'll know you're safe."

"I'll be fine."

"Promise me."

"I promise."

So it was agreed. A minute later Katharine was standing in the lobby, saying goodbye to her husband, wrapping him in a crushing embrace, kissing him and departing with a heartfelt "I love you."

Annette smiled at the desk clerk. "They're newly married," she explained.

Paris seemed preternaturally beautiful. Splashed against the bright and pleasant landscape, ever present in Katharine's mind, was the ugly specter that still burned in the flesh of her eyes: Dawes in the mess of his life-blood, his good deed unfinished. Another crime that would surely go unsolved, plastered across everything she saw, coloring the world with despair.

Katharine wandered under the shade of horse-chestnut trees that blossomed along the streets, occasionally surprised by fragrant lilacs and flowering vines, and by bursts of flowers that announced the presence of a public park. Gardenesque settings broke the spell cast by grand and imposing architecture, and everywhere there were people strolling or lounging at tables and benches, or selling wares stacked neatly in little carts. Annette gestured to a man sweeping crushed white blossoms from the streets and walkways, explaining that the city was being kept meticulously clean for the fair. Workers quickly whisked away debris and horse manure that fell into the streets; buildings all over the city had been scrubbed and polished; gardens had been expanded and were pampered daily; shops and restaurants had been refreshed and ready to offer their best; and even the little gutters in the sides of the streets were being raked clear of garbage, leaving only a bit of water from the early morning rain.

But the lined bark of the trees was the wood grain on Dawes' hotel room door, hiding a fatal surprise just beyond; the trampled blossoms were the snuffing of life and beauty; the white-fleshed statues in the parks looked like disease and death. With every step Katharine tried to see through the nightmare and hated having to do so. *If only I could tell Annette . . . if only we could talk. There are so many things I would tell her.* But she couldn't, and the woman had never seemed like such a stranger. Katharine looked at Annette sidelong, then lifted her eyes to the blossoming trees and thought of the new life she would make when she returned home.

Before they crossed the river into the fairgrounds, Annette walked her through the Tuileries Garden, where they spent nearly an hour wandering the vast and crowded walkways. Carefully plotted sections of trees and flowers grew among the fountains and elegant stone sculptures. Katharine tried to avoid her habit of scanning the crowd for malevolent faces, and let her focus become drawn up into the expressive curves of statues—some placid, others perturbing. There was something decidedly macabre about the stone animals who tore at the throats of their prey, about Theseus who raised his club to bash the head of the Minotaur—a scene that reminded her so vividly of the previous night's venture—and even the vacant, featureless eyes of Cincinnatus and Pericles lent a certain eeriness to their stately postures. A dying stone Spartacus slumped into oblivion; his gray flesh, aged and scarred, seemed to drip down his right side, from his head down to the painfully protruding ribs.

The garden, originally commissioned by Queen Catherine de' Medici, was more than three hundred years old. Within that time it had been the site of numerous remodelings, revolts, massacres, celebrations, and displays of power as well as leisure. Less than twenty years ago the Communards had burned the adjoining palace; the ruins were eventually cleared away, and the site became an extension of the garden where Parisians and travelers now spent a sunny afternoon. At one end, the vast grounds opened to the Louvre Museum; at the other they gave way to the Place de la Concorde, where hundreds upon hundreds of people had expired under the blade of the guillotine. *Another blade for the cutting of necks.*

Despite its history, Katharine found the Place de la Concorde surprisingly calming. She stopped to admire the picturesque fountains, bathing her eyes in the lovely spectacle of majestic mer-people; of the detailed folds of somber green draperies and bronze ornaments against charcoal-colored flesh; of the ever sensual flow of water. At Pont Alexandre the women crossed into the fair, entering the *Esplanade des Invalides*—the grounds of the seventeenth-century military hospital, now converted into a showcase of France's colonial possessions. Pavilions and miniature palaces lined the avenue; here were condensed imitations of Oriental and Islamic architecture, along with a Central Palace which exhibited "colonies of lesser importance"—and opposite them all was a row of French military buildings.

The Algerian Palace was at the forefront of the showcase, representing the most prized of France's African colonies. Its interior contained an upper level with ornate balconies, now over-crowded with fairgoers; and from the main level the tourists could admire lovely architectural embellishments and fine statues, walls adorned with stained glass and native hanging plants, and an enclosed, roofless courtyard. Nearby, the fresh scent of the Algerian garden was overcome by the musky smells of majestic Arabian horses and Mehari camels, who stood quiet and immobile in the grasp of their trainers; and all around were the tinkering sounds of craftsmen, pounding and weaving their wares under the watchful eyes of foreigners.

Just beyond the palace, the two women stepped into the Moor concert-café and sat down to rest. They had hardly seated themselves when Annette made an excited exclamation, and was in turn greeted by a man at a nearby table: Leonard, the friend she'd described as "an Arab from Algiers." Leonard was dressed in a cream-colored European suit; a man seated across from him, with an aged, deeply lined face, wore a long apron and hooded cloak. The two men conversed quietly for a moment before Leonard stood and moved to the women's table.

"Bonjour," he greeted Annette. He was tired-looking, with red-rimmed brown eyes shielded by wiry spectacles. "Où est votre mari?"—*Where is your husband?*

Nathan is ill, she said.

Is it serious?

I don't think so.

It is good that he is a doctor, he knows how to treat himself.

Will you sit with us?

Certainly.

Annette made the proper introductions, conveying to Leonard a few things about Katharine—that she was a newlywed, come to Paris for a post-wedding celebration, and that bad luck had kept her from seeing the fair with her new husband.

The trio commenced a trying conversation. Katharine struggled with French, and Leonard didn't speak English, though he caught enough to correct Annette's introduction. He was not from Algiers, as Annette claimed; he was from the north, near the border of Tunisia—a city called Jijel on Algeria's northern coast. He'd been born during an earthquake that had destroyed much of his city, causing his family to move westward toward the Kabylie region, and he had also lived in Tunis for some time. Upon his arrival in Paris, Nathan had treated him for the beginning stages of consumption.

Leonard spoke easily, as though reciting a series of familiar monologues. He talked a little about the Kabyle village, about architecture, about the garden. Annette was drinking Algerian wine, so he talked of the vineyards; Katharine drank cherbat, a lemonade infused with spices and rose petals, and so he spoke about Algerian cuisine, about trade and agriculture.

"He works for the fair," Annette reminded Katharine. "He's even better than the guidebook." She leaned over to peer at the *Guide Bleu du Figaro*, which Katharine had opened to the section on Algeria. It explained that France was continuing the works of civilization that the Roman Empire had tried to bestow on northern Africa nearly two thousand years past; Rome, the guide claimed, had been too timid in its colonial effort, but France had "perfected" it. Annette tapped the paragraph and added in a near whisper: "Leonard is proof."

The cherbat seemed to curdle in Katharine's stomach.

"He's only here as long as the fair is on," Annette said. "He'll have to return to Algeria afterward, but the Kabylies will keep traveling with the exhibit."

"A human zoo?" Katharine asked weakly.

It is difficult for Algerians to find work in Algeria, Annette responded in French.

Katharine asked Leonard: "Est-ce pourquoi tu es venu à Paris?"—*Is that why you came to Paris?*

He nodded. *I came here to work.*

"Settlers turned his home into a cotton plantation," Annette explained. "He worked there for some time, but his father managed to get him into a French school. Arabs aren't usually allowed. It was a great privilege, except—" She flashed a guilty look at Leonard, and changed the subject: *Leonard, what is your Algerian name?*

"Lubaid."

"Lubaid," Annette repeated uncertainly. She smiled at Katharine. "That's his real name. People had trouble pronouncing it, so someone gave him the name Leonard."

"People couldn't pronounce 'Lubaid'?"

"Well, perhaps they could; but 'Leonard' is easier. His friend who was here earlier makes pile-weave rugs. Nathan bought one for the house. We'll take it to the hotel when we move. The Algerian tapestries are so beautiful . . . ."

A few musicians, armed with flutes and bendir drums, had taken to the small concert stage. Together they kicked off a melodic set for a pair of Ouled Naïl dancers—heavily adorned belly dancers with kohl-lined eyes and tattooed limbs, glimmering everywhere with various styles of jewelry: gold and silver coins, metal plates and bracelets set with stones and jewels, a profundity of decoration from head to foot.

Leonard smiled—a good-natured smile that Katharine found instantly disarming, though it exposed two rows of hopelessly crooked teeth. "Quelqu'un fronce à vous," he said quietly, and nodded toward the tables just behind them.

Annette blushed; little spots of red swam to the surface of her pale cheeks. In a low voice she told Katharine: "We should leave. The men don't like seeing French and American women watching the belly dancers. See, we're getting looks."

Sure enough, Katharine turned to see more than one scowl fixed in her direction. She noticed for the first time how few women were in the café—and among the patrons, Leonard was now the sole non-European.

"Wait and see: there will be another editorial in the newspapers, about dainty white women watching the exotic dancers and flirting with blacks.”

Leonard excused himself; he needed to return to his work shift at the tower, while Annette became eager to check on her husband—who, she claimed, was unable to sleep or eat.

The departure put Katharine on edge. She stood and found herself trembling slightly, fatigued at the idea of having to return to the nightmarish problems of the past few days. She took Annette’s arm as they stepped back into the bustling street, crowded with stalls and people and restless animals.

“I didn’t want to mention it in front of Leonard, even if he doesn’t speak English,” Annette said, “but his father was killed—and not by the French, but by his own people. I think it had something to do with Leonard being placed in the French school. The rebels may have seen it as a betrayal.” She glanced down the avenue, to where Leonard slowly retreated past a row of Kabylie merchants. “But he does look smart, doesn’t he? I think he must be the only Arab in Paris, and he sets a fine example for what his people might accomplish. It’s unfortunate that he’ll be sent back to Algeria. . . .”

Katharine had stopped at the edge of the street. Her vision swam. The mingled smells of manure and sweat invaded her nose, encroached on her tongue.

“He wants to go back home to his mother and sisters,” Annette continued, “but he’s likely to be killed if . . . Katharine, are you all right?”

Katharine felt a sudden sense of entrapment as the masses pressed closer. An oncoming train moved at walking pace through the avenue, stuffed to its limit with fairgoers whose gawking eyes bulged from their faces. “God, this place makes me sick,” she whispered. “Good God!”

“What’s that? You feel sick?”

Katharine was about to look away and was shocked to see a face she recognized. “There’s Paul,” she said disbelievingly. The nausea dissipated; her senses sharpened. “Look—he’s there, on the train.”

“Are you sure?” Annette scanned the passengers. “Did he say he was coming to the fair?”

“No, I didn’t expect him here.” Katharine released Annette’s arm. “You go ahead and go home; I’ll catch up with him.”

“No, no, I’ll come with you. Let’s hurry.”

The train had come to a stop, and they reached it fairly quickly; but Paul was nowhere to be found.

“You’re certain it was him?” Annette asked.

Katharine was sure—or nearly sure. But she could no longer see him on the train, and no amount of searching the area turned him up.

Back at the hotel, the room was vacant. The desk clerk had not seen Paul; no messages had been left. Katharine waited in nervous bewilderment, trying to work out what might have happened. Her sudden bout of nausea may have compromised her senses; and yet she felt certain that she could not mistake another man for Paul. She knew him too well.

The ormolu struck five. Katharine watched it with a deepening sense of dread. "Come on, Paul," she whispered. "I said to come back *by* five, and no later. You promised me . . . ."

Five-thirty came and went. As the minute hand moved dutifully onward, Katharine stopped staring at the clock and sat with her hands over her eyes.

She remembered, then, how Paul had come back the previous night with liquor on his breath. He'd once told her that after Clara died, he spent two weeks in a drunken stupor, unable to cope. Katharine was beset by an increasingly strong suspicion—or, rather, a desperate hope. She imagined Paul drunkenly weaving his way through the Exposition. At last she stood with a tired sigh.

The omnibus returned her to the fairgrounds, where she commenced a search of all the cafés she could find. As the sun began to set amongst a cloudy palette of pinks and violets, she was still peering at faces, looking for the clean-shaven figure of her husband. Countless electric lights aided her search, blazing to life as the day slipped into darkness. Fountains along the Champ de Mars were lit through tinted bulbs, casting the spouting waters in vibrant colors; and above them the Eiffel Tower burst into glowing magnificence, its contours lined with radiant bulbs from top to bottom. At the top there shone the spotlight, casting its expansive beam from more than a thousand feet in the air.

As she lowered her dazzled eyes to the passing crowds, Katharine caught sight of a smooth-faced man stumbling across the pavement ahead of her. *Paul.* She quickened her step, trailing after him past Cairo Street, toward the river.

Not Paul, she corrected herself. She frowned, turning away in defeat—and found herself unable to start back toward the Pont de la Concorde. A sudden, sickening fear had overwhelmed her—a disturbing notion that she would return to the hotel and find the room still empty.

She wandered slowly; felt her muscles hardening into painful knots; felt herself stooping, shoulders curving forward.

Leonard caught sight of her from his station at the base of the Eiffel— a ticket booth tucked neatly beneath one of the vast, latticed iron legs. He waved and called to her, and Katharine approached hesitantly.

What was she doing, wandering the fair alone, he wanted to know.

More bad luck? He flashed his rows of crooked teeth.

Katharine gave him a wan smile. "Oui."

It had been, as Leonard put it, "un jour de la malchance"—a day of bad luck. One of the tower workers had died only hours ago, most likely from a fall. Leonard wasn't privy to the details. The body had been quickly removed, the incident hushed up to prevent frightening away the enthusiastic crowds.

"Bien sûr," Katharine murmured, gazing up into the luminescent ironworks.

Leonard spoke to his companion, a young Parisian who looked little more than twenty. The young man listened for a moment. "Ah, another friend of Dr. Neville," he said and smiled. "Come to see the tower at night?"

"I'm looking for my husband."

"He is missing his chance. Bring him back tomorrow night, when the lights are on. It is much different than the day."

"My husband is afraid of heights . . . and I'm afraid we're leaving Paris tomorrow."

He turned aside to speak to Leonard. Katharine was about to walk on when Leonard asked: "Avez-vous grimpé la tour la nuit?"—*Have you climbed the tower at night?*

No, she hadn't.

He encouraged her to ascend, and the Frenchman added: "The tower is closing, but we have been persuaded to allow a few late visits." He smiled. "You can go up quickly. It is *magnificent* to look down and see the fair lit up, and the city lights glowing in the dark—and without the crowds in the way. Go; you will not get another chance, unless you return before the tower is destroyed."

Katharine eyed the long staircase. She had walked so much already, and had more pressing matters to deal with. Paul might have returned late to the hotel. He might be waiting for her, worrying. And if he hadn't returned . . . .

My fault! If he is dead, it is my own fault!

Tipping her head back to survey the tower, Katharine remembered with sudden vividness the feeling of freedom she'd had up high on the first platform—the feeling of flight, of vast perspective, of separation from the weightiness of the world. She wondered for a moment if the unfortunate worker had fallen on purpose—had given in to a notion of freedom from his worldly troubles. *A quick freefall, and then oblivion. A mess discreetly cleaned up and forgotten.*

Leonard was urging her on with a smile. With a jolt, Katharine remembered Anette's words: *Leonard's home was turned into a cotton plantation . . . his father was killed . . . but he does look smart . . . he sets a fine example . . . .* At once she was able to detect the soft despair in Leonard's red-rimmed eyes, so easily concealed by his ready smile. Was his friendly composure a mask—a remembrance of his old self? A way of surviving in Paris by entertaining his Parisian peers, much the way Katharine had entertained her family's peers in Queens, when all she wanted to do was cry?

They will use him, put him on display, and discard him. How many people will Paris send to their deaths?

"Go on. Have a free visit, no cost," said the Frenchman.

"No cost," she whispered, and went to ascend the staircase. She was inexplicably drawn to the tower, to its clear and free heights, even to the cover of darkness and an escape from the crowds; to the unsteady spiral staircase that brought her up, up, far above the ground and closer to the clouds . . . .

She climbed at a quick but steady pace, her gaze angled upward into the softly glowing ironworks. The ascent was much different this time: peaceful, blinding, quiet. All around her the iron bars were painted in shades of deep red—and for just a moment, she saw an endless network of frightening red slashes jumping out at her from patches of darkness.

The beginnings of blisters formed on her feet as she reached the first platform. For a moment she stood looking around the vast promenade, carefully shifting her feet within her shoes.

The platform was empty save a lone figure on the river side. Everyone else had descended; Katharine heard them far below, withdrawing across the hard safety of the ground, a distance that at first pleased and then abruptly terrified her. After only a few moments on the promenade, she found that she did not want solitude. She wanted the press of crowds and the safety of witnesses.

The man on the platform was Mr. Damgaard.

His guise was unmistakable. Katharine had memorized his physiology, his dress, his posture, his scent, the inflections of his voice, all in detail that would likely never be forgotten. His profile was clearly illustrated by the soft glare of electric lights. Damgaard leaned on the rail, exactly where Katharine had stood three days earlier, and gazed down at the riverside landscape. He moved, and Katharine was overcome with the terrified certainty that he had sensed her. She had failed to act against him at the hotel, had crept away in silent defeat—for even though she perceived all the reasons in the world to be rid of him, she could not smash the skull of a human being who slept so defenselessly before her. And because she had failed, Damgaard might have killed Paul. And now she was alone with him, in such a vulnerable place, out of the reach of others and at such a lethal height, and he would certainly turn and overwhelm her . . . .

But he turned away instead, and leaned out over the rail. Katharine had frozen with dread upon seeing him, but now the blood seemed to flow in her muscles again, articulating with little prickles that stirred her out of paralysis. She turned and began to slide back toward the stairs, trembling with the effort to move in silence—but the effort only made her shake violently.

She snuck another look at him. His focus was occupied with something far below. Once again, Katharine stood in acute cognizance of the man who had sliced her father's life from his body; who laughed in the faces of his degraded, ruined workers; who sang outside her window while she looked on terrified, his eyes gleaming with delighted malice; who took pleasure in invading every space that was sacred to her, every friend she had dared to trust. An image flashed in Katharine's mind: *Tiger overwhelming a crocodile*—a statue at the Tuileries Garden. And another: *Tigress bringing a peacock to its young*. The massive, heaving body of a stone wildcat, presenting sustenance in her powerful fangs to two expectant cubs.

I am not going to be your prey any longer, she said silently, wickedly, to Damgaard's back. Sudden power filled her being. She saw the energetic pulsation of Damgaard's proud predation and snatched it from him, as if it were a cloak that she could simply whisk away and adopt as her own. She felt her knees bending as she began to slink toward him. Her legs seemed slender and weightless, spider-legs that crept across the iron floor. She willed her movements to silence, and with each step her mouth silently formed the word: *Quiet*.

Quiet. Quiet . . . . With fierce precision, she slipped up behind him and twined her arms around his legs. Strength surged through her body. A familiar rage flowed freely; it had found its outlet at last. An animal grunt erupted from her mouth as the man's legs were heaved up and over the rail. Damgaard, thrown off by the suddenness of the attack, barely had time to grab at the railing as he somersaulted over it—but his weight snapped his grip away from the iron rail and he hurled downward.

Katharine turned and strode toward the stairway, but she was stopped cold by the sound of Damgaard's throat-tearing shriek.

The monster fled from her. She was shaking now, holding the railing for dear life as she trembled her way down the stairs.

Someone was rushing up toward her, all panic and desperation. Leonard's face was aghast. He called out to her in French: *Madame, vous devez partir!*—then extended an arm, helped her descend.

As they went, Leonard warned her that someone—somehow—had

fallen.

"I heard a scream," she murmured.

Katharine strained to listen over the whistling wind and far-off bustle of late-night fairgoers. She imagined a horrified crowd of onlookers below; imagined the mess; wondered, with sudden panic, if Damgaard had fallen on anyone.

But the scene was silent.

On the ground, Leonard ushered her in one direction, and naturally she looked in the other. Behind her, the Frenchman and two others stood close to what she presumed to be Damgaard's body. She didn't look closely enough to be sure, didn't want to see the gruesome climax of Damgaard's mortality. She could only be too sure of what fate had met Mr. Damgaard, and in knowing, felt somewhat less frightened about her own.

Paul was pacing the room when she arrived. He turned wild eyes to her—but the moment his gaze set upon her face, he melted with relief.

The shine of apprehension took him again as he demanded: "Katharine, where in hell have you been?"

"I'm sorry. I went out." Katharine's relief matched his. Tears of gratitude pressed at her eyes, but were carefully withheld.

"You went out," Paul repeated flatly. "Did it occur to you that I'd be worried sick about you the whole damn time you were gone? It's *late*. It's—"

"I'm sorry. I was here earlier, but you hadn't come back yet."

"I was here more than two hours ago—at six, like we agreed."

"We agreed on five, not six."

"No, you said six."

"I . . . I said six *hours*, not six o'clock. We agreed on five o'clock."

He stared at her, then relaxed. His tone softened. "Fine. I probably got mixed up. Where were you?"

She glanced uneasily toward the window. Damgaard's corpse was there in the darkness, beyond her view. "I need to talk to you."

He followed her gaze; saw nothing of note. "All right, let's talk. I couldn't find the Morgan girl. I think you'll be pretty disappointed by how little I managed to accomplish. What have you been up to?"

She beckoned for him to sit. They were side by side on the bed, and Katharine explained calmly: "Mr. Damgaard is dead."

Seconds ticked by.

"He's dead?" Paul was inscrutable—but Katharine found herself unable to look on him directly. "How do you know? What happened?"

"He fell from the Eiffel. He was crushed on the pavement."

He stared at her now with some type of alarm—incredulity, fear, disbelief.

"I think we should leave," she said softly.

"Katharine, where were you just now?"

"I was there, at the tower. I saw him . . . ."

"You saw him after the fall?"

"Yes. Sort of."

"Do you think someone pushed him?"

She winced, met his gaze with difficulty. "Yes, I'm certain he was pushed."

"Did you see something?" Paul lowered his voice, but spoke with sharp concern. "I mean, was Arnaud there, or . . . what is it, what'd you see?"

She didn't move.

"Talk to me."

Katharine spoke carefully: "I want to tell you what happened. I just . . . want to make sure you want to know. If you don't want to know, I don't have to tell you."

"What is that supposed to mean? Tell me what?"

Another silence. The eyes lowered, wouldn't look at him.

"Just spit it out, please, Katharine. Let's skip this part of the drama. What, are you going to tell me that *you* pushed Damgaard?"

"He was standing there . . . ." She paused expressionlessly. "I just happened to come up behind him. The tower was closing, but Damgaard had persuaded some of the workers to let him go up. Annette's friend Lubaid let me in because he knew our trip had been interrupted. There was no one up there but me and Damgaard. And he just happened to be leaning over the railing, in the open part, when I found him. It was . . . ."

Paul was shaking his head; his eyes were focused on her, yet seemed vacant. "Are you serious?" Fear—horror—writhed in his voice.

"It's not the sort of thing I would say as a joke."

Paul closed his eyes. After a moment, he sank backward onto the bed and laid utterly limp.

"Paul." She waited, upset by his distant demeanor. "I just saw another innocent man killed by Damgaard."

"Another? You mean . . . ." He made a sound of disbelief. "Just give me a minute."

"Okay."

She sat still, perched on the edge of the bed with her hands folded, staring at the floor.

Paul sat abruptly. "Hey, I just had a really great idea," he announced with sudden fervor.

She looked at him quietly.

"Let's go home in the morning."

"All right."

He stood and started for the door. "All right. I need a drink or a nap. A drink sounds good. Would you like one?"

Katharine glanced down, gave herself a once-over for the briefest moment, then shook her head.

"No?" He paused. "I'll be back in a minute, okay? I just really need . . . ." Paul trailed off, watching Katharine, then returned to the bed. "Never mind." The edge faded from his voice. "Come here." He lay across the bed, patting the space next to him. "Lie down with me."

Katharine settled herself in his arms, her head on his shoulder.

"Good God," he whispered, and let out a long sigh. "Let's go to bed early. The earlier the better. Then we can get up at dawn and get the hell out of Paris."

"All right."

The room was silent for a few moments.

"Katharine . . . ."

"What?"

"Are you all right?"

"I don't know." Emotion was too dangerous a thing now; Katharine was afraid to delve into the workings of her own psyche. "Ask me tomorrow."

25

SATURDAY, MAY 25, 1889

Though he was eager to leave Paris, Paul slept late and dressed himself slowly. Katharine mimicked his pace. They exchanged a few banal words, and he seemed calm enough—but several times she noticed how he stopped and stared at her, as though examining her; and if she returned his gaze, she found lasting traces of disbelief written on his face.

"You're looking at me differently," she said. "Do you think differently of me now?"

He faced her without hesitation, his gray eyes mild. "I don't know how to answer that. But I don't think badly of you. Okay? I wish I'd done it myself and spared you the burden."

"I don't want you to talk like that."

"Like what?" Paul asked. "As far as I'm concerned, you're the only person who's been doing . . . the right thing." He said it with a note of doubt. He sat beside her on the bed, put an arm around her. "Are you going to be all right?"

"Are you?"

He couldn't answer. After a long pause, he asked instead: "How sure are you about Damgaard?"

"He's dead. I'm sure."

"That's not what I mean."

Katharine gave him a gently pleading look. "Paul, don't doubt me now. I'm far too certain of the things he did in Troy. And . . . perhaps this doesn't justify anything, but he's a predator. I've always worried about Mr. Damgaard—that he would find out about us, and that he would start . . . *looking* at you. I almost passed up marrying you because I thought it would be selfish on my part. I was afraid he would come to our house and kill you. Mr. Damgaard is the sort of person who, if he really wanted to destroy you . . . ."

"You don't have to think like that anymore."

"I know. This is the first morning that I woke up and . . . I don't have to worry, every moment of every day, that Mr. Damgaard is going to come creeping around to do something to you, or to me . . . or to our child."

Paul's eyes were distant; but after a moment he looked at Katharine with cautious realization.

"You haven't noticed that I'm pregnant," she said. "I didn't realize it either, until I was talking to the hotel clerk yesterday. She was telling me that they keep some extra toiletries at the desk, and then she leaned over and whispered that they had sanitary cloths if I needed them. It suddenly occurred to me that I haven't had to deal with that sort of thing since we were married. I thought I was just anxious because of the transition into married life; and then I thought I was just sea sick on the ship, and then I thought I was sick because of seeing Damgaard—"

"Katharine," Paul whispered, and his hands were closing delicately around her waist, his hand resting on her abdomen.

"I didn't want to worry about Damgaard doing something to our baby," she said. "Or about . . . ."

He kissed her. "It's okay. Stop talking."

It had seemed impossible, yet it happened for a small number of minutes: Katharine and Paul shared a feeling of genuine bliss, reveling in the excitement of the new life they'd created. Paul became himself again; he cracked jokes and worried over the immediate future of their lovemaking, while Katharine gently reprimanded him for his crass comments and smiled at his sudden profusion of whispered, tender words.

"Paul, what happened yesterday?" Katharine asked at last. The grim realities of the past few days still hung over them, waiting patiently for acknowledgment. "Did you go to the Clément?"

"Yes, I went back to the hotel," Paul replied dryly. "I don't think you're going to be very happy with the decisions I made yesterday."

She looked at him with blatant apprehension.

"I got drunk," he admitted reluctantly. "Well, at some point I got drunk. I went to the Clément first. The receptionist saw me going upstairs, and he must have told Arnaud. I knocked on the door to room 344 and there was no answer, so I started to leave. Arnaud met me on the stairs and asked if I'd forgotten anything in my room."

"What did you say?"

"I said 'No sir' and kept walking. I walked around the district for a while, trying to figure out what to do. Then I stopped for a drink. I kept thinking up different things to do, but nothing worked. So I had a few more drinks, and then I went back to the Clément. I knocked again, and then I tried to shove some money under the door, in case the girl came back. Arnaud came upstairs and demanded to know what I was doing. I said that the Morgan girl didn't have any money and I thought it would be civic-minded of us to see that she was taken care of. He said 'Miss Morgan has been checked out'—not that she checked out, but that she had *been* checked out. Then he informed me that I was at the wrong door—I was at room 342, not 344—and then he threatened to have me arrested for drunkenness and loitering. I laughed and said something like, 'Yes, I think it would be in your best interest to put me in a conference with the police.' Arnaud was furious. But then he started making this really ridiculous face, like he was trying really hard to look annoyed, but it was obvious that he was scared. I left the hotel and was walking around with a big grin, thinking about Arnaud's 'constipated' face." Paul paused, seeing Katharine's expression, and added, "I knew you'd be disappointed."

"What else?" she asked.

"Well, I wandered toward the fairgrounds, and at some point it occurred to me that I hadn't been to the fair. I knew that people back home would ask about it, and I wouldn't have the faintest idea what to tell them. So I went to the fair and hurried through some of the exhibits; then I had another drink; then I got hungry, so I stopped and had dinner at the Creole restaurant. At some point I was standing in line to listen to Edison's voice recorder, and I remembered that you were waiting for me to come back. So I started heading back to the hotel, trying to think of a way to tell you that I'd gotten drunk and that I'd lost—I don't even know her name. The Morgan girl."

They were interrupted by a loud, urgent-sounding knock at the door. Paul's face blanched. Katharine felt her body beginning to hunch forward.

"Who is it?" Paul asked.

A low voice mumbled in response. Paul frowned and stood reluctantly. "I think that's Nathan."

He opened the door just a crack, saw Nathan's pale face and bloodshot eyes.

"I need to come in. It's an emergency," Nathan said, softly, but with unmistakable desperation.

"Really, what about?" Paul replied sardonically. He gave Nathan a suspicious once-over. "You're sure you want to talk? You didn't come here to slash our throats?"

Nathan paled to a ghastly white. "That isn't funny," he whispered.

Paul opened the door and let him inside. "What do you want?"

Nathan stared at Katharine, then at Paul. His hands trembled at his sides.

"Katharine already knows everything," Paul said. "Don't restrain yourself."

But Nathan was silent, so Katharine spoke: "You must know about the British reporter who was killed—Mr. Dawes. His throat was cut."

"Yes," Nathan choked, reluctantly. His hand fluttered to his own throat, as if in morbid sympathy. "It was mentioned in the papers this morning—vaguely. That's what I came to talk to you about."

"Did Mr. Damgaard kill him?" she asked.

"What? No."

"He's a known killer—to some, anyway. If Arnaud needed the job done, he might have wanted to hire someone for it. He might have asked you . . . ."

"No, no, no."

Katharine looked at him disbelievingly. "Dawes' throat was cut at the door of his room—the same as my father. And I saw Damgaard outside Dawes' hotel just after the murder. I saw him slipping a note pad into his pocket, and Dawes' note pad—with all his notes about the Morgan case, was—"

Paul was taking her arm, trying to interrupt. "Don't tell him, Katharine. Don't say anything."

"Did you know him?" Nathan's eyes narrowed, the surfaces glinting intensely. "Did you talk to Dawes?"

"I met him at the Clément. He wanted to interview me, and when I went to his hotel . . . ." Katharine felt a sudden swell of tears.

Nathan spoke adamantly: "Damgaard didn't kill the reporter, Katharine, I swear it on my life."

"How do you know?"

"The police had him killed," he said in a broken voice. "I came to warn you to keep your mouth shut and get out of Paris, because if you go to the police, you'll more than likely end up like the reporter. I . . . I think you both understand the gravity of the situation here: France has been struggling economically for some time, and after pouring so much money into the Exposition . . . ." He shook his head. "If everyone suddenly had to be evacuated because of a plague scare, it would cause irreparable, immeasurable damage. It's not just the economy. We were on the verge of another civil war before we decided to turn our energies on the fair instead. We've managed to create enough stability to prevent ourselves from killing one another, and—"

Paul interrupted. "The *police*—you're sure the police did it? Or are you just saying that so I'll keep quiet?"

"No, Paul, please think. It's the truth."

Katharine pressed him: "How do you know?"

"Arnaud told me, without telling me. He insinuated it very plainly.
He's a friend of the local police captain. The reporter was asking
questions all around the city, and he came to the police with . . . his
plague theory." Nathan said the words almost inaudibly.

"Go on," Paul said.

"Arnaud and the captain had a conversation about how the reporter
was compromising the integrity of the Exposition, and the captain agreed
to have him taken care of. Hours later, the reporter is dead. Damgaard
wasn't involved; I swear he didn't have a thing to do with it. I believe
that you saw Damgaard outside the hotel, Katharine, and I admit that you
have good reason to think that Damgaard is a killer, but his presence at
the hotel was a coincidence. The police are what you need to worry about
now."

Katharine and Paul exchanged slow glances. Katharine's glance was
more of a wince, and after a moment she spoke in an almost defensive
tone.

"He still killed my father," she said.

Paul was inscrutable.

"Did you hear me?" Nathan leaned toward them, overwrought.
"Katharine? Forget about Damgaard."

Paul agreed: "Yes, let's forget about Damgaard, shall we?" He made
a shrugging motion and put his palms face out at Nathan. "Fine, we get
the message. Now we'll just continue on our way out of Paris. Say
goodbye to Annette for us."

"You'll forget about helping the Morgan girl?"

Katharine and Paul looked at each other silently.

"Arnaud, and the city of Paris, will go very far to keep this under
wraps," Nathan insisted. "A plague scare would plunge the country into
hell. You understand? They have money, and they have absolute need.
The reporter's dead and they have the girl over at the Salpêtrière."

"What's that?" Katharine asked.

"It's a psychiatric hospital. They're having her assessed, and if they
can't prove that she's insane, they'll try to pin the mother's
disappearance on her. They're not averse to crushing innocent people in
order to keep this quiet."

"Did Arnaud say that?" Katharine asked. "Why would he tell you all
of that?"

"Why do you think, Katharine?" Nathan stared at her. His voice
sounded dry and thin. "He said it to scare me. You should be frightened,
too. If you can't get on a ship, at least go back to Le Havre."

"Nothing to fear from us," Paul conceded. "We just want to get home and resume our lives. Goodbye, Nathan."

"Yes, goodbye," Katharine echoed, lost in thought.

26

Katharine insisted on breakfast before departing from the hotel. "The baby needs food," she insisted. Then, after breakfast, she needed to return to the room for some rest.

Paul knew she was stalling. Katharine was distant throughout the morning. Charlotte's placement at the Salpêtrière permeated all other thoughts.

Katharine remembered how, years ago, she'd suffered her own intense fear of being placed in a psychiatric hospital. Damgaard had provoked in her such desperation and panic; he deftly spread the notion that Katharine had become "hysterical," not just as a result of her father's death, but by some congenital defect, as evidenced by her previous "erratic" and "imprudent" behavior. Confinement to a hospital was one of the many fears he'd instilled in her, so potent and threatening that she had fled Troy and abandoned all but her soul in the face of his manipulations.

More than confinement, Katharine feared the treatments she might undergo. Many American doctors still believed that women's hysteria originated in the reproductive system, and that the condition could be "treated" by surgically removing the offending organ. Treatment was uncertain, experimental, and often extreme.

"Doctors don't perform clitoridectomies—or ovariotomies—in London anymore, do they?" she asked Paul.

He knew the thought behind the question. "I don't think clitoridectomies are common. Not since Isaac Brown, anyway."

Brown, a London gynecologist, had been banned from his profession after his overzealous treatments of "hysterical" women. Convinced that the clitoris was the main culprit, he had performed clitoridectomies on many of his female patients without their consent.

"What about in Paris?" she asked.

"I'd say no, or at least that it's quite uncommon in France. The American doctors, the ones like Kellogg, are the ones who haven't moved beyond their obsession with—" Here he used a vulgarity, but Katharine ignored it.

Paul and his old "friend," Dr. John Harvey Kellogg, had graduated Bellevue Medical College together. Strongly averse to such afflicting behavior as masturbation and frequent sex, Kellogg recommended burning and desensitizing an over-sexed woman's clitoris with carbolic acid; for males, he recommended sewing the foreskin over the end of the penis. His treatments were plentiful and diverse, and ranged from the nightmarishly invasive to the seemingly inane. Kellogg also believed that hot, creamy cereal was inclined to arouse a child's tendency toward self-abuse, and dreamed of creating cold breakfast cereals that would curb a young person's desire to masturbate.

Paul, who was endlessly amused by the man's quest to rid society of sexual excess, had kept an active acquaintance with him for some years—until Clara began to succumb to tuberculosis. Kellogg, who believed that a married man should refrain from "soliciting" his wife more than once or twice a month (and only when she was fertile, and only for the sake of reproduction), had written to Paul to suggest that Clara's illness resulted from "the weakening of her system through excessive sexual demand." Paul abruptly broke off the friendship.

Yet in spite of, or perhaps even because of the incident, Paul still loved to poke fun at the man's ideas. At home he kept a copy of Kellogg's pamphlet *Plain Facts for Old and Young*, a treatise on the evils of sex. Paul, with his peculiar sense of humor, would sometime read to Katharine from certain sections—namely, the sections titled "Marriage" and "A Chapter for Married People"—and then, after having a good laugh, would want to make love, and reminded her to report any weakness, feverishness, or mental fog she might suffer as a result.

He was careful to avoid the segment titled "A Cause of Consumption," in which Dr. Kellogg asserted that over-indulgence in sex could induce tuberculosis.

"Katharine, what the hell is this?"

Paul's sharp tone forced her out of her reverie. In his hand, pinched between the thumb and forefinger, he held a corner of a tattered journal. The back cover was exposed to her, stained an ugly reddish-brown. *Dawes' blood.*

"I took it from Dawes' hotel room," she said casually.

Paul dropped the book onto the bureau.

"It's a journal. It chronicles . . . ." She trailed off.

"The girl's journal?" He waited, then nodded in response to her silence. "That's fantastic. Fantastic, fantastic." He stared at the book and gave an involuntary shudder. "My wife. She steals blood-stained evidence from a crime scene, pushes Damgaard off the Eiffel Tower. What else?"

"I was going to show it to you." She winced, but chose to ignore the comment about Damgaard. She picked up Dawes' shirt and handled the book with it, delicately turning pages.

"Whose shirt is that?" Paul demanded sharply—but abruptly shook his head. "Never mind. I don't want to see it—or talk about it, because I know what you're going to do. The journal is evidence, and you want to use it to help the girl. Right? Why didn't you leave it for the police?"

She raised her eyebrows. "Yes, I'm certain they would have done a thorough investigation and arrested the culprit, and the courts would have made a fair conviction."

"Don't start. And throw that shirt away—somewhere else, not in this room. I don't want those things in here."

"Paul, I can't do that. At least let me send the journal to her family. She has relatives in London; if I can find out—"

"Nooo, no. Katharine, we are *going to get murdered.*"

"Not if I can help her anonymously. Paul, don't get so upset. I have to at least try. I can't throw the journal away. Listen."

"No."

"Be quiet and listen." She held the book open and read a paragraph aloud. "The loss of my—"

"Katharine, don't bother—"

"Listen, Paul. I won't talk about anything else until after you hear me out," she warned him, and continued:

The loss of my family is most painful, but I've come to realize that there is another, more frightening loss coming upon me—the kind of loss that my brother always understood, and that motivated him to make the church his profession. That is the loss of faith—faith in action and consequence; in justice; in meaning. I want to believe that something good can be taken from every event that is wicked, but in this I see no goodness to come. All I feel is the threat of this world-shattering despair that rolls toward my being like a monstrous wave, taking its time in coming, but leaving no doubt as to the destruction it will wreak. I pray to God to give me something to build strength upon. But the despair hisses that there is no God—or if there is, then God is a sadistic predator who entertains himself with the suffering of the innocent. Other people have fallen into the void, and more will fall still. Why not me? Am I any different from all those who have tried and despaired?

It was her last entry, dated Wednesday, May 22, 1889.

"Paul, I won't leave this girl. I can't."

His eyes flashed with pain.

"You must know that I relate to her," Katharine said softly. "She's just lost her last surviving family member, and people are covering up a crime by trying to convince her that she's mad. She's suffering in there, and she's surrounded by people who are even more confused and despair-ridden than she is. Doctors will tell her she's sick; they'll medicate her. Nathan said that the police will make it look like she had something to do with her mother's disappearance. A few days ago, you told me that you would do whatever I asked."

"I didn't think we were in danger of having our throats cut when I said that," Paul replied.

"I want you to allow me to visit her before we leave Paris."

"*Visit* her?" He gaped.

"I need one visit with her. Just one."

"And I suppose you expect me to sit here and wait while my wife and future child are gallivanting in a mental ward, in defiance of throat-slashing police."

"This is the least harmful option I can—

"What happened to sending the journal?" Paul's voice rose sharply. "What happened to anonymity? What is all this, Katharine? You say one thing, and then you do another. You talk as though you're on some sort of moral crusade, yet you only want to help this girl because she reminds you of yourself. What if she didn't? Would you still fight for her? Or are you just using her to get revenge on the world? Is revenge more important than your husband and child?"

A numbness washed over Katharine. She felt startled—not just by Paul's words, but by his challenging demeanor. "This isn't revenge."

He replied without hesitation: "So says the woman who pushed John Damgaard from the Eiffel tower."

Again, Katharine was taken aback. Her hands trembled. After some moments she realized she had stopped breathing. She forced herself to draw in a slow, difficult breath. "Maybe you're right," she said quietly. "I'm helping her to help myself. It doesn't mean I don't care. Have you ever known me to be indifferent to injustice?"

"I've never known you to risk the world for it. Even when—" Paul caught himself, lowered his gaze. "Damn it all!" He turned, walked a few paces, swiveled and paced back. Abruptly he stopped. "Let's not do this."

"I just want to warn her to stay quiet," Katharine said steadily. "I promise that after one short visit, I will go back to New York. I'll go immediately. I swear it."

Paul's face looked ashen. Even the gray eyes seemed to have paled. "If anything happens to you, I will die." His voice cracked. He sat on the bed, put his head in his hands. The knuckles went white as he pressed his fingers hard into his temples. "I feel like I'm about to be punished for my sin. Something will happen . . . ."

"I won't let it happen." Katharine hugged him, and added softly: "I handled Damgaard; I'll handle this too."

But he shook his head more emphatically, lifting his head and staring at her in disturbed awe.

"I'm sorry," she said. "Maybe I can't make you feel calm about it, but I'm going. I'll go today and see if I can get a meeting with her. I won't tell anyone my real name." She paused, watching him, but he didn't respond. "I know you don't understand, but if I don't at least try to help her, *I* will die; and if I succeed in some way, it might bring me back to life."

27

SUNDAY, MAY 26, 1889

The fiacre bumped along the busy Paris streets, moving southeast along the Seine before veering around the Jardin des Plantes. The driver stopped to let Paul off at the park, and Katharine continued toward the renowned asylum on her own.

The clerk at the hotel, with whom Katharine had become fast friends, had filled her in on the history of the Salpêtrière. The site had once contained a gunpowder factory, and was transformed into a hospital complex in the seventeenth century—the kind of hospital that served as a prison for ill and impoverished women, an unclean place infested with disease-carrying rats. Reforms in psychiatric treatment eventually began to transform the Salpêtrière into a place of medical treatment. Now it was famous for its study and treatment of female nervous disorders, led by the neurologist Jean-Martin Charcot.

The clerk made some mention of the inappropriate relations between many of the facility's male doctors and their patients, adding with an amused grin: *The doctors have replaced the rats.*

When she first set eyes on the hospital, Katharine was amazed and intimidated by its girth. Charlotte, it seemed, would be miniscule inside of it—swallowed up by a strange and massive asylum crawling with hundreds upon hundreds of tormented souls, in a strange land far from home. On closer observance, the Salpêtrière boasted lovely grounds with gardens and benches, and a quaint chapel just across from the main entrance. The driver directed Katharine to an entrance of the labyrinthine complex. She collected her nerves as she descended from the fiacre; Paul had already paid the driver, and she had nothing more to delay her from taking the next risk.

At the intake desk she faced the secretary, who didn't speak much English. He had a translator fetched from among the orderlies.

"I'm here to visit a patient named Charlotte Morgan," she explained at last, keeping her voice clear and assured. "She's English—from London—and she was committed here yesterday, or perhaps the day before, on suspicion of a nervous disorder."

After some bustling about, she was informed that "the patient is involved in an active police investigation." The translator eyed her inquisitively. "We are required to make a record of everyone who comes to see her."

"Oh, certainly. But I can visit her? I only need a few minutes; I just want her to know that someone is checking up on her. She's so far from home, and doesn't speak the language . . . ."

"You are an acquaintance?"

"Yes. We met recently, here in Paris. She approached me when she was looking for her mother, and we became friends."

"So you have not seen her mother?"

"No, I'm afraid not."

"Sign here," he ordered her.

"Certainly." Katharine signed her name *Sarah Beckett.*

"Identification?"

Katharine felt the beginning pangs of defeat. "Yes, just a moment . . . ." She rifled through her handbag; pulled out her thick, tattered copy of *Guide Bleu du Figaro*; rifled some more. "Ah . . . I think my husband has our papers," she murmured. She turned and stared anxiously down the street.

The man studied her signature, as if to detect anything suspicious in it, and waved her on. "If she is out of her room, you may have a few minutes with her," he said. "Come, I will bring you myself."

He led her deeper into the grand building. "You may have a brief visit if Miss Morgan consents to it," he explained, "and only in the open ward. The violent ones are not allowed there, so you will be safe; but if there is an outbreak of dangerous behavior, of course I may have to escort you . . . ."

Katharine found herself unable to focus on his words. She was drawn to sounds of erratic screeching; then of mournful wailing; of soft weeping. The heartrending cries seemed to multiply with disturbing speed. *Thousands—not hundreds, but thousands are imprisoned here.* At the nearer end of the female ward was a community room, filled with the same pitiful cries and moans, all against a background of somewhat milder conversation. Dozens of patients milled about here with heads drooped, or with arms hugged tightly around their chests; others curled alone in various parts of the vast room, while some patients chatted with one another in what seemed perfect amiability. But the room reeked of urine and other vaguely putrid scents, and clouds of despair seemed to twist up and out of the ghastly figures who cried and moaned, who clawed at themselves as if to scratch away the invisible residue of their pasts.

The orderly gestured toward a young woman with long brown hair gathered in a braid, slumped in a chair at the far side of the room. She sat with shoulders sagging and spine curving in a forward slouch, with fluttering eyelids aimed at the windows. Katharine inhaled deeply—suddenly realizing that her breath had been shallow since she entered the ward, as if to refrain from inhaling the energy of this degenerated place—and braced herself for what she would surely see. She remembered the way Charlotte's large brown eyes had fixed on her in the hallway of the Clément; the meek and almost apologetic smile; the friendly and charitable glow that had appeared so unexpectedly, where many a woman might have scoffed and scowled. That light would surely be gone, snuffed out by unimaginable heartbreak. *But something must still be there.* And if not, Katharine would try to help her find it.

"Miss Morgan, you have a visitor." The orderly touched Charlotte's shoulder.

The head moved; the young woman's eyes rolled up to look on Katharine, hazy and half-opened. Dry lips parted. "They put my mother behind the wallpaper, and no one believes me," she wheezed dreamily.

Katharine stared into the dead brown eyes and felt the crushing force of despair. Her own potential fate was mirrored in Charlotte, manifested in the blanched, paper-like skin in which the eyes were sunk—in the cowering, slowly imploding posture.

The orderly saw Katharine's crestfallen face and spoke quickly. "She is not quite awake." He reached out and gently shook Charlotte's arm, then placed a hand to the side of her head. "Miss Morgan, you have a visitor," he repeated.

"Hello, Charlotte," Katharine choked. Her voice came out dry and cracked. "It's me, Sarah. We met earlier, at the hotel—do you remember?"

Charlotte's face became taught with concentration; the eyes came into focus.

"Do you know Mrs. Beckett?" the orderly asked.

Vague glimmerings of recognition stirred in Charlotte's eyes. "Yes . . . ."

Katharine lowered her voice and addressed the orderly: "Thank you, I think she recognizes me."

The orderly nodded and backed away a few steps, still at attention. Katharine looked at Charlotte and chose her words carefully.

"Charlotte, do you remember me? We met at the hotel. I was telling you about what happened to my father. I never quite finished."

A spasm of confusion passed over Charlotte's face.

"Are you being treated well?" Katharine asked, trying not to give in to a feeling of helplessness. Charlotte was so young, so broken-looking.

Nearby, one of the seemingly friendly chats had turned out not to be so friendly after all. Two women were tearing at each other, shrieking hateful, spittle-flecked curses. The orderly turned and advanced on them, and Katharine quickly took advantage of his absence, kneeling close to the ghost-like young woman.

"Charlotte," she whispered, looking steadily into the large brown eyes. "Listen. I know that your mother went missing from the hotel."

"What do you know?" Awareness flickered in Charlotte's gaze.

"Be patient with me, please. I want to tell you about something else first. I have to tell you about my father. He was my only surviving family. He was murdered a few years ago and his killer was never caught. I tried to bring the killer to justice, but he was too powerful for me. He had money, connections, influence . . . I nearly went mad with grief. I think that I came very close to ending up in a place like this"—Katharine gestured around the room—"simply because I couldn't convince anyone."

Charlotte was shaking her head. The eyes were muddled, distant, but vaguely searching. "What are you talking about?"

"I knew who killed my father," Katharine said emphatically. "I *saw* him, but it didn't make any difference. No one wanted to believe it. I had to acknowledge that I couldn't beat him, and so I left. I survived. I have a husband now—a good man—and a child on the way. I've found ways to be alive again. My father died, but he lives in my memory. He would have wanted me to live, and I know that your mother wants the same for you."

"Did they send you?" Charlotte's mouth had suddenly twisted with distaste; the eyes flashed with suspicion. "They sent you to persuade me to keep my mouth shut."

"No one would bother doing that, Charlotte. It would be easier for them if you fell into despair. Despair makes you look mad."

"Who are you?"

Katharine hesitated, weighed the risk of speaking the truth. "I spoke to Mr. Dawes. He told me about you and your mother."

"Are you a witness?"

"No," Katharine lied. "But Mr. Dawes believed that you were telling the truth . . . ." She faltered.

"I will not leave this place without my mother," Charlotte said softly.

In her voice, Katharine heard such heart-rending love and grieving resignation.

"Your mother would want you safe at home," Katharine insisted quietly.

"I have no home," Charlotte spat. "What do you know?"

"Charlotte, please believe that I can understand the position you're in. I know because I've been through it. I didn't have a home either. I had to pretend I was a madwoman for a while, because a broken woman poses no threat to those in power. And when I was safe, I sought . . . well, maybe not justice, but the closest thing I could get." Katharine paused, trying to keep her thoughts in order. "Charlotte, you have the whole city of Paris against you, and right now there is nothing you can do to help your mother, except live. You understand?"

"I would rather die." The words came out hard and cold, but choked with sorrow. "I refuse to leave without her."

"You mustn't think like that," Katharine insisted. "For God's sake, Charlotte, your mother wouldn't want that." Her mind raced for words; she spoke as fast as she could think, keeping her eye on the orderly, willing him not to return. "Think of what she would say to you if her spirit was sitting here beside you. She would tell you that you are her precious child, a beautiful soul, and she can't bear the pain of watching your light go out."

Tears rolled from the soft brown eyes. Charlotte turned back toward the windows, gazing without focusing. "Her *spirit*," she whispered, almost inaudibly, but with unmistakable bitterness.

Katharine glanced back at the orderly, felt her attention caught for a moment by a hunched-over form that wandered listlessly across the floor.

"Do you have anything else to say?" Charotte asked softly.

"Yes. I want to tell you to do what I did. Be calm; don't argue. Leave quietly with your uncle. If he knows you, he'll know you're not lying."

"Howard will say that I was confused . . . at the least."

"Maybe not. Sometimes we can't predict who will believe us and who won't. Later, maybe in a few weeks' time, you might discover what happened. You will be able to speak more freely than you can in a place like this. You're here because people have played a cruel game against you, and if you want to get out, you'll have to play your way out. Play the part of the helpless woman, get to a safe place, collect your wits and tell your story to those you trust—and when you're ready, strike back. If isn't fair, but it's necessary." Katharine stared at Charlotte's blank profile and sighed. "I don't know if I'm saying the right things," she whispered. "I can't think of anything else to do. But remember this: human beings are easily duped. These people cannot see you. They will tear your soul to pieces, and perform monstrous acts against you, without even realizing they're doing it."

"I know," Charlotte whispered.

"Albert Dawes was murdered. You know that, right?" Katharine searched Charlotte's distant gaze for some sign of understanding. "He was collecting witnesses for you, and he ended up dead—and the same will happen to your other witnesses, because now it's not just a disappearance that's being covered up. It's a murder. No one will bother to kill *you* as long as you're not a danger, and right now no one feels threatened by you. Keep it that way—and when you're safe, I will do what I can to help you get justice. Not just for you and your mother, but for Albert Dawes. I swear it. I can help you; I just can't do it here, in Paris."

Charlotte turned and looked at her then. She was focused, but indiscernible. "How can . . . ." The glint of recognition lit her eye, more sharply this time. "You . . . the woman from the hallway," she said slowly. "Mr. Dawes said . . . ." She frowned, perturbed. "You *were* a witness. You saw my mother."

The words stirred the beginnings of alarm in Katharine. The orderly was returning now, and Katharine spoke quickly, hating the words as she uttered them: "I'm sorry; you're mistaken. I didn't see your mother, and if I had, I would never admit it in Paris, because I *don't want to get my throat cut like Mr. Dawes*." She said the last words in a sharp whisper, and abruptly stood.

Charlotte ignored the implications of those last words—or perhaps hadn't heard them. The young woman was getting to her feet, pushing herself from the chair with effort, her eyes burning with desperation. "No, I am certain—you were there, in the hall. I remember you."

Katharine shook her head. Softly, calmly, she said: "No, dear, I'm sorry. I can't help you with that." She felt a natural impulse to escape before Charlotte gave her away, felt the increasing vulnerability of each passing moment. But Katharine knew that she didn't need to run; she did not need to hide. All she needed was to maintain the right demeanor, the right expressions—to remain composed and assured while Charlotte unraveled before her. It was a lesson she'd learned from Damgaard.

"Sir . . . sir," Charlotte said, reaching for the orderly. She gripped his arms, as though she could physically force him to believe her. "This woman saw my mother at the hotel. She was in the room next to us. She can prove it."

Katharine heard the strength of conviction in Charlotte's voice, power flowing through a body weak with grief and over-exertion. She recognized the sound of that voice; she remembered it from her own past. In the days after her father's death, that voice had pleaded with police, had alerted neighbors and friends, until at length she realized she had been defeated. Katharine had vowed not to speak to anyone in that voice ever again.

The orderly raised his eyebrows questioningly at Katharine. She shook her head, her eyes exuding genuine pity. "I'm afraid she's confused," she said gently.

The burning desperation in Charlotte's eyes seemed to fall away inside her, into unseen depths. She stared at Katharine in mute helplessness.

"Goodbye, Charlotte," Katharine told her quietly. "Please remember what I said, and take care. I'll be in touch." She turned to the orderly with a polite "Thank you," and walked away.

Two patients were pacing before her, broken and listless. She quickly weaved her way between them toward the hall, but their despair seemed to stick to her, to invade her lungs as she breathed. *I'm afraid she's confused*. A woman with an aged and sallow face; a young one with limp hair plastered above eyes that betrayed a bottomless sadness. Katharine felt incredible pressure in her chest, pressure behind her eyes. *I'm afraid she's confused*. The words sounded over and over again in her head. Her vision blurred as tears spilled out over her cheeks—one after another, faster than she could wipe them away. The orderly caught up with her. He questioned her as they walked, expressed concern for her tears. "Are you unwell? What else did she say to you?"

"Do you have any idea how long she'll be here?" Katharine asked him. "Has her uncle said when he'll arrive?"

"We expect someone to come for her in a couple of weeks. Not the uncle, though; we received a telegraph from him, saying that he was sending someone else. His son-in-law, I think. A doctor."

"I see. In the meantime, please take good care of her."

Minutes later she was back at the Jardin des Plantes. The "garden" was also a zoo—not one that exhibited humans, but instead contained a menagerie of otherwise wild animals, contained in cramped and stifling cages. Katharine found Paul standing motionlessly in the wild beasts exhibit. He stared at a sickly-looking tiger who looked back at him with matted, dripping eyes. The air seemed to thicken with humidity as Katharine approached. She smelled once again the acrid stench of urine.

Paul saw her and gestured toward the two empty cages beyond the tiger. "The other animals are dying from consumption," he choked, and Katharine realized that he was crying.

She embraced him and doused his shirt with her own tears.

"Did you see her?" he asked.

"Yes."

"And?" he asked cautiously.

Katharine shook her head. Paul squeezed her and whispered in her ear. "All right, let's go. Are we catching the train to Le Havre?"

"Yes."

He kept his tone calm. "Are we in worse trouble than before?"

"No." Katharine drew away and wiped her face. "I was able to get in without giving them my name. But we're leaving now."

As Paul searched for another fiacre, he kept Katharine close, walking with an arm around her. "Don't cry, Katharine," he soothed her. His own tears had dried, and he kept them safely at bay. "You did the best you could."

She shook her head silently.

They were quiet on the ride back to the hotel. They caught a carriage back to the train station, and as they waited on the platform, Paul gave Katharine another squeeze and murmured in her ear. "At least we accomplished one good thing," he said, placing a hand on her belly. He muttered: "Well, you accomplished two, in fact."

"You mean Damgaard," she said softly.

"For a start. Look, Katharine, I need you to know that I can't blame you for what happened—though I can't quite believe it yet."

"Nevertheless . . . I feel like I did everything wrong. I feel safer, for the time being, but I didn't solve anything. Mr. Damgaard isn't the problem."

28

"Are you mad?" George Jr. stared at Paul incredulously.

"Not that I'm aware of, but perhaps I'm not the best judge of my own sanity."

The Gardiners hadn't spent two days at home before Paul announced that they intended to leave again. He had sent word to his cousin Abigail, whose home had been destroyed by a flood, to come and live at the house during his absence. George was more than supportive of the gesture—until he learned where the newlyweds were heading.

"I'm serious, Paul," he said. "It's a kind gesture on your part, but Johnstown is no place for a pregnant woman."

"Nevertheless," Katharine said, "there are plenty of pregnant women in Johnstown."

News of a terrible flood in Pennsylvania had reached Katharine and Paul even before they reached port. They had arrived back in New York on June 3rd, three days after the South Fork dam collapsed in a heavy downpour and sent twenty million tons of water down the path of the Little Conemaugh River. The torrent devastated a number of towns, wiping away the entire village of Mineral Point, carrying away much of what it destroyed—rocks, trees, animals, people, hundreds of buildings, train cars, towers, parts of factories, and more—before crashing down on Johnstown. By that point it had become a 50-foot-high locomotive of tumbling wreckage, and by all reports, thousands of people were presumed dead, crushed by the wave of debris or caught in islands of burning rubble. Even the most organized and daring rescue efforts were grossly impeded by the sheer amount of debris, much of which was tangled together with miles of barbed wire from the Gautier Wire Works. As the country grieved, people began to cast blame on the South Fork Hunting and Fishing Club, a group of wealthy Pennsylvania industrialists whose original members had purchased the dam and the adjacent reservoir; the area had been transformed into an exclusive resort, the dam modified to suit its needs. Now the club's members faced accusations that their alterations of the already-compromised dam had substantially weakened it.

Among those members was the famous philanthropist Andrew Carnegie, who, at the time, was at the World's Fair. The day's paper mentioned that he was supporting a Paris fundraiser for victims of the flood.

"Might you not take more time to consider the risks?" George's brow was lined with worry. "Especially since . . . you'll forgive me for saying so, Katharine, but since your mother had such difficulty with pregnancy . . . ."

"But I've had no difficulties. I won't push myself. And if it's too much, of course we won't stay."

"I'm not sure you can do much good. Johnstown needs people who can lift, who can help clear the wreckage. It's dangerous work."

"Exactly," Paul replied. "Those people will need medical care. Katharine was already planning to volunteer with the Red Cross Society, and she's had some experience with nursing. I'd like to have her on hand to assist me."

George raised his eyebrows in perturbed surprise. "*Assist* you? Have you read the papers? There are all sorts of risks you'll be exposing yourselves to: disease, contaminated water, not to mention the wreckage of people's lives. The things that have happened . . . ."

"We've seen terrible things before," Katharine said calmly.

"Not like this."

"Perhaps not," Paul said, "but someone has to go, and we're both willing. Clara Barton is almost seventy years old, and she's already on her way there. If she can do it, I don't see why two relatively young and healthy people shouldn't follow in her steps."

"Excuse me," Katharine said, standing. "I'm just going to get some water. Would you like anything, George?"

"No thank you." George studied his half-brother in troubled silence as Katharine left the drawing room. He searched Paul's face, looked him over as if for clues to an unsolved mystery. "Paul, did something happen in Paris? You seem . . . somber."

"I got married," Paul deadpanned. "I'm married and I'm expecting my first child. That will sober up a man if anything will." He smiled, but George looked unconvinced.

"And Katharine?"

"Katharine is a tigress. She'll be fine. Look, I know we haven't said much about Paris—but once we found out about the baby, the World's Fair seemed incredibly unimportant."

"Just unimportant? I think Katharine found it offensive. Did you hear what she told me?"

"No, I missed it."

"She said that the fair crushes and exploits people to lift itself, like a heartless opportunist—but that it was very well dressed."

"That's not inaccurate," Paul replied. "Was that all?"

"Basically. She didn't seem to care for much of anything, except the tower. She thought the tower was magnificent."

Abigail arrived the following day with her seven-year-old daughter in tow. She helped Katharine pack, gave advice, described the needs of her ravaged community—but Katharine's mind often strayed to other matters. When her luggage was arranged, she retreated to the bedroom and turned her attention to the stack of envelopes on the bedside table. They were addressed to a number of newspapers, among them *The Daily Telegraph* and *The Times of India.*

Katharine had listened to Abigail's stories without flinching—but when she picked up the envelopes, her hands trembled.

She had not felt shaken in the least until that moment. The fits of nausea had ceased with her final departure of the Eiffel Tower. No longer was Katharine hunched forward, her body wrought with tension. Her shoulders had eased back, and her spine straightened as she made space for the child she carried; the baby seemed to nestle comfortably within her womb, as though the whole system of her body had resolved its troubles. The bog monster, too, had vanished from the dreamscape, and no longer preyed on her fears.

Damgaard was not the only specter that had lost its power over her. Once out of Paris, Katharine no longer feared the consequences of revealing the truth about Elizabeth Morgan.

In Le Havre, just before boarding the ship, Katharine had mailed Charlotte's journal to London's *Daily Telegraph.* On the inner cover she'd written a short, anonymous note: *Property of Charlotte Morgan, whose mother Elizabeth Morgan disappeared on May 21, 1889, after arriving in Paris with symptoms of the Black Death. This journal was found in the hotel room of Daily Telegraph reporter Albert Duwes. Following his murder, witnesses to Elizabeth's Morgan's presence in Paris have refused to speak up for fear of having their throats cut. Please forward to London Metropolitan Police.*

She felt it unnecessary to explain the bloodstain.

But that was not the end of it. Earlier, on the train from Paris, Katharine had copied notes from Charlotte's diary: names, dates, any relevant detail that could help prove Charlotte's story. With them she had prepared a narrative of Elizabeth's disappearance. She started making copies during the voyage across the ocean. Paul knew what she was doing, and accepted it with quiet resignation. These communications would not be anonymous. Katharine had included her own name and her husband's name, and described their roles in the events.

Paul entered the room and closed the door softly behind him. "George will be here soon with the coach." He stood close to Katharine, looking at the envelopes over her shoulder. "Are they ready?"

"Yes." Katharine set the stack down, so that he wouldn't see the trembling in her hands. She glanced up at him. "Are you sure you don't mind?"

"No, I don't mind pursuing justice for an innocent murdered man—or the Morgan girl, for that matter."

Katharine noted his use of the word "innocent." Paul hadn't said a word about Damgaard since leaving Paris, and seemed not to judge her; but every once in a while Katharine caught him staring at her with a cautious, probing look in his eyes, as though he was seeing a stranger.

Sometimes she wished she hadn't told him.

Paul placed his hand over hers. "Are you nervous?"

Katharine's thoughts turned back to Charlotte. "I'm afraid that nothing will happen. That no one will care, and Dawes' murderer will never be caught, and . . . ."

"And?" He waited, but Katharine stood silently, her head lowered. "What else?"

"Time," she said at last. "The look on Charlotte Morgan's face when I left her. She wasn't on good terms with her relatives. She was alone. I'm afraid that I've waited too long . . . and that I helped break her." She looked at Paul with haunted eyes. "I told the orderly that Charlotte was just confused."

"Yes, you've mentioned that. More than once."

"I keep thinking about it. I tell myself that I did it to save us, but . . . sometimes I think . . . I may have been angry."

"Angry at what? At Charlotte Morgan?"

"Maybe."

"For what?"

"For being so naïve. For giving up. Perhaps I was angry at myself; I sat there and preached about revealing the truth, but I lied to Charlotte, and I lied to the orderly. How was she supposed to trust me?"

"You can't hold yourself accountable. Christ, Katharine, you make me feel like an ass! Aren't you concerned for yourself?"

Katharine's gaze was distant, distracted. "I'm going to be a mother. I want to know myself. Especially after . . . things I did." She paused. "Thanks to me, Damgaard's victims will never get justice."

"They never would have. And now there won't be any more of them."

"I've been debating what I should teach our child about justice. I've thought about it this whole time. I don't want to raise a bitter and hopeless child; yet in honesty I want to teach that people are cowards, and the justice system is a hierarchy of privilege that stomps on the powerless . . . and that I myself resorted to vigilante justice."

"It will be a few years before we'll have to address those issues," Paul replied tersely. "I have more present concerns."

"So do I, but . . . I'm trying to figure out how to live. I think I can encourage our child to be shrewd, and yet to have hope; to avoid putting faith in the justice system, but to never stop working for justice. I want to keep our daughter or son from ending up like Charlotte, or . . . like me." She paused, her gaze becoming suddenly distant. "You know, when Damgaard came to the window that night—that night when he threatened to have me dead within the week—he must have congratulated himself on playing such a clever trick. But that was what did him in, because it made me certain of his guilt. If he hadn't confessed, and threatened me, I would have always maintained just enough doubt. I never would have . . . ." Katharine glanced at the door. Her voice dropped to a near whisper. "I never would have been able to push him. The fact that I did that, so impulsively . . . sometimes it scares me."

She looked anxiously at Paul, wanting to see his reaction. He averted his eyes; his face was unreadable. Finally he sighed. "Hell, Katharine, think of what he put you through—you and countless other people, and he did it all with a smile on his face."

"It's the impulsiveness that scares me. When I was young and went up against Damgaard, I thought I would get justice because I was right, because so many reasonable people knew that Damgaard was a scoundrel . . . but now I know better. People don't react with reason to such things. I'm afraid that the pressure will expose the monsters in everyone—that they will impulsively blame, torment, and kill to protect themselves— that Nathan will end up with his throat cut, and Charlotte—"

"The city is beyond that now," Paul interrupted, with a faint note of doubt. "The plague scare has petered out, and they have nothing to gain by causing more suspicious deaths. Listen, I'm going to admit something: I did have doubts about revealing the truth. I kept telling myself that I let you handle all this"—he gestured to the envelopes— "because you wanted to do it yourself. But after a while, I realized I was resisting it. I feel safe now that we've left France, but I'm afraid that the scandal will cost me. I'm afraid of not being able to provide a secure life for my child. I don't want my reputation smeared, my private life scrutinized, my mistakes flaunted so that Paris can discredit me. I don't want to be ostracized. It would be a kind of small death—but you've had your life yanked out from under you, and you've taught me how to cope." Paul lowered his voice a notch, and spoke gently. "I want you to make sure you've hesitated, though, and really thought this through. Once you send these letters, it's all out of our hands. What if Charlotte *is* broken, to the point that she can't corroborate anything? What if the carriage driver fears for his life and denies everything, and Nathan dismisses you as a madwoman? What if it's just us against the powers that be?"

"I have to do it anyway," Katharine replied.

"Well, at this point, so do I. I know doctors who lied and created cover-ups to save their reputations, and . . . I don't want my child to discover, someday, that I didn't help someone because I was afraid of tarnishing my image."

He took a breath, as if to continue, but halted and lowered his eyes. Katharine knew he was thinking again of Damgaard. She recognized the troubled look that often followed his cautious scrutiny of her, and she braced herself for what he would say.

"Did you—" Paul jumped as a knock sounded at the door. "Come in."

Abigail cracked the door open and peeked through. "George is outside," she said timidly.

"All right." Paul squeezed Katharine's shoulder. "I'll take care of the luggage."

Abigail remained in the doorway, wringing her hands, after Paul had gone. She had hardly stopped wringing them since her arrival. Her gray-blue eyes darted anxiously around the room, as though she expected the walls to implode at any moment. Suddenly she stopped and looked at Katharine with shining eyes; she smiled and spoke in a strained voice. "Thank you for being such a great friend to us. We've lost nearly everything, but my daughter is safe because of you, and my husband and others will get well because of you. There's a lot of disaster still to be met in Johnstown. I hope you'll stay away from danger, and keep yourselves safe."

She entreated Katharine to visit her husband, who was recovering in a hospital, and promised to take the most excellent care of the house while the Gardiners were away.

Katharine embraced her. Then she excused herself and collected the envelopes.

On the way to the train station, George stopped the carriage at the post office. Katharine went inside with her stack and found the front room nearly empty, aside from a lone clerk struggling with several heavy packages. He heaved them onto a cart and turned to the desk. "What can

I do for you?"

Katharine presented the stack and paid the shipping fees. The clerk set the envelopes on top of the cart and wheeled them toward the back room. Katharine didn't linger to watch them drift out of sight. She turned away and set her foot toward the carriage and Johnstown.